Jean de La Bruyère

The Morals and Manners of the Seventeenth Century

Being the character of La Bruyère

Jean de La Bruyère

The Morals and Manners of the Seventeenth Century
Being the character of La Bruyère

ISBN/EAN: 9783337418922

Printed in Europe, USA, Canada, Australia, Japan

Cover: Foto ©Andreas Hilbeck / pixelio.de

More available books at **www.hansebooks.com**

THE MORALS AND MANNERS OF THE SEVENTEENTH CENTURY, BEING THE CHARACTERS OF LA BRUYÈRE.

TRANSLATED BY

HELEN STOTT

LONDON
DAVID STOTT 370 OXFORD STREET
1890

THIS TRANSLATION IS DEDICATED TO A DEAR MEMORY AND AN EVER PRESENT INFLUENCE. "THE DEAD ARE NOT DEAD, BUT ALIVE."

H. S.

London, May 29th, 1890.

CONTENTS.

	PAGE
Biographical Introduction	vii
Introduction	1
Intellect and Learning	5
Personal Merit...	28
About Women	40
The Heart	57
Society and Conversation	67
The Benefits of Wealth	85
Paris	102
The Court and Courtiers	112
The Nobility	136
The Sovereign and the Republic...	153
Men...	173
Judgment and Criticism	208
Fashions	243
Some Customs	261
The Pulpit	277
Of Unbelieving Minds	289

BIOGRAPHICAL INTRODUCTION.

JUST two hundred years ago Jean de la Bruyère issued the little volume which at once gàve him his place in that illustrious throng of learned intellect which made the close of the seventeenth century and the reign of Louis XIV. so great and glorious. Racine, Molière, Bossuet, Fénelon enjoyed with him the favour of the King, and La Rochefoucauld, La Fayette, and Madame de Sévigné were also of the Court.

Little is known of La Bruyère's youth, and we have few details of his family, or of his personal life; indeed, it is through his characters and reflections alone that we can form any intimate knowledge of him ; but it does not require much imagination to build or to idealize the hidden life, even the carefully shrouded love, which his own thoughts reveal to us. Once he lifts the veil of obscurity in which his family history is enveloped, when he tells us, with terse humour, of that Geoffroy de la Bruyère of the Crusades; and it has been said that an ancestor of his exercised the duties of Civil Lieutenant during the time of the barricades of Paris in the reigns of Henri III. and IV. Guizot says that he was born at Dourdan in 1639, but no entirely authentic record of his birth has been discovered, although from one of the parish registers of Paris we learn that Jean de la Bruyère was christened there on the 17th of August, 1645. We find him first at Caen, in an official capacity under Government, and we must suppose he had some previous acquaintance with Bossuet, Bishop of Meux, as it was through his influence he was appointed historical tutor to M. le Duc, the grandson of the great Prince of Condé, with a only compensation is in the knowledge that we have had the moral strength to renounce them."

His appreciation of the picturesque and beautiful in nature is very uncommon for the time in which he lived; as, for instance, when he describes the little town which in the clear air looked like a beautiful picture painted on the hillside; and what a gracious comparison we find in the story of the prince, and the shepherd, and the flock; what exquisite feeling in the thought, "There are some places we admire, others we love; wit, passion, taste, and sentiment depend on the place we live in."

Ideas ever new and fresh carry the reader along, germs of thought which our own minds expand, and we wonder how such deep and subtle knowledge of the workings of the mind was gained.

"At a first glance," says Sainte-Beuve, "you may think you have taken up a book of fragments arranged in successive order, and you find yourself in a labyrinth of wisdom to which there is no end." Each thought is corrected, enlarged, and made clearer by surrounding thoughts, and all are bound together by a golden thread gleaming out here and there in some nobly uttered reflection. "Her talent," La Bruyère says of Catherine Turgot, "was like a well-set diamond," an expression which is itself an exquisite gem. Read the glowing eulogism on Cardinal de Richelieu, and the wonderful character of a glorified Louis XIV., to whom, however, he offers advice but thinly veiled in praise when he speaks of the "difficulty a religious prince has in reforming his Court, and making it pious."

More serious and less bitter than La Rochefoucauld, as brilliant as Cardinal de Retz, and more firm in his opinions, La Bruyère was a more sincere believer than either. "I feel that there is a God," he says, "and I do not feel that there is no God: that is enough for me; all the reasoning in the world is useless as far as I am concerned. I am convinced. Are men good enough, faithful enough to be worthy of our whole confidence, to prevent us longing for a God to whom we can appeal against injustice, and in whom we can take refuge when men persecute and betray us?" Is not this the reasoning of a mind convinced that the world can be governed by justice alone?

D'Olivet writes of him as a philosopher who loved a quiet life among his friends and his books, able to make a good choice of both, neither seeking nor evading pleasure, disposed to simple enjoyments and ingenuously creating them, polished in his manners and wise in his discourse, and so afraid of notoriety that he modestly hid even his talent.

Much light is thrown on his character by the story of the publication of his "Characters," as told by M. Walckenaer, who relates that "Monsieur de la Bruyère used to go nearly every day to the shop of a bookseller named Michallet, where he would sit down and turn over all the new books, amusing himself at the same time with the pretty little daughter of the bookseller, to whom he had taken a liking. One day he drew a manuscript from his pocket, saying to Michallet "Will you publish this? I don't know if it will pay you, but if it is a success the profit will be for my little sweetheart here." The bookseller, more uncertain of the result than the author, undertook to publish an edition, and no sooner was it issued than it was sold, and he had to print it over and over again, and made two or three hundred thousand francs by it. And in this unexpected way the bookseller's daughter got her marriage portion : and when long afterwards she married a man in a good position, she took her husband a fortune of more than 100,000 *livres*. So the book, with all its bitter and misanthropical experiences, became by a strange contrast a girl's dowry."

In 1693 La Bruyère was made a member of the Academy of France; his oration was most eloquent, and, following the custom, he eulogized great living members, praising Bossuet, Fénelon, Racine, and La Fontaine, etc., but bringing upon himself the animosity and jealous criticism of those he did not notice. His sensitive nature was deeply wounded, and he retired to his quiet life at Versailles, where three years afterwards he died, disappearing in the height of his glory before biographers had thought of interviewing him.

Saint Simon, writing soon after 1696, says, "The public has lost in La Bruyère a man who must ever be illustrious for his originality, his wit, and his knowledge of human nature; he has surpassed Theophrastus, whose work he translated, he was a simple, genial, honest man, with nothing of the pedant or self-seeker in his nature. I knew him well enough to regret him, and the work which, from his comparative youth, might have been expected of him."

If the translator may be allowed to add a sentence to this epitomized account of the philosopher and his work, she would first quote his own words, when he says that, "Among all the varied expressions by which we may render a single thought, only one is correct; we cannot always find it either in speaking or writing; it exists however, and any other form of expression is feeble, and does not satisfy the student who would be understood." In this spirit she has attempted her work, but it is difficult to convey the fine and delicate shades of meaning of the incomparable original into the concise English, which would be in keeping with La Bruyère's style; for it has been well said that his motto might have been "The best in the least."

THE MORALS AND MANNERS OF THE SEVENTEENTH CENTURY:

BEING

THE CHARACTERS OF LA BRUYÈRE.

THE material for this book I have borrowed from the world at large. Justice demands that having accomplished my work to the best of my ability, and with such due regard for truthfulness as the subject merits, I should acknowledge my obligation and restore what was lent to me. The public may regard at leisure the picture I have drawn of it from nature, and, if it recognizes and admits some of the faults I describe, correct them. This is the only aim a man ought to have in writing, although he must not always expect to succeed. As men do not weary of wickedness, neither must we grow lax in rebuking them. But for our censure and reproof they would probably be worse ; therefore, preaching and writing do much good, and to those who wield such powers appreciation is keenly gratifying, although were an orator or an author to seek praise only, he might blush for shame. The improvement or reformation of those who read or who listen is the highest approbation, the most enduring praise. We ought neither to speak nor to write, save for the instruction of others, and if at the same time we chance to please, we may rejoice, for by this means we instil instructive lessons in an agreeable and gentle manner.

When any thoughts or reflections slip into a book having neither the brilliancy nor the spirit of the context, but which appear to have been introduced for the purpose of variety, or to relax the mind and render it more receptive to that which follows, we must take care that they are expressed simply and intelligibly, otherwise the author would do well to expunge them, lest even the unlearned, who ought never to be neglected, condemn them. This is one good rule. There is another which, for my own interest, I ask you to observe. It is this, do not lose sight of my title, and remember throughout the perusal of this book that I am describing the characters or the manners of this age in which we live. And although my observations are most frequently drawn from the Court of France and from my own countrymen, it has nevertheless been impossible to restrict them to any single court or country, for by such restriction I could not have carried out my purpose, which is to portray men in general, and my book would thus have lost much of its breadth and usefulness. These are some of the considerations which guided me in the arrangement of my chapters, and in a certain unconscious order the reflections of which they are composed.

After this perhaps necessary warning, the meaning of which will be easily understood, I think I may be held innocent of any special application of censure, and I protest against all complaint or wrong interpretation on the part of those readers who may be maliciously disposed towards me.

People ought either to be able to read and keep discreetly silent, or else to relate with perfect accuracy what they have read, and neither more nor less ; this method ought invariably to be observed. Without these conditions, which an exact and scrupulous author has a right to require from certain minds as the sole reward of his labour, I question if he ought to write at all, for he must ever set truthfulness before zeal, and consider his own gratification less than his usefulness.

I confess that since the year 1690, before publishing the fifth edition, I hesitated between my anxiety to make my book fuller and larger by the introduction of more characters, and the fear that some people might say, " Will these 'Characters' never be finished ? Shall we never see anything else by this author?" Some sensible people said to me, "Your subject is solid, useful, agreeable, inexhaustible ; may you long discourse on the same theme—you could not do better. The follies of mankind will each year provide you materials for a volume."

.Other friends with equal judgment told me to beware of the whims of the multitude and the fickleness of the people (with whom, however, so far I have good reason to be contented). Those friends also hinted to me, that as for the last thirty years people had read only for the sake of amusement, they must be amused by new books with new titles. That this frivolous humour had flooded the shops with a dull and lifeless literature, without aim or style, meaning or moral, written and perused in equal haste, and only for the sake of novelty ; but that if I could do no more than add to a book already tolerably long, it would be wisest to rest from my labours.

Of this opposing counsel I adopted a medium course, agreeing a little with each. I did not question the propriety of adding a few new remarks to those which had already enlarged my work to double the size of the first edition ; but in order that the public might not be obliged to look through the whole book to find out what was new in it, and that they might readily find what alone they wished to read, I was careful to distinguish for them this second addition by a peculiar mark, and the first enlargement by another simpler mark, which also conveniently showed the progress of my characters, and helped the reader in his choice of a chapter. And lest it might be feared that there would never be an end of those additions, I added to my formalities a sincere promise to venture on nothing more of the kind. If any one accuses me of breaking my word in continuing to insert new remarks in later editions, he will nevertheless see that in mixing those new remarks with the older ones, and in suppressing all distinguishing marks, I have thought less of novelty than of the possibility of leaving my work in complete and regular form to posterity.

Finally, I have not been endeavouring to write maxims; those are like laws of morality, and I possess neither the genius nor the authority of one who makes laws. I am aware that I have even transgressed against the accepted mode of forming maxims which are short and concise, after the manner of oracles. Some of my remarks are in this form, others are more lengthy. Different things are thought out by different methods and explained by diverse expressions, it may be by a sentence, an argument, a metaphor, or some other figure, a parallel, a simple comparison, by description, or by portraiture. In this way the length or the brevity of my reflections arises. Those who lay down maxims desire to be considered infallible. I shall, however, be contented though it is said of me, " His remarks are not good," provided always that those who say so make better remarks themselves.

INTELLECT AND LEARNING.

EVERYTHING has already been written. We have been born too late, for men have lived and thought for more than seven thousand years, and all the grandest or most beautiful thoughts regarding the morals or the manners of men, have already been culled. We can only glean after the old philosophers, and the abler of our modern minds.

We must only endeavour to think and to speak honestly ourselves, without attempting to convert others to our tastes and sentiments ; that would be too ambitious an enterprise.

As much craft is necessary for the writing of a book as for the making of a clock. More than intellect is required of an author. A judge attains the highest dignity by the force of merit ; he is keen and practical in all points of law, and he instils rare moral lessons while he seems to ridicule.

It is not so easy to make ourselves a name by a perfect work as to make an indifferent work valuable by the reputation one has already acquired.

A satire when circulated privately will, even if it possesses little literary value, pass for marvellous ; but printing will prove it.

Take certain works of moral philosophy, extract the advice to the reader, the dedication, the index, the preface, and the approving notices ; and there will

seldom be a sufficient number of pages left to make a
book.

———

Poetry, music, painting, and oratory are some of the
arts in which mediocrity is unendurable. What a
weariness it is to listen to a dull speech pompously
delivered, or to a weak poet declaiming his indifferent
verses.

———

Many poets in their dramatic flights indulge in long
words, and sounding verses which seem very powerful and elevating and full of noble sentiments, and the
people listen greedily, and stare and gape, believing
they please the poet. The less they understand, the
more they admire and hold their breath, being impatient even of the noise of applause. In my early
youth I imagined those passages must be clear and
intelligible to the actors, as well as to the pit and the
gallery; that the authors had some hidden meaning in
them which with all my careful attention I could never
discover, and I thought I must be to blame for my want
of comprehension. I am now undeceived.

———

Up to the present day, a masterpiece has seldom
been produced from the joint labour of several minds.
Homer wrote the "Iliad," Virgil the "Æneid," Livy
his "Decades," and the Roman orator (Cicero) his
"Orations."

———

There is an acme of perfection in art, as in nature there
is an extreme degree of goodness or of maturity. One
who feels this and loves it has perfect taste. He who
does not feel it, and can rest satisfied with anything
short of it, has defective taste. So there is good and
bad taste, and consequently there is a basis for disputes of taste.

Men generally possess more ardour than judgment, or in other words, there are few men whose talent is guided by perfect taste and judicious criticism.

The lives of heroes have enriched history and history has glorified the actions of heroes ; therefore, I know not which are most beholden to the other, the historians to the heroes who furnished such noble material, or those great men to their historians.

A heap of epithets is weak praise ; simple facts and the style of narrating them commend a man.

An author's talent is shown by clear definition and vivid portraiture. Moses, Homer, Plato, Virgil, and Horace, are superior to other writers only through their expressiveness and their imagery. To depict with truthfulness a man must feel naturally, strongly, and delicately.

Style in literature ought to have been treated as architecture has been treated ; the Gothic order, which a rude age had introduced for palaces and temples, has been abandoned ; Doric, Ionic, and Corinthian styles have been reintroduced. What was once to be seen only among the ruins of ancient Rome and old Greece is now become the modern architecture, and enriches our porticos and peristyles. Likewise, in writing, we need not expect to attain perfection ; and, if it is possible to surpass the ancients, it will only be by imitating them. How many centuries passed before men returned to the tastes of the ancients, and before they recovered the simple and the natural in matters relating to art and science.

Our minds are strengthened by the study of the ancients and the abler minds of our own time. We extract all we can from them, we enlarge upon and draw inspiration from their work, and when at last we are full-fledged authors ourselves, and feel that we can sail along unaided, we rise up and abuse them, as an infant grown strong and vigorous through good nourishment will turn against its foster mother.

A modern author generally tries to prove that the ancients were inferior to us in two things, reason and example; the reason he draws from his own peculiar taste, the example from his own writings. He confesses that an ancient author, however unequal and incorrect he may be, has a few good lines, which he proceeds to quote ; and they are so good that, for the sake of them, people read his criticism.

Some learned men pronounce in favour of the ancients as against modern writers, but we suspect they have interested reasons, so obviously are their own works formed on models of antiquity.

It is best to read our works to those who know enough of the subject to be able to appreciate and suggest corrections. Not to tolerate advice or correction is pedantry. An author should receive praise and criticism with equal modesty.

Among all the different modes in which a single thought may be expressed, only one is correct ; and this does not always occur to us in speaking or writing. Nevertheless, it exists, and any other is weak, and never contents a man of talent who wishes to be understood.

A careful writer often finds that the expression he has sought in vain for a long time and found at last is most simple and natural, and one which apparently ought to have struck him at once without effort.

Those who write as the whim moves them often touch up their work ; therefore, it is irregular, varying according to their moods, and usually they end by altering the very expressions or words they liked best at first.

The same sound judgment which enables an author to write well makes him value his work modestly.

A person of middling abilities believes that he writes divinely, while a man of real talent thinks his production but tolerable.

" I was engaged," said *Aristus*, "to read my book to *Zoilus*, and I did so. It made some impression on him at first before he had leisure to discover its inferiority. He indeed gave it some cold praise in my presence, but since then he has ignored it to every one. I must excuse him, and ought never to have expected more from an author. I even pity him for having been obliged to listen to many beautiful passages of which he was not himself the author."

Those who from their position are exempt from the jealousies of an author have other cares and passions to distract them and render them indifferent as to how another man's conceptions will be received. Scarcely anyone is so well-disposed in mind, heart, and fortune, as to be in a condition to freely enjoy the pleasure a perfect composition can give.

The pleasure of criticising often deprives us of the pleasure of being deeply touched by the beauty of some passage.

Many people who feel the merits of a manuscript when they have it first read to them, will say nothing in its favour till they see what effect its publication has on the world, and what verdict is pronounced on it by men of letters. They will not risk their commendations till success is certain, they must be guided by public opinion, led by the multitude ; then how eager they are to explain their early appreciation of the work, and to express their pleasure that the world at large agrees with them.　Such persons miss the opportunity of convincing us of their intelligence and judgment, and of their ability to bestow appreciation when it is due.　Something very good falls into their hands, an author's first work perhaps.　He has no name, no influence, nothing can be gained through him or his friends by praise of his effort.　Self-interest does not require you to pronounce it a masterpiece of genius, to declare that nothing could excel it, and that in future a man's appreciation of this work ought to be made the test of his capacity.　Strained exaggeration such as this would only be detrimental to what is really commendable.　But why cannot they simply say, it is a good book !　They end by saying so when everybody else does, when it is praised by Frenchmen and by foreigners alike, and translated into every European language.　But such tardy acknowledgment receives no gratitude.

Some people having read a book, quote certain passages which they do not in the least understand, garble their meaning by infusing something of their own, and, thus distorted, they expose these passages to censure, maintain them to be bad, and, as they quote them, the world accepts and condemns.　But injustice does not destroy the true beauty of the passages they have pretended to quote.

" Well," says some one, what do you think of *Hermadotus's* work ? "　" It is very poor," replies *Anthimus*. " Poor !　I don't understand you."　"Very poor," continues *Anthimus*, "so poor that it is not worth notice at all." "But have you read it?" "Oh, no," is the reply. Why does he not add that *Fulvia* and *Melania* condemned it unread, and that he is the friend of *Fulvia* and *Melania*.

Arsenus from the height of his intellect contemplates mankind, and feeling himself so far removed from them, he affects to be afraid of the littlenesses he beholds.

Lauded to the skies by certain friends with whom he has formed a compact for reciprocal admiration, having a little merit, he believes himself the possessor of more than he will ever have. Full of sublime ideas of his own wisdom he has scarcely time to utter his oracular sayings.

He is elevated far beyond ordinary human feelings and opinions, and leaves it for common mortals to value a regular united life. For all inconsistencies he holds himself accountable only to those particular friends who see in them something more to admire; and as by his coterie he alone is deemed capable of thought and judgment, so he also alone can write, or ought to write, and no other work, no matter how highly approved of by the public, will he condescend to read. Therefore, as he will never read this sketch, he will never benefit from it.

Theocrines is well informed on unprofitable subjects. His sentiments are always peculiar; he is more systematic than learned; he makes little use of any faculty except his memory, is absent-minded and disdainful, appearing ever to laugh to himself at those who do not see his worth. By chance I once read to him something of mine; he listened, then talked of his own. You want to know what he said of mine? I have told you already, he talked of his own.

No production, let it be ever so highly finished, would survive criticism if the author took heed of every censor, and allowed each to strike out the passage which pleased him least.

Experience tells us that if there are ten persons who would blot out a thought or an expression from a book, an equal number will oppose the rejection, exclaiming " Why would you suppress that thought? it is new and beautiful, and well expressed ; " others declare that it ought either to be omitted or at least another turn given to it. The first critic remarks, " I notice one expression in your book which is very clever, and exactly hits off your meaning." " I observe a word," says another, " which it seems to me is rather doubtful, and besides it does not convey all your meaning." Both persons are speaking of the same word, the same expression, yet both are considered good judges. What then can an author do but follow the advice which approves ?

An earnest writer is not obliged to trouble his head with all the coarse and silly remarks which are passed, or to concern himself with the inept applications which are made of portions of his work ; much less ought he to suppress them, for it is quite certain that however scrupulously exact a man may be in his manner of writing, supercilious jests and sneering strictures are inevitable, since in certain quarters the best things are turned into ridicule.

There is an immense difference between what is called a fine work and one which is perfect and regular. I doubt, indeed, if anything deserving the latter description exists, for it is less difficult for genius to reach the grand or sublime than it is to avoid all errors. " The

Cid," from its first appearance, was with one voice commended. Its power was stronger than politics or authority, which tried in vain to crush it. People of every class and of the most varied sentiments and opinions were unanimous in their favourable estimate of the tragedy, and everybody knew it by heart, so that when repeating it the actors were not infrequently prompted by the audience. "The Cid," in fact, is one of the finest poems in existence, and perhaps the criticism on it is the best that was ever written.

If you find that the perusal of a book elevates your thoughts and inspires you with great and noble sentiments, seek no other rule by which to judge of its merits. It is good, and shows the master's hand.

It is the journalist's business to inform us that a certain book is published, and by whom; to describe it and its style and character, and say where it can be bought. It is foolishness in him to make any criticism of it.

His chief business is to write a lengthy, empty argument on the political situation of the day. But he may lie down at night relying on some piece of news which the morning proves to be a false report.

The philosopher wastes his life and energies in observing men and exposing vice and folly. If he gives the public the benefit of his observations, it is less for the pride of authorship than to throw the light of day upon some discovery, so that it may make the impression he desires. Yet some people think he is well rewarded if they read his book and say authoritatively that there is wisdom in it. He does not value their praise, this was not the object of his sleepless labour. He has higher aims, and acts on a nobler

principle. He exacts from mankind a greater acknowledgment than praise or reward. He requires reform.

Fools read a book, but understand it not. Men of
little understanding think they comprehend perfectly,
while the wise man cannot understand entirely ; but
distinguishes between what is clear and what is
obscure to him. A wit, on the other hand, tries to make
a mystification where it does not exist, and pretends
not to understand what is perfectly intelligible.

An author tries in vain to excite admiration by his
productions. Fools sometimes admire, but then they
are fools. A sensible person is by nature pregnant with
truth, and his moral perceptions are keen ; so nothing
is quite new to him. He seldom admires. He approves.

I do not think it would be possible to find in any
other letters greater talent, more liberality, or a more
agreeable style, than we find in those of Balzac* and
Voiture. It is true they do not contain those popular
sentiments, for the creation of which we are indebted
to our female writers, who excel us in this kind of
writing. Words and expressions which come to us
after long labour and weary research, flow easily and
gracefully from a woman's pen. She makes a happy
choice of words, and arranges them so tersely, that
ordinary phrases have all the charm of novelty, and
seem both apt and original. Only a woman can put
a volume of meaning into one word, and express a
delicate thought in words as delicate. She has an inimitable faculty of linking together, in an apparently
effortless way, the most diverse subjects. If women

---

* Jean Louis Guez de Balzac (1594-1655), author of a series of
' Familiar Letters."

were only more correct, I am not afraid to assert that there is nothing in our language better written than some of their letters.*

The fault one finds in Terence is his coldness, but nowhere do we find greater accuracy, elegance, and politeness than in his characters. From Molière we could have desired greater purity, and the avoidance of vulgar words and barbarisms : but what vivacity we find and what simplicity joined to keen sense of humour ; his characters are portraits overflowing with wit. Had those two comic writers been one man, what a genius he would have been.

I have read Malherbe and Theophile. They both understood nature, but with this difference : the first, in a copious, regular style, sets before us at once the beautiful and noble and what is simple and natural ; he makes a picture for us with his pen. The other, with erratic mood, carelessly and inaccurately charges his descriptions with tiresome details, anatomizing, at times drawing on his imagination, until he exaggerates and goes so far beyond the truth that his writing becomes romance.

Ronsard and Balzac have produced each in a different fashion as much bad and good as would model heroes in prose or verse.

Judging from his manner and style of diction, Marot would seem to have written later than Ronsard, for between his style and that of our day there is only the difference of a few words.

---

* An allusion to the Letters of Mme. de Sévigné.

Ronsard and his contemporaries have done more harm than good to our language. They retarded its progress to perfection and exposed it to the danger of permanent defect. It is surprising that Marot's works, which are so easy and natural, did not make Ronsard, otherwise so full of vivacity and enthusiasm, a much greater poet than either : and that on the contrary Belleau Jodelle and Du Bartas were so soon followed by a Ragan and a Malherbe, and that thus our language was scarcely corrupted ere it was purified.

Marot and Rabelais are inexcusable for indulging in ribald language. Both had sufficient genius and wit to have been independent of such aid, even had they only aimed at the amusement of those who will laugh more often than admire. Rabelais, especially, is incomprehensible ; his book is an enigma, we might say a fabulous fancy, a woman's lovely face with feet and tail like a serpent, or some more hideous anomaly— an insidious mixture of ingenuous morality and monstrous coarseness. Where it is bad it is abominable, and fit only for the *canaille*, while the good parts are just as surpassingly excellent, and afford exquisite pleasure to the most refined.

Two writers in their works have condemned Montaigne. I do not hold him exempt from blame, but they appear to consider him worthy of no esteem, and allow him no credit at all. The one thinks too little to be capable of enjoying an author who thinks much, and the thoughts of the other are too subtle to be pleased with what is natural.

A grave, earnest, scrupulous style will live long. Amyot and Coeffeteau are still read, but which of their contemporaries ? Balzac in his phrases and expressions belongs to a later day than Voiture. But if the talent and natural style of the latter is not modern, and does not resemble our modern literature, it is because our authors have found it easier to neglect than to imitate him, and the few who followed him could not come up to him.

"Le Mercure Galant"* is just of less value than nothing. There are many other works of the same importance. There is as much device in growing rich by a silly book as there is want of sense in buying it. Ignorance of the public taste sometimes prevents the publication of silly things.

Opera is the outline, the faint idea, of some magnificent spectacle.

I do not understand why it is that an opera, with its perfect music and its splendid accessories, has yet the power of thoroughly wearying me.

There are some parts in an opera which make us long and long for more, and others which make us wish to escape from the whole performance, just as we are pleased or not with the plot and the actors.

Opera as it at present exists is not a poem, but a metrical dialogue, nor is it any longer a show, since automatic puppets have been discontinued by the economy of *Amphion*† and his kind. It is a vocal and instrumental concert ; and I think it is unfair to tell us that automatons are fit only for children's marionettes. In my opinion they increase and beautify the romance and keep up a delightful illusion in the minds of the spectators, and throw an element of the marvellous into the performance. Neither

---

* A now forgotten work by de Visé.
† Lulli and his school.

wings, triumphal cars, nor transformations are wanted in tragedy, but in opera they are necessary, its chief design being to hold eye and ear in a spell of enchantment.

Connoisseurs, or those who consider themselves such, assume the power of giving an opinion for or against all public productions. Dividing themselves into cliques, they are swayed by anything but public interest or fairness : they admire a certain poem or a certain musical composition and condemn all others. Their partizanship is so hot that they cannot properly defend their opinions, and so injure the reputation of their favourites. They discourage poets and musicians by their inconsistencies and contradictions, and retard the progress of science and art by withdrawing the stimulus of emulation from those masters who, according to their different talents, could produce excellent work.

What is the reason that people laugh so easily, yet are ashamed to weep at a theatre ? Is nature more easily swayed to mirth than moved to pity ? or is it the disfigurement of tears which keeps them back ? Immoderate laughter is more unseemly than the bitterest grief, and we ought to be as much ashamed to let others see us laugh as cry. Are we afraid to be thought soft-hearted, or weak-minded, or easily imposed on by unreal things ? We shall not take into account those strong-minded persons who never give way to either excessive laughter or to tears, but let us consider for what reason we go to listen to a tragedy. Is it to laugh ? Is truth not as vividly portrayed there as in comedy ? Will anything but truth, let it be in comedy or tragedy, move the soul ? Will people be satisfied with the improbable ? Therefore, as it is no unusual thing for a theatre to ring with spontaneous laughter at some amusing hit in a comedy, so also the violent efforts people make to control their tears and break into forced laughter at some touch of pathos, clearly prove that giving way to natural emotion should cause no other embarrassment than that of drying our eyes, and having agreed to indulge our feelings in this way, experience will teach us that there is less fear of being moved to tears at a play than of being made to feel ashamed.

A tragedy arrests the attention at its very commencement, and during its progress we almost hold our breath, and can think of nothing else ; or if our attention is diverted for a moment it is only to be plunged anew into yet deeper absorption ; we are moved to pity, then to alarm, and so we are swayed by alternate tears, sobs, hopes and fears, horror and surprise, to the end. Tragedy should not then be a mere concoction of pretty speeches, tender situations, and soft words, or sometimes of pleasant jests, to be certainly followed by a last scene in which some riotous persons appear and kill some others—why, we do not understand, as already there seems to have been enough bloodshed.

It is not enough that the manners of the stage are not bad, they ought also to be seemly and instructive. Some of the things one sees there are either so low and gross, or so dull and poor in themselves, that they are not worthy a poet's attention, nor can any audience be diverted by them. The peasant or the drunkard may be made a subject for a comic farce but ought never to enter into the action of a true comedy. " But," says some one, "these characters are natural." " Yes, but by the same rule our attention might be engaged by bringing on the stage a whistling lackey or a drunkard sick and snoring ; there is nothing more natural."

It is the custom of an effeminate youth to rise late and spend the best part of the day over his toilet, looking at himself in his mirror, perfuming, powdering, and laying on his patches, then receiving his love notes, and replying to them.   But try putting this *rôle* on the stage ; as the play goes on from act to act, the truer to nature, the more life-like it seems, but the more dull and stupid it also becomes.

It seems to me that plays and romances may be equally useful or hurtful to those who read them.   In them are to be found many fine examples of constancy, virtue, tenderness, and disinterestedness, many beautiful and noble characters ; so that when a young man casts his eyes around him and sees so much that is base and unworthy his ideal, I am surprised that he is able to retain any weakness for his fellows at all.

Corneille cannot be equalled in those parts in which he excels ; in them he is inimitable, as well as original, but he is unequal.   His first plays are dry and heavy, and give us no reason to expect that he would afterwards rise to such a height ; just as his later plays make us wonder how he could have fallen from it.   In some of his best pieces there are unpardonable faults of style ; as, when he declaims, the action stops, and there is a carelessness in the rhythm and expression such as we can scarcely understand in so great a man. But his genius is sublime, and we are beholden to him for some of the happiest verses which were ever written.   We are also indebted to him for first opposing the ancient rules in the direction of a theatre, and lastly for the admirable manner in which he unravels his eventful plots, though in this he does not imitate the grand simplicity of the Grecian taste. He is likewise to be admired for his great variety; among all the numerous poems he composed he rarely repeats himself.

In Racine's poems more similarity is apparent; the same idea pervades many of them, but he is more equal and sustained throughout, both in the design and in the working out of his pieces, which are appropriate, regular, full of nature and common sense. His versification is correct, rich in rhyme, elegant, harmonious. He is an exact imitator of the ancients, whom he scrupulously follows in simplicity of action, although he does not come far short of Corneille in the sublime and marvellous, as well as in the touching and pathetic.

Where can we find greater tenderness than is diffused through the "Cid," "Polyeucte," and the "Horaces?" What grandeur we find in Mithridates, Porus, Burrhus.

Terror and pity, the favourite passions of the ancients, were well understood by those two poets, as Orestes, in the "Andromache" of Racine, and his "Phædra," and also the "Œdipus" and the "Horaces" of Corneille prove. If however I might be allowed to make comparison between the two, and to distinguish each by what I discover in his works, perhaps I would speak thus: Corneille subjects us to his characters and ideas, Racine conforms himself to ours. The former paints men as they ought to be, the latter describes them as they are. In the first there is more of what we ought to admire and imitate, and in the second more of what we know there is in others, and of what we feel to be in ourselves. Corneille elevates, astonishes, instructs, and influences us; Racine pleases, moves, affects and penetrates. The former overcomes

us by touching what is grand and noble in our nature,
the other through our most refined and delicate sentiments.   One is full of maxims, rules, and precepts, the
other is occupied with agreeable and pleasant tastes.
Where Corneille arrests our attention, Racine moves
or disturbs our minds ; Corneille is more moral,
Racine more natural.   The one seems to imitate
Sophocles, the other Euripides.

In ordinary language, the power of being able to
speak for a length of time, gesticulating and loudly
attesting with much lung power, is called eloquence.
Pedantic persons affirm that eloquence can be displayed only in public speaking, and they are unable to
distinguish between true eloquence and those rounded
periods full of symbols and long words by which it is
simulated.

Logic is the art of convincing others of some truth,
while eloquence is a gift of the soul, which makes us
masters of the hearts and minds of others, and
enables us to inspire them or persuade them as we
will.

Eloquence may exist in any discourse, or in any kind
of writing.   We rarely find it when we look for it,
but sometimes when we do not expect to find it.

Eloquence is to the Sublime what the whole is to
one of its own parts.

What is the Sublime? It does not seem ever to have
been defined.   Is it a figure of speech, or is it derived
from figures, or at least, from some figures?   Is any
kind of writing capable of being sublime, or is sublimity found only in great works?   Could anything be
more touching than the beautiful simplicity of a
pastoral? and what is more pleasing in letters and
conversation than natural delicacy?   Now, may it not
be, that simplicity and delicacy form the Sublime in
those works in which such qualities are the per-

fection, for what is the Sublime and where does it begin ?

Synonyms are words or phrases having the same signification. Antithesis is the opposition of two truths which by contrast explain each other.

Metaphor or comparison borrows from an outside object to give a natural image of the truth. Hyperbole expresses more than the truth that the mind may realize it better. The Sublime describes the whole truth nobly and entirely, both in cause and in effect, and it expresses it in a manner worthy of truth.

Little minds cannot express themselves fitly in one word, and therefore use synonyms. Young men are dazzled by the brilliancy of antithesis, and often use it. Greater men who take pride in exactitude of speech prefer comparison and metaphor. A lively imagination is often carried beyond justice into the use of hyperbole. As for the Sublime, only the highest genius is capable of it.

He who would write correctly ought to put himself in the place of his readers, examine his work as something he has never read before or had anything to do with, but which has been submitted to his criticism. Then let him discover if he understands his writing only because he wrote it himself, or because it is really intelligible.

An author must not write only to be understood, but he must inform us of the things that ought to be understood. He must, it is true, possess pure diction and correctness of expression, but his correct expressions ought to convey high and noble thoughts, full of sound good sense.

It is making a bad use of pure, clear language to use it on some frivolous, unprofitable subject, having

neither wit, novelty, nor purpose, which, although
easily understood, has no other merit. It is better to
be a little uncertain of an author's meaning, than tired
of his production. If sometimes we throw more depth
into our writings, more variety of expression, or it may
be greater delicacy, we err from having formed a high
opinion of our readers.

In reading books written by members of some clique
or party, there is this disadvantage: we do not always
get the truth from them. Facts are disputed, and
both sides of the question are not handled with equal
force or correctness, and if we have time and patience
we may read a great deal of strong language used by
grave and reverend men, who, on some point of
doctrine or controversy, make personal quarrel. Some
books have this specialty: they deserve neither the
extraordinary sale they have for a time, nor the
profound oblivion they afterwards fall into. As soon
as the heat and antagonism of partisanship ceases,
they are forgotten like an old almanack.

Some men deserve glory and reward for having
written, others for not having done so.

During the last twenty years the style of composition
has been careful and accurate, construction has been
properly attended to, and the language has been enriched by many new words. We have thrown off the
yoke of Latinism and confined ourselves to a phraseology purely French. Indeed we have almost
recovered the harmony which Malherbe and Balzac
first revealed to us, but which their numerous
successors suffered to be lost. Our language has now
all the method and distinctness it is capable of, and
this will in the end add wisdom to it.

There are some scientific men whose genius is as vast as the art or science they profess. By their ingenuity and invention they repay with interest all they have borrowed from the principles of science. They break away from rules of art only to ennoble it, and they set aside example when it does not appear likely to lead to greatness. They go on alone with no followers, but they aim high and push forwards, self-confident and strengthened by the success which is sometimes a result of want of system. Men of ordinary talent cannot overtake them, and do not even admire or understand them, much less imitate them. These go on quietly, reaching only that certain point which forms the limit of their capacity. They can go no further, as they cannot see beyond; and at the best they only attain a foremost place in excellent mediocrity.

There are certain minds, if I may be allowed to say so, which are distinctly inferior or subordinate. Their place seems to be to collect, enroll, and chronicle the fruits of other people's genius. They are plagiarists, compilers, translators, whatever you choose to call them. They do not think for themselves, but only write what others have thought. A good choice of thoughts is, it is true, a kind of invention, but such men are seldom just in their choice, they prefer rather to make it large than excellent. They infuse no originality into their work, and, understanding little of what they purloin, they purloin what the world could do without. Theirs is a useless calling, neither pleasant nor profitable, either as regards conversation or commerce. It is like bad money. We wonder at the extent of their reading, but soon get tired of their company and of their work. The rich and vulgar confound such poor ability with wisdom, but the better informed know it as pedantry.

Criticism can scarcely be called a science; it is a trade at which more health than wit is required, more work than intellect. It is more a matter of routine than of genius. The criticism of a man who reads more than he can discriminate, perverts both his own and his reader's judgment.

———

Any author who has only the faculty of imitation, or who through extreme modesty is a copyist, I would advise to choose for his models such as are full of wisdom, imagination, or learning. If he does not equal his ideals, he will at all events come somewhat near them, and he will at least be read. On the other hand, he ought to avoid as a rock of destruction any desire to copy those whom caprice or sentiment inspires to express on paper their innermost thoughts. These are dangerous models, and those who follow them will fall into a dull, uninteresting, vague style. Besides, how laughable it would be to see someone trying to speak in our exact tone of voice, or to resemble us physically.

———

A man who is born a Christian and a Frenchman is restricted in his exercise of sarcasm. Great subjects are forbidden him, though sometimes he attempts them. He therefore turns to little things and raises and ennobles them by the beauty of his genius and his style.

———

We should avoid foolish trifling things, for fear of resembling *Dorilas* and *Handburg;* although in some kinds of writing certain expressions may be risked if they depict vividly; and we pity those who cannot feel the pleasure this freedom gives, and who cannot use it judiciously.

He who in his writing regards only the age he lives in, thinks more of himself than of his work. We should ever aim at perfection: then that justice which is often denied us by our contemporaries will be yielded to us by posterity.

We must never attribute a jest where none exists. It is bad taste, and depraves our own judgment as well as other people's. But when banter is intended, draw it out in a pleasing and instructive manner.

"Horace and Despréaux," you say, "made such a remark before you." I take your word for it, but I said it as original. May I not think a truism as well as they, just as others may do the same after me?

PERSONAL MERIT.

WHO among us, even if he possesses the rarest talent and the most exceeding merit, is not convinced of his uselessness, when he considers that when he dies he will leave a world which will not feel his loss, and in which there are so many people to fill his place.

Some people's worth lies only in their names. When you come into close contact with them you find they have no merit. They only impose on us at a distance.

I am convinced that those who are chosen for different employments, each according to his talent or professional training, do well: yet I shall venture to say that there exist many persons, known and unknown, who are not employed at all, and who would acquit themselves as well; and I am drawn to this induction by the extraordinary success of some whom chance alone has brought to the front, and from whom till then no great things were expected. How many admirable men of great talent have died without ever being heard of; and how many are living now of whom no one talks, or ever will talk.

How difficult it is for a man who belongs to no society or party, who has no partizans or promoters, but who stands alone upon his merits, to make his light shine out of obscurity, and to put himself on a level with the influential fool.

It is seldom that a man discovers for himself the

merit of another. Men are generally too much occupied with themselves to have leisure to study others,
and therefore a man of great merit, if he also possesses
modesty, may long remain unknown.

Sometimes it is the genius and the talent which
are absent, sometimes the opportunity. Some may
deserve praise for what they have done, and others for
what they could have done.

It is not so rare to meet with wit, as with people who
make a good use of what wit they have of their own,
and know how to bring out other people's.

There are more tools than workmen; and of the
latter, more bad than good. What would you think of
a man who tried to saw with a plane, and who took up
his saw to plane with?

There is not in all the world so tiresome a trade as
that of trying to win renown. Life is over, and you
have scarcely sketched your work.

What is to be done with *Egesippus* who is seeking a
post? Shall we put him into one of the public offices,
or into the army? It does not matter which, he will
make as good a financier as soldier; therefore, interest
alone should decide. His friends say he is capable of
anything, which generally means that he is fit for
nothing. He is, like many other men, entirely taken
up with himself; in his youth he consumed his time in
every kind of pleasure, and now that he is older,
fondly imagines the country has only to be made aware
of his indigence or uselessness, to exert every effort to
aid him and establish him in some office; and he never
thinks of the important fact that men ought to employ

the early years of their life in becoming, through work
and study, so valuable that the state would soon discover the need she has of their knowledge and intelligence. In this way men would become a necessary
integral in the fabric of the country, which will
be obliged for its own advantage to advance their
fortunes. We must work if we would merit high
employments. Other things do not matter ; let them
be the concern of other people.

It requires great firmness, as well as vast intellect, to
refuse high posts, and remain contented in obscurity.
Very few possess the merit to play this *rôle* with dignity, nor enough depth of mind to fill up time without
what is commonly called business. The idleness
of a wise man should however be called by another
name; and his meditation, discourse, reading, and
repose ought to be called work.

A talented man in office never troubles others
through his vanity: for he is less proud of the post he
occupies than humiliated by the thought of a greater,
of which he considers himself worthy. He is more
chagrined than haughty, and is too depressed to
despise anyone.

It is difficult for a man of real talent to flatter, but
not for the reason you may suppose. True worth is
very modest, and he would never imagine it could
give pleasure to another to see him continually putting
himself in his way. He would be more likely to consider himself importunate in so doing ; and it requires
the pressure of duty and custom to make him resolve to
appear at all. He, on the other hand, who has a good
opinion of himself, and whom the vulgar appreciate,
likes to be seen ; and makes his court with all the more

confidence, that it never enters his mind to imagine that the great people before whom he appears think less of him than he does of himself.

An honourable man is repaid for his strict application to duty by the pleasure it gives him to perform it : and this makes him independent of the praise, esteem, and acknowledgment, which is often withheld from him.

. If I dared to make comparison between two altogether unequal conditions, I would say that a courageous man sets about performing his duty just as a slater would set about performing his work. Neither of them seeks to expose himself to danger, but neither will the fear of it deter him from duty. Death is an accident which might happen to either, but the thought of it is never an obstacle. The brave man is no more proud of having been in the trenches, of making a breach, or forcing an entrenchment, than the workman is of having finished work at the top of a steeple or at some equally perilous elevation. They each think only of doing their duty well, whilst the boaster only tries to make people say he did well.

Modesty is to merit what shading is to a figure in a picture. It makes it stand out in strong relief.

A plain exterior seems fit and proper for a common man, but it is an ornament to one whose life is full of great deeds; I would compare it to unconscious beauty, which is only the more charming.

Some people, being highly pleased with the tolerable success of something they have done, and having heard that modesty is becoming to great men, try to imitate those who are truly and naturally modest, but they are like those persons of ordinary height who stoop as they enter a door in case they should strike their heads against the top of it.

In our choice of friends some special virtue ought to attract us: we should not examine as to whether they are rich or poor; but if we are persuaded that we could follow them into adversity, then we may boldly cultivate their friendship in their greatest prosperity.

If it is usual to be deeply touched by rare things, how does it happen that we pay so little attention to virtue?

If it is happiness to be well-born, it is not less so to be so estimable that nobody inquires if we are well-born or not.

From time to time there appear in the world men of such rare virtue that the brilliancy of their preeminently noble qualities sheds light all round them; like those wonderful stars whose origin we know not, any more than we know what becomes of them when they disappear. Those men have neither ancestors nor posterity. They alone compose their race.

Good sense tells us our duty, and our obligation to perform it; and even if there be danger, to face the danger. It either inspires us with courage or takes the place of it.

If a man excels in his art and enriches it by every perfection of which he is capable, he puts himself into it, so to speak, and raises it to all that is highest and noblest in himself. Vignon is a painter, Colasse a musician, Pradon a poet; but Mignard is Mignard, Lully is Lully, and Corneille is Corneille.

A single man can, if he has wit, raise himself above his station, and mix in the world above him on a footing of equality; but this is less easy if he be married, for marriage seems to settle everyone in his proper rank.

Next to personal merit, we must confess that eminent dignities and titles give most distinction and *éclat* to a man. He who cannot be an Erasmus ought to aim at being a bishop. Some, to increase their importance, obtain peerages and orders of various kinds, and, after the cardinal's hat, would like the Pope's tiara. But what need has *Trophimus* * to be made Cardinal ?

With us the soldier is brave and the lawyer learned; and we wish no more. With the Romans the lawyer was brave and the soldier learned: a Roman citizen was both soldier and lawyer.

A hero should be one thing only—a brave man; whilst a great man should know everything, whether of the robe, the sword, the cabinet, or the court; but both together are not worth one honest man.

In war, the distinction between a hero and a great man is difficult to define. Both possess all the military virtues : nevertheless the first must be young, daring, of great valour, bold, adventurous, and of dauntless courage : the other excels rather by his profound good sense, his vast foresight, great capacity, and long experience. We might call Alexander a hero, Cæsar a great man.

---

* Bossuet.

*Æmilius** was born a hero ; he had all the qualities
which men do not generally attain without learning, meditation, and exercise. In his childhood he had only to
fulfil the powers which were natural to him, and to
follow the bent of his own genius. He acted himself,
and influenced others to act, before he knew ; or rather
he understood before he had learned. Need I tell
you that his youthful games were a series of victories ?
A long and prosperous life would be rendered illustrious
solely by the acts achieved by him in his youth.
After that period he seized every opportunity to excel or
to conquer ; and when no opportunity existed, his
star seemed to predominate, and his valour created it.
He was admired as much for what he could have done
as for what he did. He was looked upon as a man
incapable of giving way to an enemy; numbers and
obstacles never made him yield : a being of the highest
order, he was inspired by greater light and knowledge to see further than other men. To have him at
the head of the legion was a sure presage of victory ;
for he alone was worth many legions. He was great
in prosperity, and greater still in adversity. The raising
of a siege, a retreat, gained him more honour than a
victory, and has been lauded almost as much as a
victorious battle or the taking of a town. He was as
grandly noble as he was modest ; and has been heard
to say, " I fled," with as much grace as he might have
said, "We gained the battle." He was devoted to the
state and to his family, and sincere towards God and
man; as great an admirer of merit as if it had been
less familiar to himself ; a true man, naturally brave
and noble ; in whom only the least of all the virtues
might be found wanting.

---

* The Great Prince of Condé, to whose grandson La Bruyère
was tutor.

The children of the Gods, so to speak, are exempt from nature's rules. They have nothing to learn from age or experience. Their merit is beyond their years; knowledge comes with their birth, and they arrive at perfect manhood before ordinary beings are out of childhood.

Shortsighted people, that is to say, people with so little imagination that it cannot reach beyond their own sphere, cannot understand that universality of genius which is sometimes observable in the same individual. Where they see amiability, they exclude solidity; and where they find personal grace, activity, and dexterity, they will not grant mental endowments, judgment, prudence, wisdom. They ignore that history relates of Socrates that he danced.

There are few men so amiable or so necessary to their fellow-men that their loss could not be endured.

A simple, straightforward man, even if he be clever, will readily be ensnared. He thinks no one would try to make a dupe of him, and this confidence makes him incautious, and the wag takes advantage of him. But he who tries it a second time will come off badly; he is cheated only once.

I would avoid offending any one, as is right; but especially a clever man, if I care for my own interests.

The greatest cunning or simplicity will not guard a man from exposing his peculiarities. A fool neither comes in, nor goes out, nor sits down, nor rises up, nor is silent, nor uses his legs, like a man of sense.

D 2

I came to know *Mopsus* from a visit which he paid me, although he had no previous acquaintance with me.

It is his custom to ask people he does not know to allow him to accompany them to visit persons who do not know him. He also writes to ladies he knows only by sight, or gets into conversation with individuals who have no idea who he is ; and, not waiting till his opinion is asked, he rudely interrupts, speaking absurd nonsense. Another time he will attend a public meeting, and sit down anywhere, paying no attention to anybody: when asked to move from a seat retained for some minister of state, he goes and sits down in a place reserved for a duke. Everybody laughs, but he preserves a stately gravity, and does not even smile.

He reminds one of the dog driven out of the king's chair, which jumps into the pulpit. He takes no heed of the world's opinion, is neither embarrassed nor ashamed, and could no more blush than a fool.

Celsus belongs to the middle classes, but is tolerated in the highest. He has no learning himself, but is allied to learned men, and although he has little merit of his own, he knows people who have a great deal; he is not clever, but he has a smooth tongue and feet to carry him where he will.

He seems to have been born to run backwards and forwards on other people's business, listening, reporting of his own accord, and getting no credit for it ; conciliating people who fall out at their first interview ; succeeding in one thing and failing in a thousand ; taking to himself all the glory of success, and casting on others the odium of defeat. He knows all the gossip and scandal of the town, originates nothing, only repeats other people's stories, in other words he is a newsmonger. He knows all the family secrets, worms himself into the deepest mysteries, can tell why that

person has withdrawn from society, and why the other
has entered it again.   He knows the cause of the many
disputes between those two brothers, and of the
rupture between the two ministers.   Did he not
predict of the first what would be the end of their sad
misunderstanding, and of the latter that their harmony
would not last long?   Was he not present when
certain things were said ?   Did he not try to patch the
matter up ; but would they believe him, or listen to
what he said ?   Who but *Celsus* ought to know about
all these things?   Who has more knowledge of all the
Court intrigues than he, and if he has not—if he only
dreams or imagines it, can he not at least make you
believe it, and put on the mysterious, important air of
one who has just returned from an embassy?

Menippus is the daw decked with peacock's
feathers.   He neither speaks nor thinks himself, but
repeats other people's sentiments and conversation ;
and it comes so natural to him to use other people's
minds that he even deceives himself into thinking
that he is expressing his own taste and uttering his
own thoughts, when he is only the echo of some one
he has just parted from.   He is a man whom you can
tolerate for a quarter of an hour : but after that he palls
upon you; the glamour is removed, and you see his
brilliant wit is only a little memory which soon wears
threadbare.

He himself, however, is quite unconscious how
far below the sublime and heroic he is, and does not
know how high it is possible for talent to reach, as he
innocently supposes that he has as much as it is possible
for a man to have, and he therefore has the air of one
who is quite satisfied with himself and envies no one.
He usually speaks to himself, and does not try to conceal the habit ; and he is so much engaged with his

own thoughts that to salute him in passing is to throw
him into a state of great perplexity as to whether he
ought to salute you or not, and whilst he is deliberating
you are quite out of sight. He vainly assumes to himself every befitting virtue, and raises himself far above
his natural merit. To see him is to know that his
whole mind is occupied with his own person ; he has
the air of being satisfied that all he does is right, that
his finery is well-chosen and adjusted ; and that all
eyes are upon him, and every new-comer is an
admirer.

False greatness is unsociable, inaccessible, and, as if
quite aware of its weakness, hides itself, or at least
does not push forward more than is necessary to
preserve its assumed position, for fear of betraying its
real littleness. True greatness, on the contrary, is
free, kind, familiar, popular, allows itself to be seen
and touched, loses nothing by close observation,
and the better known the more admired. It good-
naturedly bends to inferiors, and without effort assumes
again its natural manner. It can even put off all
appearance of superiority, but never loses the power
of resuming its proper dignity, even when laughing
and jesting with perfect carelessness. In our intercourse with such a character we may exercise frank
familiarity, but must also reverence the nobility which
is so courteous that even princes who are exalted to
the height of greatness may be approached with a confidence which prevents us from feeling our own humble
condition.

The wise man is cured of ambition by ambition
itself. He aims at such great things that he is not
contented with what is called wealth, preferment, and
favour : he sees nothing in such poor advantages good

enough or important enough to satisfy the longings of his nature, or worth caring for ; he has even to make an effort not to show how he despises such things. The only honour which can tempt him is that glory which springs from virtue pure and simple : but as that is seldom found in the world, he has to do without it.

He is good who does good to others ; if he suffer for the good he does, he is very good ; and if he suffer from those to whom he did that good, he is so good that nothing can increase his goodness but an increase of his sufferings, and if they end in his death his virtue can reach no further : it is perfect and heroic.

ABOUT WOMEN.

MEN and women rarely agree as to the merits of a woman ; their interests are too diverse. It does not please a woman to find in another the very perfections which captivate a man. The many charms which awake in us the tender passion cause in them mutual antipathy and dislike.

The superiority of some women is simply artifice, a movement of the eyes, a toss of the head, a graceful carriage, or a superficial sparkling wit, which is all the more esteemed because it is not deep. But there are some women who possess a simplicity and natural grandeur independent of gesture or movement. This springs from the heart, and is the result of good birth. They are gifted with a quiet, unassuming superiority, and many virtues, which the greatest modesty cannot hide from those who have eyes to see.

I have often wished I could be a girl, a beautiful girl of course, from thirteen to twenty-two ; after that, a man again.

Some young persons are not sufficiently grateful for the advantages bestowed on them by kind nature, and do not know how they ought to cherish them. Rare and fragile are those gifts from heaven, but they weaken and spoil them by affectation. Their tone of voice, their mien and gesture are artificial ; they are constantly examining themselves before a mirror, and endeavouring to be as unlike themselves as possible. And they take all this trouble to make themselves less agreeable.

If women only desire to be beautiful in each other's eyes they may, of course, follow their own caprice or taste, as to the way in which they dress and adorn themselves ; but if they desire to please men, if it is to charm them they rouge and paint, I can assert, in the name of mankind, or at least of those men whose votes I have taken, that white and red paints make women look old and hideous, that it is as disgusting to see women with paint on their faces, as with false teeth in their mouths and waxen balls to puff out their thin cheeks ; and that far from countenancing it, men solemnly protest against all such arts, which infallibly tend to cure them of love. If women were by nature what art makes them, if they were to lose in a moment their fresh complexions and their faces were to become as brilliant or as leaden-hued as they make them by rouge and paint, they would be inconsolable.

A coquette never loses her passion for admiration, or the high opinion she has of her own beauty. The passing years are regarded by her only as periods which wrinkle and disfigure other women ; she forgets that age is written on the face, and that the dress which enhanced her youthful beauty is most unbecoming to her now, serving only to heighten the ravages of age. A mincing affectation attends her sick bed, and till the end she is decked out in brilliant ribbons.

A beautiful face is the finest thing we can see, and the sweetest music is the sound of the voice we love best.

Liking is optional. Beauty is a reality, and is independent of taste and opinion.

———

There are some women of such radiant loveliness and such perfect goodness that to see them is to love them, even if we can never hope to converse with them.

———

A beautiful woman with the acquirements of an accomplished man is the most delightful acquaintance in the world, for her conversation has the charm of both sexes.

———

Impulsive little attentions from the fair sex are very bewitching and highly flattering to those to whom they are addressed. Men are rarely impulsive, their endearments are voluntary or deliberate, they speak and act from choice, and are seldom persuasive.

———

A woman's caprice very often counteracts the effect of her beauty, and is the antidote to the heart-sickness she creates.

———

Women attach themselves to men by the favours they grant. Men are lured by these same favours.

———

A woman is capable of forgetting a man she no longer loves to the extent of forgetting even the benefits she has bestowed on him.

———

A woman who has only one lover thinks herself no coquette. She who has many lovers thinks herself only a coquette. Such a woman may avoid being a coquette by an attachment to one in particular, but will be called a fool for having made a bad choice.

An old love is of little consequence; he must give way to the new husband, whose supremacy, alas! lasts such a little while that a new lover jostles him out of his place.

The old lover fears or suspects the new rival according to the character of his mistress, and he frequently owes his continued favours to the fact that he is not the husband.

An *intriguante* is more than a coquette, and a male flirt is worse than gallant. A male flirt and an intriguing woman are a match for each other

Few intrigues are secret. Many women are not better known by their husbands' names than by their lovers'.

An intriguing woman desires to be beloved, a coquette is satisfied if she is thought worthy of love and is acknowledged to be a beauty. One seeks to make an engagement, the other to make a conquest. The first breaks many engagements, the second has several flirtations in hand at once.

Passion and pleasure are dominant in one, vanity and frivolity in the other. Intrigue is a fault at heart, probably constitutional obliquity; coquetry is irregularity of mind. The intriguing woman is feared, the coquette inspires dislike. From the two characters might be formed a third worse than either.

A weak woman receives reproach with self-torment-ings, her heart is always at war with her reason. She would fain be cured of her failings, but will never have the strength of mind to surmount them herself, or at all events will do so very tardily.

An inconstant woman is one who is no longer in love ;

a false woman is one who already loves another ; a fickle woman knows neither whom she loves nor if she loves at all ; an indifferent woman does not love at all.

Treachery, if I may name it, means falsehood of the whole nature. In a woman, it means putting an action or a word in a wrong light, perverting everything, and often involves the breaking of most sacred promises.

A faithless woman, if she is known to be such by the person concerned, is simply faithless ; but if she is trusted in she is perfidious. The only good thing a woman's treachery does, is to cure us of jealousy.

Some women have two characters to keep up, two parts to play in the world, both equally difficult. One requires nothing but a contract, the other nothing but a heart.

To judge of that woman by her beauty, her youth, her pride, and her *hauteur*, one expects that nothing less than a hero will captivate her. But behold her choice is made. A little monster without a grain of sense !

Women who have passed the springtime of life seem naturally to fall to the lot of young fellows who have no great fortune. I know not who is most to be pitied, the woman advanced in years who requires a lover, or the young man whose needs force him to marry an old woman.

The riffraff of the Court will be received in the city boudoir, where he ousts even the judge in his gala dress, and routs the citizen in sword and wig, possessing himself of the field and receiving all the attentions. It is impossible to resist a gold scarf, a white plume, and a man who talks to the king and associates with his ministers. He no doubt makes enemies, male and female, but has many admirers, although not four leagues off he is pitied.

A provincial woman regards a man about town as a city lady does a *habitué* of the Court.

———

A vain man with little wit and a voluble tongue, who speaks of himself with assuming confidence, and of others contemptuously, who is proud, brusque, and adventurous, without breeding or honesty, morality or sense, requires no more to make him admired by certain women than good features and a fine figure.

———

Is it love of something clandestine or a depraved taste that makes one woman love her valet, another a monk, and *Dorina* her physician?

———

Some women can be generous to the church and to their lovers at the same time, both charitable and artful. They have even at the altar rails a place to read their love notes, while they are supposed to be at their devotions.

———

What kind of woman is she who is directed, as it is called? Is she a woman who is more dutiful to her husband, kinder to her servants, devoted to her family, careful of her concerns, sincere and zealous towards her friends? Is she not at all the slave of moods, not selfish or luxurious? I do not ask if she loads her children with gifts ; they may have no need of them; but out of her superfluity does she provide them with every necessary which is their right?

Is she exempt from self-love and neglect of others, or free from worldly employments and entanglements? "No," you answer, "she is none of these things." But I insist on knowing what is a woman who is directed? Oh ! I now understand, she is a woman who has a director.

If the confessor and the director cannot agree upon some rule, what third person can a woman ask to arbitrate the point?

———

A woman's chief thought should not be to provide herself with a director, but to live so discreetly that she has no need of one.

———

If a woman could, along with her other weaknesses, tell her confessor that which she has for her director, and the time she wastes in his company, perhaps it might be made her penance to renounce him.

———

It is too hard for a man to have a wife who is both a coquette and a bigot. Surely one of these qualities is enough for a woman.

———

I have now something to say which I have had difficulty in suppressing so long; but now it must come out, and I only hope the frankness of my words may be useful to those women who, thinking a confessor is not enough to guide them, use no judgment in. their choice of a director. I cannot express my admiration and surprise at beholding some people who shall be nameless. I gaze wonderingly at them; they speak, I listen, I inquire; I am told certain things, and I meditate upon them.

I cannot comprehend how persons in whom I seem to see everything directly opposed to common sense, sound reason, worldly experience, knowledge of mankind, religion and morality, should presume to assert that heaven would, in their persons, renew in our generation the miracle of the Apostleship; making ignorant, pretty creatures like them capable of the ministry of souls, an office which, above all others, is noble and sublime. More than this, if those persons consider that they have been born to fill such high and holy functions, which very few are qualified for, and if they are persuaded that in doing so they are following their vocation and exercising their natural talents, then I understand the matter still less.

I can see plainly that it is pleasant to them to be made the depositaries of family secrets, and to be thought indispensable in all social and domestic difficulties, and, generally speaking, to find every door open to them, a place at every table, even the highest. It is also pleasant to drive about town in somebody's comfortable carriage, and enjoy a delightful country retreat, to see many people of rank and distinction so interested in their health and prosperity ; and it may also be a congenial occupation to manage the affairs of other people as well as their own : and I can only infer that these are the considerations for which the care of souls is made the plausible and irreproachable pretext, and out of which have sprung up in the world that inexhaustible supply of directors.

A woman is easily guided, provided a man gives himself some trouble. One man is frequently the chosen guide of many women. He cultivates their minds and memories, determines their religion, and he even undertakes to regulate their hearts. They will neither approve nor disapprove, praise nor condemn, till by look or gesture they are assured of his opinion. He is the guardian of their joys and sorrows, their desires, their jealousies, their loves, and their hates. He makes them quarrel with their lovers, makes mischief, and reconciles them again to their husbands ; and profits by the intervals. He takes care of their business affairs, petitions in their law suits, sees the judges for them ; finds a doctor for them, tradesmen, workmen ; dictates as to their lodging, their furniture, their equipages ; drives

out with them in town, is to be seen with them in
country walks, in their pew at church, their box at the
play ; pays visits to the same people at the same time,
travels with them to their favourite watering-places,
and has the best room in their country houses. He
grows old without losing his authority, having a little
wit and much leisure in which to preserve it.

Children and servants all depend on him. He began
by being esteemed, and ends by being feared; and
this old and necessary friend dies at last without being
regretted; and the dozen or so women over whom he
tyrannized inherit liberty.

In the play an actor exceeds nature ; a poet exaggerates in his descriptions, and an artist who paints from
nature heightens the sentiment, the contrast or the
postures, while he who copies, when he measures
exactly the sizes and proportions, will enlarge his figures,
and give to every part of his picture greater bulk than
belongs to the original. In the same way, prudence
imitates discretion.

There is a kind of false modesty which is vanity ; a
false pride which is trifling; a false grandeur which is
meanness; a false virtue which is hypocrisy; a false
wisdom which is reserve.

A prudish woman is accounted so from her bearing
and language; a wise woman is known from her conduct ;
one follows her humour and inclination, the other her
reason and affection ; one is serious and austere, the
other is on all occasions precisely what she ought to be.
The first hides her failings under a plausible exterior,
the second hides her depth of feeling under an air of
natural frankness. Formal prudery constrains wit, and
hides neither age nor wrinkles ; it rather gives cause
to suspect them. Wisdom, on the contrary, conceals

bodily defects and ennobles the mind ; it makes youth more piquant and beauty more dangerous.

Why should men be blamed because women have little learning? By what laws and restrictions have they forbidden them to use their eyes, and to read and retain what they read and show it in conversation or literary effort? Is it not rather they themselves who have introduced the fashion of ignorance, either through weakness of disposition or laziness, or care for the preservation of their beauty, or by inherent levity which prevents them studying anything thoroughly? Or is it the natural genius they have to employ their fingers, and the distractions of domestic detail, or an aversion to anything difficult or serious ; or because their minds are occupied with gossip or any pleasure but that of exercising the intellect? But to whatever cause men may attribute women's ignorance, they must rejoice that, as the sex have the pre-eminence in so many other ways, they should in this show to less advantage.

We regard a learned woman as we would fine armour ; it is artistically chased, rarely polished, of most fine and curious workmanship : but, suited only for a museum of art, it would be of no more use in the camp or hunting-field than a circus horse, let him be ever so well trained.

If I find learning and wisdom united in one person, I do not wait to consider the sex, I bend in admiration; and if you tell me that a wise woman is seldom learned, or a learned woman wise, you must already have forgotten what you have just read, namely, that constitutional defects have turned women from learning. Judge then for yourself if women who have the fewest of those defects will not likely be the wisest. Therefore, a wise woman is the more likely to become learned, but a learned woman being such by reason that she has

E

overcome many defects, surely shows herself the wisest.

———

It is difficult to remain neutral when two women who are equally our friends fall out about something which does not concern us. We are often obliged to choose between them or to lose both.

———

There are women who love their money better than their friends, and their lovers better than their money.

———

It is strange to discover in some women something stronger than love, I mean ambition and play. Such women make men virtuous, because they have nothing womanly but their clothes.

———

Women are extremes, they are either better or worse than men.

———

Most women have no principle : they are led by their hearts, and their morals depend on those they love.

———

Women love more devotedly than most men, but in friendship men have the advantage.

Men are the cause of women not loving each other.

———

. A man is more faithful to the secret of another than to his own. A woman, on the contrary, keeps her own secret better than another's.

———

A young woman's heart is never so engrossed by love as to have no room for ambition or self-interest.

———

There is a time when even the richest women ought to marry. They cannot allow their youthful chances to escape them without the risk of a long repentance. The importance of their reputed wealth seems to diminish with their beauty. A young woman, on the contrary, has everything in her favour, even in men's eyes ; and if added to youth she possesses other advantages, she is so much the more desirable.

To how many women has great beauty been of no service but to raise in them hopes of a great fortune.

A beautiful woman who treats her lover badly commonly gives him his revenge, for she throws herself away on an ugly, old, or unworthy husband.

Most women judge of a man's merit or good looks by the impression he makes on them, and will allow neither merit nor good looks to one who does not impress them at all.

A man who is anxious to discover what change age has made in him need only consult the eyes of the lady he addresses, and listen to the tone of her voice as she talks to him ; he will soon learn what he fears to know. But it is a hard school !

The woman who has eyes only for one person, or whose eyes constantly avoid him, leads us by both actions to the same conclusion.

It costs a woman less to say what she does not feel than it costs a man to say all he feels.

Sometimes when a woman is trying to hide from a man the love she feels for him, he is pretending for her a love he feels not.

A man may deceive a woman by a feigned attachment, provided he has no real one elsewhere.

A man blazes out against a woman who no longer cares for him, then consoles himself. A woman makes less noise, but her regret endures.

Idleness in women is cured either by vanity or love; but, on the other hand, in a naturally active woman idleness is the precursor of love.

It is pretty certain that a woman who writes with great warmth is touched, though it is not so certain that she is truly in love. A strong, tender love is more likely to be pensive and silent, and her most fervent desire is to be assured of her lover's devotion, not to convince him of hers.

There is a certain lady who seems to have buried her husband, or at least, expunged him, for there is never any mention made of him in society. No one knows if he be alive or not, and in the household he is a mere cipher, of no use except as an example of timid silence and perfect submission. The income is all settled on the wife, and she might almost be taken for the husband, and *vice versâ*. For months together they live in the same house without the least danger of meeting each other, less indeed than if they were only neighbours. He pays the butcher and the baker, but it is madam who entertains. They have nothing in common, not even their name, for they follow the Roman and Greek fashion, and have separate names ; and only time and a thorough knowledge of town talk acquaints you with the fact that Monsieur B. has been for more than twenty years the husband of Madame L.

Other wives have different methods of tormenting their husbands. They have no irregularities, but annoy them by continual reference to their high birth and good connections and the large dowry they brought, their beauty and attainments, and what they call their virtue.

Few women are so perfect that they do not give their husbands cause, once a day at least, to regret that they possess a wife, or to envy those who do not.

Dumb, stupid grief is out of fashion. Women weep, and talk, and lament, and are so affected by bereavement that every detail of their sorrow is repeated to you.

Is it impossible for a man to discover the way to make his wife love him?

The woman who has no susceptibility is one who has not yet met the man she must love.

In Smyrna there lived a beautiful young girl who was called *Emira*, and who was less known throughout the city for her beauty than for the propriety of her conduct and manners, and more especially for the complete indifference she displayed towards men; whom she saw with no more concern or feeling than she had towards her brothers or her girl friends. She could not credit the thousandth part of the follies which people told her love had been the cause of in old times; and those she saw herself she did not understand. Friendship was the strongest sentiment she had any comprehension of, and she owed her enjoyment of this experience to a young and charming girl of her own age, who was so sweet and made her so happy that her only desire was that the friendship should last for ever, not imagining that any other senti-ment could supervene to weaken the esteem and con-fidence she cherished so dearly. She was continually speaking of *Euphrosyne*, which was the name of that faithful friend, and all Smyrna talked of her and of *Euphrosyne.* Their friendship became a proverb.

Emira had two brothers, both young and handsome, so that all the women of Smyrna were in love with them, and she herself loved them truly, as became a sister.

There was a priest of Jupiter who had access to her father's house, and who, being struck by *Emira's* beauty, ventured to declare his passion to her, but was rejected with scorn. An old man, who, trusting to his noble birth and great wealth, had the same audacity, met with the same repulse. She was now triumphant, for surrounded by brothers, a priest, and an old man, had she not proved herself insensible? But it seems heaven had still greater trials to expose her to, which, however, only served to make her yet more boastful, and to confirm her reputation as a girl whom love had no power to touch. Of three lovers whom her charms had successively gained her, and at whose ardour she was not dismayed, the first, in a transport of love, stabbed himself at her feet ; the second, filled with despair that she would not listen to his suit, went to seek his death in the Cretan wars ; while the third languished and died from sleepless depression.

He who was to avenge all these had not yet appeared.

The old man who had been so unfortunate in his addresses cured himself at length by reflecting on his age and the character of the young person in whose eyes he had wished to find favour, and, desiring to see her sometimes, he obtained her consent to visit her. One day he brought with him his son, a young man of agreeable countenance and noble mein. *Emira* regarded him with unusual interest, but, as he was very silent in his father's presence, she judged he had not sufficient confidence, and wished he had had more. Next time he saw her alone, and then he talked enough,

and with plenty of spirit and humour ; but as he paid
little attention to her, and spoke even less of her and
of her beauty, she was surprised and a little indignant
that a man so handsome as he could show so little
gallantry.   She discussed him with her friend, who
expressed a desire to see him, and from that time he
had eyes only for *Euphrosyne*, displaying in many
ways his admiration of her beauty. And *Emira* the
indifferent become jealous, realized that *Ctesiphon*
meant all he looked and said, and that he was capable
not only of gallantry, but of tenderness.

From this time she was more reserved with her
friend, yet she longed to see them together again, so
that she might solve the matter.   The second interview
revealed more than she had feared, and changed sus-
picion into certainty.   She evaded *Euphrosyne*, and no
longer saw in her the virtues which had charmed her
before, and she lost all taste for her society.   She no
longer loved her, and this change made her feel that
love had at last taken the place of friendship. .

Ctesiphon and *Euphrosyne* met every day, loved,
became engaged, and married.   The news spread over
all the city that two persons who loved each other were
blessed with the rare felicity of happy marriage.

Emira hears the news, and is in despair, for she is now
sensible how great her love is.   She seeks *Euphrosyne*
again for the sole pleasure of beholding *Ctesiphon*, but
the young husband is still the lover of his newly wedded
wife, and only sees in *Emira* the friend of her who is
dear to him.

The unfortunate girl can neither eat nor rest ; she
becomes weak, and her mind becomes disturbed, so
that she mistakes her brother for *Ctesiphon* and
addresses him as a lover; then recollects herself and
blushes for her distraction, relapses into greater blun-
ders, but no longer blushes, for she is unconscious.

Her heart is awake at last, but too late; it is only folly
now.   She has intervals of reason, but only to lament
its restoration ; and the youth of Smyrna who had
found her so proud and hard-hearted, think now that
the gods have punished her too severely.

THE HEART.

In pure friendship there is a sensation of felicity which only the well-bred can attain.

Friendship may exist between a man and a woman, quite apart from any influence of sex. Yet a woman always looks upon a man as a man, and so a man regards a woman. This intimacy is neither pure friendship nor pure love. It is a sentiment which stands alone.

Love is born suddenly, without deliberation, either through temperament or weakness: some grace or beauty attracts, determines us. Friendship, on the contrary, grows by degrees through time and long familiar acquaintance. How many years of affection, kindness, and good service it takes to do what a lovely face or a beautiful hand will often do in a moment!

Time which strengthens friendship weakens love.

So long as love lasts it is self-subsisting, and is even fed by the very things which might rather seem powerful to extinguish it—caprice, severity, neglect, jealousy. Friendship, on the contrary, requires care, confidence, kindness, and congeniality, without which it would perish.

Perfect friendship is more rare than excessive love.

Love and friendship exclude each other.

He who has had the experience of one great love neglects friendship, while he who has spent all his devotion on friendship has made no progress on the way to love.

Love begins with love, and the very strongest friendship can only be changed into feeble love.

Nothing so resembles intense friendship as those intimacies we cultivate for the security of our love.

We never love truly except once, and that is the first time. The attachments which succeed are more voluntary.

Sudden love lasts longest.

The love which increases by slow degrees is too much like friendship ever to be a violent passion.

He who loves so passionately that he wishes he could love a thousand times more than he loves already, yields only to him who loves more than he would love.

Granted that in the intensity of a great passion it is possible to love another more than oneself, who has the truest pleasure—he who loves, or he who is beloved?

Although we are so fastidious in love, we pardon more faults in that than we will overlook in friendship.

He who loves deeply finds a sweet revenge in acting so that his beloved one shall appear ungrateful.

It is sad to love if our fortune is not enough to enable

us to heap benefits on those we love, and to make them so happy that they have nothing more to wish for.

A woman with whom we have once been deeply in love may, later in life, render us the greatest possible service ; but if she has been indifferent to our love, she will not receive much gratitude from us.

Deep gratitude is a sign that we have much liking and friendship for the person who has benefited us.

To be with those we love is happiness ; even if both are silent, the mere fact of being together is sufficient : we may each be dreaming of the other, or thinking of quite different things.

Hatred is not so remote from friendship as antipathy.

In friendship we confide our secrets ; in love they escape us.

It is possible to have a person's confidence without having his love. He who possesses the heart has no need of confidential information, all is open to him.

In friendship we perceive only those faults which may be prejudicial to our friends ; in those we love we see no faults, except those from which we suffer ourselves.

Jealousy is greatly dependent on temperament, and does not always mean passionate love. Yet a great love is always exclusive, and this is a paradox.

Our susceptibilities seldom disturb any one but ourselves. Jealousy makes others as well as ourselves uneasy.

Friendship does not cool without cause ; love diminishes for no other reason than that we have been too well beloved.

We are no more able to love always than to prevent ourselves loving sometimes.

Love is killed by disgust and buried in oblivion.

The beginning, as the end, of love is manifested by our anxiety to be alone.

To cease loving is one clear proof that the heart of man has its limits. To love is weakness, but often it is weaker still to try to cure love. We are cured as we are consoled. The heart cannot grieve for ever or love for ever.

There are certain losses for which our hearts ought to contain inexhaustible sources of grief. It is seldom through either moral excellence or strength of mind a great sorrow is overcome. We weep bitterly and are sorely touched, but at last either we are so weak or so fickle that we are comforted.

When an ugly woman inspires love it is a passion, for either the lover is strangely weak, or she has some secret and invincible charm more potent than that of beauty.

To try to forget a person is to continually think of him. Love has this in common with conscience that it is fed by the very arguments and considerations which are used to free us from it. We might weaken love if we could disregard it.

Our desire is that all the good fortune of those we love, or, if that is impossible, all their evil fortune, should come to them from our hands.

It is happier by comparison to mourn one we love than to live with one we hate.

However disinterested we may be with regard to those we love, we must sometimes force ourselves to give them pleasure by accepting their gifts. He who is capable of receiving a gift delicately displays as much generosity as he who gives.

To give is to act, not simply to allow our benefits to slip from us, nor to yield to the importunate demands of those who ask.

If we have been generous to those we love, we shall never be tempted by anything which may happen later to reflect on our benefits.

A Latin author has said that it costs less to hate than to love, or if you prefer it, that friendship is more costly than hatred. It is true, we are not expected to be liberal towards our enemies, but does revenge cost nothing? Since it is easy and natural to do evil to those we hate, is it less agreeable to do good to those we love? Should we not rather find it difficult and troublesome not to be kind?

There is pleasure in meeting the glance of one we have lately benefited.

I doubt if a benefit which falls on an ungrateful, and therefore unworthy, person, does not change its name, and if it is a thing which deserves gratitude

Liberality consists less in giving much than in giving appropriately. If it is true that pity and compassion are drawn from us by a kind of selfish fear lest we should ever be in the same circumstances, how does it happen that the unfortunate extract so little help from us in their misery?

It is better to run the risk of ingratitude than to neglect the distressed.

Experience teaches us that luxurious self-indulgence and hard-heartedness towards others is one and the same vice.

A laborious, hard-working man who does not spare himself will not be considerate for others, except for some very potent reason.

However unpleasant it may be to feel ourselves responsible for the maintenance of an indigent person, we seldom relish the better fortune which at last withdraws him from our patronage. In the same way, the pleasure which we feel in the exaltation of a friend is counterbalanced by the slight annoyance of seeing him become our equal or superior. He does not suit us so well thus, for we like to have dependants who do not cost us anything. We wish good fortune for our friends; but when it comes, our first feeling is not one of pure delight.

Some people delight in giving invitations to their house and table, and in offering their means and their services; all this costs little, and is of small value if they are not as good as their word.

One faithful friend is enough; it is even much to meet with one, yet we cannot for the sake of others have too many friends.

When we have done all we can to conciliate, and yet do not succeed, there is one resource left, which is to leave such persons alone.

To live with our enemies as if they might one day be our friends and with our friends as if they might be our enemies, is neither in accordance with the nature of hatred or the rules of friendship. It may be a good political maxim, but it is a bad moral one.

We ought not to make enemies of those who, if better known, might rank among our friends. We ought to choose as friends persons of such honour and probity that, should they ever cease to be our friends, they would never abuse our confidence, nor give us cause to fear them as enemies.

It is as pleasant to see our friends from inclination and esteem as it is irksome to cultivate people from interested motives. This is importunity.

We ought to court the favour of those we desire to oblige, rather than those from whom we expect benefits.

He who knows how to wait for what he desires will not despair if he happens to have to do without it. On the other hand, he who impatiently longs for a thing has been too much engrossed with the thought of it to feel that success rewards him for all his anxiety.

The things most wished for never happen, or if they do they come at such a time or in such circumstances as spoil the enjoyment of them.

We must laugh before we are happy for fear we should die before we have ever laughed at all.

Life is short if we only count the time when it is pleasant; and if we were only to reckon the hours we spend agreeably, it would take a great number of years to make up a life of a few months.

How difficult it is to be quite satisfied with any one!

It is hard for a proud man to forgive one who has found him out in some fault and who has good reason to complain of him: his resentment is never healed till he has regained his advantage by putting the other in the wrong.

As we become more and more attached to those we oblige, so we cordially dislike those to whom we have given great offence.

It is as difficult to stifle the resentment of an injury at first as it is to preserve the feeling after a certain length of time.

It is weakness which makes us hate an enemy and wish to be revenged, and it is laziness which pacifies us and makes us not pursue revenge.

A man will allow himself to be governed as much through indolence as from weakness.

There is no use attempting suddenly to control a man, and especially in matters of importance to him and his. It requires some address to prevent him feeling that you are trying to gain a moral power over him; shame or caprice would move him to resist the restraint. Let him first be guided in little things, and from thence the progress to greater things is certain. Even if at first your influence is only such as will persuade him to go to the country, or to return to town, it will end in your dictating the terms of the will by which his son is disinherited.

To direct or govern any one absolutely and long, it is necessary to hold a light rein, and to let him feel his dependence as little as possible. Some people will allow themselves to be controlled up to a certain point, and from thence are quite unmanageable, and will no longer be led. All at once the power of moral suasion is lost, and neither through reason nor affection can you move them ; some act thus from conviction, others from caprice. There are men who will not listen to reason nor to good advice, and willingly go wrong through fear of being controlled.

Others will allow their friends to dictate to them in little things, so that they in their turn may assume the right to dictate in affairs of more importance.

Drance would like to be thought his master's governor. His master, however, is not of the same opinion any more than the rest of the world. A servant who incessantly chatters to him he serves, laughs loudly in his presence, interrupts his conversation with others who have come to pay their court, seats himself as near his master as possible, or lounges about familiarly in his presence, even presuming to pluck his sleeve or tread upon his heels, is more likely to be thought a vain fool than a favourite. A wise man neither suffers himself to be governed nor seeks to govern others ; he desires solely and always to be governed by his judgment.

For my part, I would not object to yield myself up entirely to the guidance of another, provided he were a person of sound judgment. I would thus be sure of doing right without the trouble of deliberating, and should enjoy all the peace and tranquillity of one who is governed by reason.

———

All our passions are deceitful ; we conceal them as much as possible from the eyes of others, and even try to disguise them to ourselves ; there is no vice which

F

has not some spurious resemblance to virtue, and takes advantage of this.

The best and most agreeable conversation is that in which the heart has more influence than the head.

There are certain sublime sentiments, certain grand and noble acts, which are called forth more by our moral strength than by innate goodness.

There is scarcely any excess in the world so commendable as an excess of gratitude.

He must be a dull person indeed whom neither love, hate, nor necessity can inspire with wit.

There are some places we admire ; others we love.

It seems to me that wit, humour, passion, taste, and sentiment depend on the place we live in.

Only those who do well deserve to be envied ; but there is a still better course to take, which is to excel them.   This is a sweet revenge to take over those who give us the opportunity.

Some people keep from loving and from rhyming as two weaknesses they dare not encourage—one of the heart, the other of the head.

It sometimes happens in the course of life that our most ardent pleasures or most cherished attachments are forbidden us, and it is natural that we should regret them, for they cannot be surpassed: our compensation lies in the knowledge that we have had the moral strength to renounce them.

A PERSON with no character is insipid.

A fool is always troublesome, while a sensible man sees at once if his company is agreeable or if he is in the way ; he knows the exact moment to take leave before he has become tiresome.

There are many offensive wits, many more slanderous and satirical, and few delicate. A man must have polished manners, graceful language, and a good deal of imagination to carry off a light and playful conversation with success, for his airy jests are created out of nothing.

If we were to pay serious attention to all the vain and silly remarks in ordinary conversation, we should be ashamed to take part in it at all, and might take a vow of perpetual silence which would be more injurious to society than the most unprofitable talk. We must therefore accommodate ourselves to all minds, permit as a necessary evil false reports and vague political reflections, and listen patiently to the grand notions some men are continually airing. We must allow *Arontius* to utter his wise sayings, and *Melinda* to talk of herself, her nerves, her ailments, and her want of sleep.

We often meet with people who in conversation irritate us by using absurd phrases and novel or inappropriate words used by nobody but themselves and twisted into meanings quite at variance with the signification their inventors intended. They observe neither custom nor reason in their language, but follow their own fantastic genius. The desire to be thought witty gradually turns this jargon of theirs into their natural phraseology, and their ridiculous originality is accompanied by odd gestures and affected pronunciation.

However, they are quite pleased with themselves and their wit, which we admit they are not devoid of; but we regret they have not more, for we suffer from its puerility.

———

If we go much into society we cannot avoid meeting certain vain persons who are easy, familiar and assertive; they are the talkers, the others must listen. We hear them in the antechamber but need not fear to interrupt them, for their eloquence flows on without the slightest regard for those who come in and go out, or for the rank and quality of the company. They silence any one who begins to tell a piece of news, so that they may be left to report it in their own way, which is of course the only right way; did they not hear it from *Zamet,* or *Ruccelay,* or *Concini,** persons they never even spoke to and whom they certainly would not dare to address without some title of respect. At other times they will accost the most important guest, and in a confidential undertone inform him of some fact known to no one else, and which they would on no account tell to any one else. They suppress names to disguise the story and prevent applicability. And so the mystery grows. You beg them to be explicit, but it is

---

* Three of the Italian retinue of Marie de Médicis, the last being the unfortunate Marquis d'Ancre.

useless, there are certain things they cannot tell, certain persons whose names cannot be mentioned, their word has been given, it is a secret of the utmost importance ; to insist would be to demand an impossibility, for in truth they know nothing whatever of either the persons or the facts they speak of.

Arrias has read and seen everything ; at least he would make you believe so. He lays himself out as a universal genius, and would rather lie than be silent, or seem ignorant on any subject. At table a great man at some northern court is mentioned ; at once the words are taken out of the speaker's mouth, and *Arrias* refers to that distant country as if he had been born there ; speaks of the manners of its court, of its women, its laws, and its customs ; tells little stories of things which happened there, finds them amusing to himself and laughs heartily over the recollection. Some one ventures to contradict him, and to say flatly that what he affirms is untrue. *Arrias* is not put out by this, but gets angry with his opponent, saying, "Sir, I assert nothing I do not know to be true ; I heard it from *Sethon*, the French ambassador at that court, who returned thence a few days ago, and who is such a particular friend of mine he would keep nothing from me." Then, with greater confidence than ever, he resumes the thread of his discourse, when one of the guests informs him that he is *Sethon*, and that he has just returned from the Embassy !

I hear the voice of *Theodectus's* in the antechamber. The nearer he comes the louder he talks, and he enters, laughing noisily, and grinning from ear to ear. He is no less remarkable for the things he says than for the tone in which he says them. His noisy tumult is only quieted when he is stammering out some of his folly and vanity. He has so little regard for persons, place, or decorum, that he hits off everybody in turn, with the confidence of ignorance. No sooner is he seated than, quite unconsciously, he has annoyed the whole company. Dinner served, he is first at table, in the place of honour, ladies on his right and left, he eats, drinks, talks, jests, and interrupts, with no consideration for host or guests, abusing the toleration shown him ; indeed, any one would suppose he had given the feast, he assumes so much authority ; and it is less trouble to let him have his own way than to argue with him. Eating and drinking do not improve his manners, while at play he wins and laughs at the loser till he gives offence. The frivolous are on his side, and they excuse in him any amount of folly.

At last I give it up and disappear, unable longer to endure *Theodectus* and those who tolerate him.

Troilus is very useful to those who have too much money. He relieves them of their superfluity, and saves them the trouble of hoarding, locking coffers, carrying about keys, or fearing dishonest servants. He assists them in the pursuit of pleasure, and is even serviceable to them in their love affairs, which he regulates for them. He is the household oracle, his word is law, his every wish is anticipated. He orders that this slave shall be punished, ·that one whipped, and the other freed, and it is done. If it is noticed that a sycophant does not make him laugh, it must be that he displeases him, so he is dismissed. The master of the house must think himself fortunate if *Troilus* graciously leaves him his wife and children. At table his taste decides which dishes are dainty, which insipid. He is seldom to be found elsewhere than in the house of this rich man, whom he governs ; it is there he eats, sleeps, digests, quarrels with his valet, sees his work-people, dismisses his creditors. He rules with a high hand in the audience-chamber, where he receives the homage of those who are clever enough to know that they will best reach the master through *Troilus.* If some one comes in whose expression of countenance does not please him, he frowns and turns away from him; and if he comes up to him he sits still and takes no notice; he sits down beside him, talks, but is repulsed; if the new-comer persists, *Troilus* will move into another room, make for the staircase, and would rather jump down the whole flight, or even leap out of the window, than be forced to speak to a man whose face or voice he dislikes. He is himself fortunate in both, and they serve to insinuate and gain his ends, till at last every-thing is beneath his notice and he scorns to preserve his supremacy by the least of the efforts through which he gained it. It is quite a favour if occasionally he rouses himself from his silent reserve to contradict or even to criticize, unless it be once a day to show his wit. There is no use expecting that he will condescend to listen to any expression of your opinions or com-mend anything you do, or indeed that your courtesy and compliance with his wishes will be recognized.

The great gift in conversation lies less in displaying talent ourselves than in drawing it out of others. He who leaves your company pleased with himself and his own cleverness is perfectly well pleased with you. Most men would rather please you than admire you, and desire less to be instructed or even amused than to be approved and applauded, and the most delicate pleasure is to give it to another.

Too much imagination is not necessary either in our conversation or in our writings; it often produces vain and silly ideas which neither tend to make us wiser nor

better. Our thoughts ought to be guided by good sense
and right reason, and resolved by our judgment.

It is a very sad thing to have neither wisdom enough
to speak well, nor sense enough to be silent. This is
the origin of all impertinence.

To speak of a thing in tones of moderation, to say
simply that it is good or bad and to say why you think
so, requires good sense and a happy turn of expression;
and is not such an easy matter as it is to say with an
air of conviction which carries with it the proof of your
assertion, that the thing is execrable or that it is mira-
culously good.

Nothing can be more displeasing to God and man
than the habit of supporting the smallest subjects of
conversation by a jarring oath. An honest man who
says yes or no deserves to be believed, his character
swears for him, gives credit to his words and gains him
every confidence.

He who is continually saying he is a man of truth
and honour, that he wrongs no one and is quite willing
that any harm he has ever done to others should recoil
on himself, and swears in order that he may be believed, does not know how even to imitate an honest man.
A really honest man, with all his modesty, does not
know how to prevent people saying of him all that a
dishonest man says of himself.

Cleon says rude or unjust things, one or the other,
but he adds that he cannot help it : he was born *brusque*,
and what he thinks he says.

There is a knack of speaking well, speaking easily,
speaking justly, and speaking appropriately, or in good

taste.   It is offending against the latter to enlarge on the subject of some grand banquet you have just given before those who are reduced to poverty, to boast of sound health before the ailing, to entertain a man who has neither house nor lands with an account of your wealth, your estates, and your belongings, in short, to speak of your blessings before the miserable.   Such conversation is very hard for them, and the comparison they draw between your condition and theirs is hateful.

"Oh you!" says *Eutiphron*, "you are rich, or at least you ought to consider yourself so.   Ten thousand livres a year invested in land, why it is delightful; you are certainly fortunate."   Now he who speaks thus has fifty thousand livres a year, and thinks he has not half as much as he deserves.   But he reckons up how much you are worth, and what your expenses are, and if he considers you worthy of a better fortune, even of what he himself aspires to, he does not fail to say that he wishes you may get it.   He is not the only one who makes such ill-judged calculations and unkind comparisons; the world is full of *Eutiphrons*.

There are some people who cannot speak without giving offence.   They are sharp and piquant, their style is a mixture of gall and wormwood, sneering abuse and insults fall freely from their lips, and it would have been a blessing had they been born dumb or stupid.   The little wit and cleverness they possess does them more harm than other people's foolishness; sharp answers do not always satisfy them; they prefer to be the aggressors, and will attack with virulence; every subject they touch upon is treated with extreme bitterness, and while those present have their feelings wounded, the absent do not escape; they are like battering rams falling foul of every one.

We do not expect by this portrayal to reform such ill-natured people: when we see them, the best thing we can do is to fly from them with all our might, without ever looking behind us.

There are men of such disposition and character that we must be careful how far we trust them. We must say as little against them as possible, as it would never be believed that we were doing them justice.

I hate a man whom I cannot accost or salute till he has just recognized me, without the risk of being thought contemptible or contemptuous. Montaigne would say, " I must have perfect freedom, and be as courteous and affable as I like without being obliged to weigh the consequences. I cannot go against my inclination or act contrary to my nature which makes me meet people half way, provided they are my equals, and not my enemies. I reciprocate their reception and make enquiries as to health and occupation, and I offer my services if it seems they can be of use, without hesitating to think how much or how little, or to value my favours as some people do. He displeases me who, through the knowledge I have of his ways and manners, would like to deprive me of my frank liberty. How can I remember in an instant when I see such a man afar off that I must put on a grave and important expression, so that he may know that I consider myself as good as he is, nay, better? To do this I would have to call to my mind all my good qualities and his bad ones, and compare notes. This is too much trouble for me; I am not capable of such swift and subtle examination, and even if I could do this once, I am sure I should fail the second time. I cannot force myself to be constrained and proud for any man."

A man may have capacity and every virtue, and be well-conducted, and yet be unbearable. Manners which are often neglected as of no importance are frequently the points upon which a good or bad opinion of one is formed. A little care taken to be gentle and polite will prevent a bad impression. It requires very little to gain a reputation for pride, incivility, and disdain, and it requires even less to gain esteem.

Politeness does not always inspire kindness, justice, generosity, and gratitude ; it only makes a man appear to have those virtues which he ought to possess.

We may define the spirit of politeness though we cannot determine its practice. It has certain recognized rules according to time, place, and persons, and there are different rules for the sexes and for different conditions. Wit alone cannot attain it, but it may be gained by imitation, and practice perfects it. There are certain temperaments which are impressible through politeness, and there are others which can only be reached by talent or solid virtue. It is true that a polished manner sets off merit and makes it more agreeable, and that it is necessary to have very eminent qualifications to be bearable without it.

Politeness seems to consist in taking a certain amount of care about our words, and our manner of saying them, so that other people may be pleased with them and with us.

It is not polite to praise immoderately before those who have just been singing or playing for our amusement, some one else who possesses the same talent, or to commend another poet in presence of one who has just read his verses to you.

When we give an entertainment, make presents, or procure any pleasure for another, we may do it grandly or in accordance with their tastes. The latter way is the better.

It is rude to reject with indifference every kind of praise. We ought to appreciate that which is honestly given by people who praise in us what they see worthy of it.

A talented man who is naturally proud loses nothing of his pride and reserve by being poor ; on the contrary, if anything can soften him and make him more pleasant and sociable it will be a little prosperity.

It does not show a good disposition if we cannot bear with the many bad tempers we meet with in this world. In commerce copper is as necessary as gold.

To live with people who are continually at variance, and who make you hear first one side and then the other, is like living, so to speak, in a court of justice, hearing cases from morning till night.

There were two persons who spent their lives in close union. Their goods were in common, they had one dwelling, and never lost sight of each other. But after four score years they perceived that it was time to part and put an end to their intimacy. They had only one day more to live, but they could not risk passing it together. They were in such haste to break with each other before death came to part them that their forbearance could not last till then. They lived too long for good example : a moment sooner and they had died good friends, and left behind them a rare instance of a lasting friendship.

Family life is often torn by jealousy, distrust, and dislike, whilst outwardly the members seem happy, con-

tented, and peaceable, and we suppose they enjoy a
tranquillity which they do not know. There are few
households which can bear close examination; the visit
you make, stays a domestic quarrel which only waits
your departure to begin again.

Only those who have, or who have had, old relations
from whom they have expectations, can tell what they
cost them.

Cleantes is a very worthy person. He chose as his
wife one of the best and most sensible women in the
world, and each in his or her way gives much pleasure
in the society they frequent; such politeness and excellence is rarely met with ; they part to-morrow,
and the deed of separation is already prepared at the
notary's. There are, no doubt, certain virtues which
are incompatible and were not meant to be together.

A man may seemingly count on his wife's portion,
jointure, and settlement, but cannot be certain of his
peace. This depends on such a fragile thing as harmony between a daughter-in-law and a mother-in-law,
and often ends during the first year of married life.

A father-in-law loves his son-in-law and his daughter-
in-law. A mother-in-law loves her son-in-law but not
her son's wife. There is a law of reciprocity in everything.

A step-mother loves her husband's children less than
anything else in the world ; the more she dotes on
her husband, the more she is a step-mother.

Step-mothers make whole towns and villages miserable ; the country owes its beggars, vagabonds,

servants, and slaves to them more than to poverty itself.

G * * * and H * * * are neighbours, their estates adjoin, and the neighbourhood is very solitary, far from any town or society; one would expect that solitude and the natural yearning men have for society would draw them together. It would be difficult to say what trifles have prevented their friendship and roused an implacable hatred in their hearts against each other, a hatred which their children inherit. No family quarrel ever arose out of so little.

If there were only two men in existence and the whole world were divided between them, I am convinced that very soon some subject of dispute would arise between them, if only about their proper bounds.

It is frequently easier as well as better to agree in another man's opinion, than to bring him over to ours.

I am approaching a little town, I have reached an eminence from which I discover it; it is situated half way up the hill, a river runs beside its walls and flows into a lovely valley; it is sheltered from the cold, northerly winds by the thickly-wooded hill. The air is so clear that I can count its turrets and steeples; it seems to me like a beautiful picture painted on the hill-side; and I exclaim how delightful it would be to dwell there under such a heavenly sky! I descend into the town, and have not been there two nights till, like those who live there, I wish to get away.

There is one thing which never has been seen and apparently never will be seen on this earth. It is a small town which is not divided into cliques; where families

are united, relations trust each other; a marriage does
not stir up civil war; where disputes about precedence
do not crop up at every moment, from which all lying,
scolding, and gossiping are banished ; where one may
sometimes see the mayor and the sheriff talking amic-
ably together; where the people and the tax-collector are
not at daggers drawn; the bishop lives at peace with the
dean, the dean with the canons, the canons do not
disdain the chaplains, and they in their turn are able to
endure the curates.

Countrymen and fools are always ready to take
offence, and think you are laughing at or despising
them. It is best not to venture on the most innocent
joke unless it be among men of refinement and sense.

We seldom shine among great people ; their grandeur
keeps us at a distance, nor among the common people ;
they are so matter of fact that they repulse us.

Merit is discriminating ; it is mutually felt and distinguished. If we would be esteemed, we must
associate with estimable people.

He who holds himself apart and will not take a jest
should never make one.

We all have little failings which we do not mind
being bantered about, and we should choose similar
defects in others when we banter them.

It is the privilege of fools to laugh at talent. A wise
man is to the world what a fool is at Court, of no
consequence.

Mockery is often poverty of wit.

You believe a man to be your dupe ; but if he is only pretending to be so, who is the greater dupe—he or you ?

If you carefully observe those people who never praise, but are always finding fault, and are never contented with any one, you will find that they are people with whom nobody is content.

Pride and scorn have the opposite effect to that desired, if it be esteem.

Among friends the pleasure of society is increased by similarity of tastes as regards inclinations, and by some difference of opinion as to learning; thus in matters of taste we feel ourselves supported, whilst our minds are stimulated and instructed by argument.

Two persons cannot be great friends if they cannot forgive each other's little failings.

How many fine and useless reasons are laid before him who is in great trouble, to try and calm him. But circumstances are often too much for reason or nature. It is cold advice to be told to eat and drink, and not to kill oneself with sorrow, to live and be reasonable, it is not wise to grieve so deeply. Is this not equal to saying—are you not a fool to be so miserable?

Counsel is necessary in business affairs, but in society it is sometimes prejudicial to him who tenders it, and useless to the recipient. You remark, perhaps on some bad habit which is either not admitted as such or looked upon as a virtue. You mark out a passage in an author's writing, the very one in which he considers he has surpassed himself. In this way you lose the intimacy of your friends without making them better or wiser.

Some time ago a weak and silly kind of conversation was fashionable ; it turned mostly on trivial questions as to love ; and what is called passion or tenderness. Reading certain romances first started the habit among the best people of the Court and city ; but they soon discarded it, and the middle classes have now assumed it with all its doubtful witticisms.

If we sometimes pretend to forget names which we look upon as obscure, or if we affectedly mispronounce them, it can only be because we have such a high opinion of our own.

Sometimes, in a humorous mood or in the freedom of friendly conversation, we say silly things which we mean to be silly, and which are amusing simply because they are so ridiculous. This undignified style belongs to the people, but it has already infected the youth of the Court. True, we need not be afraid that it will take deep root, it is too stupid and crude an amusement to extend far in a country which is the centre of good taste and politeness. We ought, however, to show those who practise it that it is objectionable ; for although it is not a serious matter, yet in ordinary conversation it fills the place of something better.

I cannot choose between the people who say absurd things and those who repeat, as new, clever things which we all know already.

Lucan says a good thing ; there follows a happy expression in Claudian ; then a passage from Seneca ;

G

and then a long Latin quotation, cited to those who although ignorant of every word of it pretend to understand. It would be better to have sense and talent of one's own ; for then we might dispense with ancient quotations, or, having read carefully, we would choose the best and only quote them appropriately.

Hermagoras does not know who is King of Hungary, and is surprised when some one mentions the King of Bohemia. Do not speak to him of the wars of Flanders or of Holland, or at least do not expect him to reply, for he is confused as to dates, and does not know when they began or ended. Battles and sieges are all new to him, but he is well up in the wars of the giants ; he can tell you all about them to the smallest details. He can with equal ease pierce the mist of that dreadful chaos in which the Babylonian and Assyrian monarchies existed ; he is deeply read in Egypt and its dynasties. He never saw Versailles and never will see it, but he nearly saw the tower of Babel ; he has counted the steps and knows how many architects were employed, and has discovered their names. I believe that he supposes Henri IV. to be the son of Henri III.; at all events he has not thought it worth while to know anything about the houses of France, Austria, or Bavaria ; mere trifles ! he says, while he can recite from memory the long list of Kings of Media and Babylon, and such names as Apronal, Heregabal, Noesnemordach, and Mardokempad, are as familiar to him as those of Valois and Bourbon to us. He asks us if the Emperor is married, but he knows all about Ninus and his two wives. You tell him that the King enjoys perfect health, and he remarks that Thetmosis, a King of Egypt, was healthy, and that he inherited a good complexion from his ancestor Alipharmutosis. What does he not know ? What in

all venerable antiquity is hid from him? He will tell
you that Semiramis, or, as some call her, Serimaris,
spoke so like her son Ninyas, that their voices were
not distinguishable; but he dare not decide whether the
mother had a manly voice like her son, or the son an
effeminate voice like his mother. He reveals to you
that Nimrod was left handed, whilst Sesostris could
use both hands with equal ease; and that it is a mistake
to suppose that one of the Artaxerxes was called
Longimanus because his arms reached to his knees,
and not because one of his hands was longer than the
other; and he adds that there are authors who gravely
affirm that it was his right hand, but he has good
reason to believe that it was the left.

Profound ignorance makes a man dogmatic; he who
knows little thinks he may teach others what he has
just learned himself; whilst he who knows a great deal
can scarcely imagine that others can be ignorant, and
therefore he speaks with more impartiality.

Great things should be simply spoken, emphasis
spoils them. Little things must be said in a dignified
manner, they require the support of a deep-toned
delivery.

We can generally say things more wittily than write
them.

An honourable birth, and a good education, are almost
the only things which make a man capable of keeping
a secret.

Confidence is dangerous if it is not entire. With but
few exceptions it is best either to tell the whole truth or

nothing. We have already told too much to a man from whom we think it necessary to conceal one circumstance.

Nicander entertains *Eliza* with stories of the tender, kindly manner in which he lived with his wife from the day of their marriage till her death. He has already told her how much he regrets that she left him no children, and he now repeats it. He talks of his houses in town and his estate in the country, and he calculates the income it yields. He describes the situation and the plan of the house, and enlarges on the convenience of the rooms, and also on the beauty and elegance of the furniture. Assures her that he likes to live well and in good style, with carriages and horses ; and regrets that his wife did not care more for play and society. "You are so rich," remarks a chosen friend, so that *Eliza* may hear, "so rich, why don't you buy that post, or why don't you add such and such a domain to your own ?" "Oh," replies *Nicander,* modestly, people credit me with greater wealth than I possess." He does not forget to refer to his connections either— *the treasurer, my cousin; my kinswoman, the chancellor's wife,* this is his style. He tells her a story which shows how dissatisfied he is with his nearest relations, even his heirs, and asks *Eliza* to judge if he has not been deeply injured, and does she think he can be expected to do them more kindness. Then he hints that he is in a feeble languishing state of health, and speaks of the vault where he desires to be interred. He insinuates himself into the good graces of all those who are very intimate with this lady he courts. But *Eliza* has not the courage to be made rich at the cost of being his wife ; and whilst he is still talking a cavalier is announced whose presence alone is enough to knock down the battery raised by this citizen : he rises disconcerted and chagrined, and departs to tell some one else that he is anxious to marry again.

———

Wise men often avoid the world, so that they may not be wearied by it.

A RICH man may eat of fine dishes, decorate his ceilings and alcoves, enjoy himself in his palatial country residence or in a splendid town mansion, have a great retinue of servants, marry his daughter to a Duke, and buy a title for his son—this is all right, and within his power; but contentment belongs to another man.

High birth or great wealth sets of merit, and makes it sooner appreciated.

If anything can justify a foolish man's ambition, it is the trouble he takes, after he has made his fortune, to discover some imaginary merit great enough to give him the importance he considers himself worthy of.

As wealth and favour desert a man it is discovered that he is a fool, although nobody discovered it in his prosperity.

If we did not see it every day could we ever imagine the extraordinary disproportion a few pieces of money more or less make between men?

This more or less decides whether a man is to follow the profession of arms, the church, or the long robe; and this is almost its sole vocation.

Two merchants were neighbours, and engaged in the same business, but in the end their fortunes were very different. Each of them had an only daughter, and they were brought up together, and lived in such intimacy as was natural for young persons of the same age and condition. Years later one of them in great distress sought to find a situation, and at last entered the service of a very great lady, one of the first rank at Court. This was the companion of her childhood !

If the financier misses his aim, the courtier says of him—he is only a citizen, a nobody, quite a low-bred fellow. If he succeeds, the courtier asks for the honour of his daughter's hand.

Some men in their youth have served an apprenticeship which has well fitted them to exercise a very different one for the rest of their lives.

A man is ugly, deformed, and weak-minded. It is whispered in my ear, he has fifty million livres a year. That concerns him alone, and I shall never be the better or the worse for it. What a fool I should be were I to begin to look at him with different eyes, and not remain master of my own judgment.

It is vain to attempt to turn a rich fool into ridicule ; the laughers are all on his side.

Clitiphon, I have need of you, and have risen early from my bed to go and see you. Would that my misfortunes did not require me to trouble and annoy you ! Your slaves tell me that you are invisible at present, and cannot see me for a whole hour. I return before the time mentioned and they tell me you have gone out. What are you doing, *Clitiphon*, in your private room, that you will not see me, what is the important labour which prevents you listening to me?

Are you filing your accounts, comparing your memoranda, signing papers, writing explanatory notes, or what, whilst I wait with only one question to ask you, to which you would have but one word to answer, yes or no? If you desire to be important, render service to those who require it of you, and you will be more esteemed than by making yourself so scarce. You are a man of note at present and full of business, but the time may come when you will have need of my services; come then into the privacy of my apartment, the philosopher will be accessible. I shall not put you off till another day. You may find me occupied with Plato on the immortality of the soul, or pen in hand calculating the distance between Saturn and Jupiter: for I admire the Creator in all his works, and I endeavour by acquiring a more perfect knowledge of the truth to regulate and improve my mind. Come in, all the doors are open, my ante-room is not a place of weary waiting, come straight in to me without any ceremony. You bring me something more precious than silver or gold, if it is the opportunity of obliging you. Tell me, what do you wish me to do for you? Must I leave my books, my studies, my writing, the line I have just begun? Ah, but I am very happy to be interrupted if I can be of use to you!

The monied or the business man is a bear, we dare not approach his den; even at home we cannot see him without a great deal of trouble. What am I saying? He is not to be seen at all, for at first we are told we cannot see him yet, and then that we can see him no more. The man of letters is quite different, he is as common as a mile-stone, and can be seen at any time, anywhere, by anybody; he is of no importance, and does not wish to be.

———

Let us not envy some people their great wealth; the

burden of it is very heavy, and would not suit us at all. To possess it they have sacrificed health, rest, honour, and conscience, and this is too high a price ; there is no profit in such a bargain.

The P. T. S.* rouse all evil passions in us one after the other. First we despise them on account of their obscurity, then we envy them, then hate, then fear, and sometimes we esteem and respect them ; and if we live long enough our concern with them will end in compassion.

Sosia rose from a footman's livery through a receiver's office till he got a sub-lease of the revenue taxes ; and by extortion, violence, and abuse of trust is now advanced on the ruin of several families to a high station. Ennobled by his position, all he now lacks is honesty.

Arfuria used to go alone and on foot to church, and had to listen to the sermon of the bishop or the priest from behind a pillar where she lost half the words, and only saw the preacher indistinctly. Her virtue was obscure, but her devotion was as notorious as her person. Her husband has got into one of the public offices and has in less than six years made an immense fortune. She now comes to church in a coach, and her heavy train is carried by pages, the preacher pauses while she seats herself, for she now sits well in front, and loses not a tone or gesture. There is a plot among the priests as to who shall confess her; they all desire to give her absolution, but the curé has the privilege.

Wealth has not only gained another name for *Sylvanus,* but also good birth. He is lord of the manor

---

* An enigmatical reference to certain partisans.

where his ancestors were vassals. Formerly he was
not good enough to be the page of *Cleobulus*, now he is
his son-in-law.

Dorus is carried in a litter along the Appian way,
his freedmen and slaves precede him to make the
people turn aside to make room for him. He lacks
nothing but lictors. He enters Rome with his retinue,
and thinks that he triumphs over the meanness and
poverty of his father *Sanga*.

No one can put a fortune to better use than *Periander;*
it brings him rank, credit, and authority. People no
longer try to gain his friendship, they implore his protection. He begins to say of himself, "A man of my
position," and sometimes, "A man of my quality."
When he assumes these airs, there are none who
borrow money from him or who partake of his dainty
hospitality would think of disputing them. His
residence is magnificent, the external decorations
are Doric; the entrance is a grand portico, and
people mistake it for a temple rather than a private
house. He is the lord paramount of the neighbourhood, the man everybody envies, but whose fall they
would rather rejoice to see. His wife's pearls have
made even the ladies his enemies. Everything succeeds with him; as yet there has been nothing to
detract from all this grandeur, which he has acquired
by his own exertions. What a pity his decrepit old
father did not die twenty years ago, before the world
had heard anything of *Periander*, for how will he
endure the opening up of that old parish register:
odious papers these are, which make a man's extraction
so clear to the world that the widow and heirs are
often quite ashamed. He cannot hide it from the eyes
of a jealous town, and will be at the mercy of the

thousand or so malicious mourners who will insist on their privilege of attending the funeral. He could wish that on this account he were able to call his father a nobleman or even a gentleman ; for is he not now the esquire ?

How many men are like well-grown trees transplanted into a beautiful garden. It surprises us to see them there, as we never saw them growing ; so we have no knowledge of their beginning nor their progress.

If some who are gone were to return again to this world, and see their names and titles, estates and ancient castles in the possession of people whose fathers were probably their tenant farmers, what opinion could they have of our age ?

Nothing will more readily make us comprehend how valueless in God's eyes are wealth and grandeur, and the other advantages He bestows on mankind, than the dispensation He makes of them, and the kind of men who are best provided.

If you were to go into your kitchen, where all that skill and method can do is employed to please your taste, and tempt you to eat more than is necessary ; and if you were to examine too particularly all the dishes which compose the feast you give ; if you knew how many hands they pass through, and all the different processes they undergo before they arrive at the neatness and elegance which charm your eye, puzzle your choice, and force you to try them all ; if you were to see the whole repast anywhere else than on a well appointed table—how disgusted you would be. If you were to go behind the scenes at a theatre,

and see all the wheels, and weights, and ropes, and
consider how many people are necessary to put the
machinery in motion, what an amount of muscular, as
well as nerve power, it all means, you would say : are
these things the mainsprings of that most natural
scenery and beautiful spectacle, which appeared to act
of itself? and you would exclaim : what violent efforts
are required! In the same way, as regards men in
office, do not inquire too narrowly into the sources of
their fortune.

This fine, strong, healthy youth is patron of an abbey
and of two other benefices ; all together bring him in
26,000 livres of revenue paid to him in gold. Somewhere else I know 106 poor families who are never warm
throughout the whole winter, have no clothes to cover
them, and who often want bread to eat : their poverty
is extreme and shameful. How unequal this is ! Does
it not clearly prove that there is a future ?

Chrisippus was a newly created noble, the first of his
race. Thirty years ago his earnest desire was to have
some day an income of 2000 livres a year : this, he
said, was his highest ambition, and he repeated it so
often that many still remember it. He succeeded, I
know not how, in gaining such enormous wealth that
when one of his daughters married her dowry was the
sum which formerly was the utmost he aspired to have
as his own entire income. A similar sum is set aside for
each of his children, and he has many to provide for. This
is only the first of their inheritance ; there will be a great
fortune to divide at his death, and now at an advanced
age he is still employed in labouring to be yet richer.

That man who made your fortune, and that of several
other people, was not able to maintain his own or to

secure sufficient for his wife and children after his death. They live in miserable obscurity, and though you are well informed of their condition, you do not try to alleviate it. You have no time, in fact, you are too busy entertaining, and building a house of your own. Your gratitude moves you to preserve the picture of your benefactor, removing it, however, from your private room to the ante-chamber. How condescending ! Its next removal will be to the store-room.

A man who has been clever and capable enough to fill his coffers comes at last to think he has a head fit for government.

When we are young we are generally poor, for we have neither acquired wealth nor come into our inheritance ; we get old and rich at the same time ; so seldom is it that man can enjoy all his advantages at once ; and if it does happen to some, we cannot envy them ; for they may through death have lost so much that they deserve our compassion.

A man must be thirty years of age before he is fit to begin to make a fortune. He may have completed it at fifty, and he begins to build in his old age, and dies by the time his house is ready for the painters and glaziers.

What is the fruit of a great fortune, if it be not to enjoy the vanity, industry, labour, and expenditure of those who lived before us, and to labour ourselves in our time—planting, building, and acquiring for our posterity.

Men display their goods every morning to cheat the public; and pack them up at night, after having cheated all day.

In all conditions of life the poor man is nearer to honesty than the rich, who is not far removed from knavery. Quick wits do not bring riches. Whatever your profession or trade may be, a great display of honesty will help to make you rich.

The best and the quickest road to fortune is to convince others that it will be their interest to serve you well.

Men are forced by the necessities of life, and sometimes by the craving for riches or glory, to cultivate profane talents or to engage in doubtful occupations, the perilous consequences of which they disguise even to themselves. They generally abandon them in the end to embrace a circumspect devotion, which they never thought of till after they had gathered in their harvest, and were in the enjoyment of a well-established fortune.

There are miseries in this world which strike cowardice to the heart. Some are denied even necessary food ; they dread the winter and fear to live ; whilst others eat the earliest fruits, the seasons are forced forward, and the earth is made to yield its riches in advance to furnish them with delicacies. Obscure citizens, simply because they are rich, have the audacity to swallow in one morsel the living of a hundred families. I am not pleased with such extremes, and would not choose to be either so poor or so rich, but would find refuge in moderation.

The poor are troubled because they want for everything, and nobody comforts or relieves them. The rich are annoyed if they have to wait for the least thing, or if any one attempts to thwart them.

He is rich whose income is more than his expenses ; and he is poor whose expenses exceed his income.

Some people, although they had an income of two millions, would manage to have five hundred livres a year too little.

Nothing holds out so well as a moderate fortune; and nothing flies so quickly as a large one.

Nothing comes so near to poverty as great wealth.

If it is true that we are rich by as much as we have of unnecessary things, a wise man must be the richest man.

If he is poor who is always wanting something, the covetous and ambitious man must languish in extreme poverty.

The passions tyrannize over man, but ambition suspends every other feeling for the time, and gives him the appearance of virtue. *Tryphon*, who is possessed of every vice, I once believed to be sober, chaste, liberal, and humble, even devout. I would have believed it still had he not made his fortune.

There is no limit to a man's desire for riches and greatness; sickness overtakes him, death approaches, but even then with shaking limbs and withered lips he mutters of his *fortune*, his *position*.

There are but two ways of rising in the world; one is by your own industry, the other by the weakness of others.

Features may disclose the disposition and manners, but a man's appearance indicates his fortune; his expression will tell if he has more or less than 1,000 livres a year.

Chrysantes, a wealthy and insolent man, was ashamed to be seen with *Eugenius*, a man of great merit, but poor *Eugenius* had exactly the same feeling for *Chrysantes*, so there seemed little chance that they would often run against each other.

———

When I now meet certain persons who in former times used always to anticipate my civilities, they wait till I first salute them, and are very punctilious : I say to myself, "Oh, very well, I am delighted things are so flourishing with you ;" for I am quite certain he is living in a grander way than formerly ; that he has got into some lucrative post and has already advanced his fortune. God grant that it may continue, and in a short time he will be in a position to despise me.

———

If thoughts, books, and their authors were dependent on the wealthy and those who have risen to wealth, what a hard fate they would be under ! How seldom the learned would be heard of ! They would be domineered over and dictated to, and treated with contempt as poor wretches whose merits have not advanced their fortunes, and who do nothing but think and write down wisdom. We must confess the present time is for the rich, and the future for the virtuous and learned. Homer lives still and will live for ever, when the treasurer and tax-collector are no more. Have they ever existed ? we ask. Were their names or their country known ? Were there any revenue farmers in Greece ? What has become of all the important personages who despised Homer, who took care to avoid him in the public places, who scarcely returned his salutation, and scorned to invite him to their tables, who regarded Homer only as a man who was not rich, and had written a book ? What will become of the hawks of the State, they who farmed the king's revenues ? Will they be handed down to posterity like Descartes, who was born in France and died in Sweden ?

The same pride which makes a man hold himself so much above his inferiors makes him cringe and fawn on his superiors. It is characteristic of a vice which is founded neither on personal merit nor on virtue, but on riches, position, and useless knowledge, to despise those who have less of these things, and to over-estimate those who have more than ourselves.

Whilst *Orortes* was increasing in years, wealth, and estates, a daughter was born in a certain family. She grew up and increased in beauty till she entered her sixteenth year. He at fifty desires to marry this young, beautiful, and accomplished girl : a man without birth, learning, or the slightest merit, and she prefers him to all his rivals.

Marriage, which ought to be the fountain of all good things, is often by the turn of fortune a heavy burden under which a man succumbs. This is the case when wife and children become a temptation to fraud, falsehood, and unlawful gain ; he finds himself hemmed in between poverty and knavery : strange solution of a problem. To marry a good Frenchwoman, who is a widow, means to make your fortune, though it does not always turn out what it seems to mean.

Dine well, *Clericus*; have a good supper ; pile the wood on the fire ; buy yourself a fine cloak ; hang your room with tapestry. You know you don't love your heir ; you do not know him, indeed, or you have not one at all.

When we are young we provide for our old age : when we are old we save for death. The prodigal heir pays for an ostentatious funeral, and devours the rest.

H

The dead miser spends more in a single day than he spent living in ten years; and his heir more in ten months than he has been able to part with in all his life.

What one wastes he steals from his heir; what one sordidly saves he steals from himself. A medium course is just, for ourselves and others.

Children would perhaps be dearer to their parents, and parents to their children, were it not for the title of heirs.

It is a sad condition to be in, and it makes life distasteful, if we have to drudge for, and watch over, and be dependent on some one for a little money, or if we have to owe our fortune to the death of our nearest. He who has never longed to step into his father's shoes is a singularly honest man.

Very courteous and obliging is the person who expects to be our heir. We are never more flattered, better obeyed, paid more attention to, courted and caressed during all our lives than we are by him who believes he will gain by our death, and wishes it would come.

Titles, posts, and successorships make all men regard themselves as each other's heirs, and consequently self-interest makes them continually cherish a secret desire for each other's death. In every condition of life the happiest man is he who has most to lose by another's death, and who will be most missed by his successor.

Not even in the House of Assembly, or in the Court of Justice, will you behold anything so grave and

serious as a table of gamblers playing high. A melancholy severity sits on their countenances. Inexorable
towards each other and unrelenting to their enemies,
whilst the play goes on they recognize neither relationship, friendship, nor distinction. Chance alone, blind
chance, that fierce divinity, presides at that table, and
exercises an absolute control, and they honour her by
a profound silence and engrossed attention, which elsewhere they would not be capable of. All other passions seem suspended to make way for this. The
courtier is no longer a pleasant flatterer, or even attentive.

In those who have made their fortunes at the gaming-
table we can trace no sign of their former condition.
They lose sight of their equals, and associate with
people of higher rank, although it often happens that
the accidents of the die or the exigencies of lansquenet
put them back again in their original position.

Thousands have been ruined by gaming, and yet you
say calmly that people could not get on without play.
What foolishness ! Is there any passion, however
shameful or violent, which might not put forth the
same plea ? Would we be allowed to say we cannot
live without murders, robberies, and suicides ? Why
then should play be allowed, hideous play, unbounded,
unceasing, where nothing is thought of but the ruin of
an adversary ; where one is transported by the desire
for gain, desperate over loss, consumed by avarice, and
where, on the turn of a card, we risk our own fortunes
and those of wife and children ? Is this a thing which
you cannot live without, which even ought to be tolerated ? And these are not the worst consequences of
this folly; utter ruin follows, till food and clothing of
families are sacrificed.

I would have no one be a cheat, but I would allow only
a cheat to play high. I would forbid an honest man ;
it would be too foolish to expose himself to a great
loss.

There is only one lasting affliction, and that is the
loss of fortune. Time, which softens all others, increases
this ; we feel it each moment in our lives in which we
are short of money.

If a man does not lay his money out to the best advantage, pay his debts and marry his daughters ; it
signifies nothing to any one except to his wife and
children.

Neither the troubles, *Zenobia*, which disturb your
Empire, nor the wars which, since the death of the
king your husband, you have so courageously waged
against a powerful nation have impaired the magnificence of your kingdom. You have chosen the shores
of the Euphrates on which to raise a stately palace.
The climate is healthy and temperate, the situation
charming. The western side is shaded by that sacred
wood, and the Syrian gods, who, it is said, frequent it,
could not choose a more beautiful abode. All the
country round is peopled with labourers hewing, carv-
ing, going and coming, conveying the wood of
Lebanon with brass and porphyry. The air is filled
with the noise of tools and the grinding of machines ;
and travellers, on their way to Arabia, hope, on their
return, to see the palace completed, with all the splendour you intend for it before you consider it fit for you
and the princes your children to dwell in. Spare nothing,
great queen, neither gold nor the most excellent workmanship. Let the Phidias and the Zeuxis of your age
display their art on your walls and ceilings. Lay out

great and enchanting gardens, which will seem too
luxuriously lovely to have been formed by the hands of
men : spare no industry and no wealth on this incomparable edifice. And then, *Zenobia*, when you have
perfected it, one of the shepherds who dwell on the
neighbouring sandy flats of Palmyra, enriched by the
toll-tax on your rivers, will disburse some of his riches
to buy your royal house, beautify and adorn it, and
make it more worthy of him and his fortune !

That palace, with its beautiful furniture, its gardens
and fountains, charms you, and at the first sight of this
delightful abode you exclaim how great must be the
happiness of the master. He is no more, his life was
neither so pleasant nor so tranquil as yours ; he never
knew a quiet day nor a peaceful night. He was inun-
dated with debts, contracted to adorn the building you
admire so much, his creditors drove him out, he turned
round to take one last look at it, and grief killed him
that instant.

If you have neglected no effort to make your fortune, how great your labour must have been ! If you
have neglected the smallest thing how great your
repentance !

PARIS.

IN Paris we meet without any previous appointment, as if it were a recognized *rendez-vous*. Punctually every evening in the drive or at the Tuileries we scan each other's faces and disapprove one of the other.

All the same we cannot do without this society, although we dislike it and make fun of it.

We wait for each other in the public drives, and pass in review before each other's eyes. Carriages, horses, liveries, nothing escapes the eyes which are curious or malicious to observe, and we carefully distribute our respect or our disdain, according to the grandeur or simplicity of an equipage.

Everybody knows the long bank* which bounds and confines the Seine, where it is joined by the Marne as it enters Paris. Men are fond of bathing at the foot of the bank in the dog-days; you may see them throw themselves into the water and come out again ; it is an amusement. The townswomen never think of walking there excepting during that season, and when it is over they no longer walk there.

In this public promenade, where the ladies assemble only to show off their fine clothes, and to enjoy the triumphs of the toilet, people do not choose their company for the sake of conversation. They walk together to talk over the play, to show themselves socially, and to strengthen themselves against criticism. This is

---

* The Quay St. Bernard.

where people talk without saying anything, or rather, they talk for the benefit of passers-by, on whose account they raise their voices, jest and bow, and pass and re-pass.

The town is divided into several cliques, which are like as many little republics, each of which has its own laws, customs, jargon, and jests; and so long as one of these little societies is popular, nothing is well said or well done, or enjoyed outside of it; and those who are not initiated in its mysteries are despised. If chance brings into it a stranger, even if he be a talented man of the world, he feels as if he were in a strange country, whose ways, and language, and manners, and customs he does not know. He sees people who buzz, and talk, and whisper, and laugh, and presently fall into a doleful silence. He feels quite lost, does not know where to put in a word or even when to listen. Even here there is always some man who, with his insipid jokes, makes himself the hero of the company, and seems to feel accountable for a certain amount of mirth on the part of the others, and is able to make them laugh before he opens his mouth. If at any time a woman comes among them, who does not join in their merry-making, the jolly company wonders why she does not laugh at things she does not understand, and appears insensible to nonsense which they would see no fun in themselves were it not their own; so they criticize her voice and her silence, and spare neither her face, her figure, or her dress, her manner of coming in or going out. Those clubs never last long, however; two years is the longest time a coterie keeps together. In the first year the seeds of division are sown: the next year dissension follows. A dispute about some beauty or some gambling incident it may be, or the extravagance of the feasts, which from modest beginnings soon degenerate into pyramids of dishes, costly banquets, causes dissatisfaction, which means ruin to such cliques, and in a very short time no more is heard of them than of last year's flies.

In the city there are members of the greater magistracy, and of the lesser; and the first avenge themselves on the second for the mortifications they endure at Court. It is not easy to discover where the greater ends and the lesser begins, there being a considerable number who refuse to belong to the second order who are not allowed to be in the first. They will not yield, however, and try by their gravity and expenditure to equal the council to whom they unwillingly give place. They are often heard to say that the nobility of their employment, the independence of their profession, their talent in speaking, and their personal merit, balance at least the bags of money which the sons of partizans or bankers paid as a premium for their posts.

What mean you by sitting idly dreaming in your carriage? Quick, take up your books and papers, study them, and scarcely salute those who bow to you from their grand equipages; they will believe you have an extraordinary amount of business, they will say, "That is a most laborious, hard-working man; he reads and studies even in the streets." Observe the smallest attorney, how he makes himself appear to be overwhelmed with business, draws his brows and thinks very deeply of nothing; pretends he has no time even to eat and drink, can very seldom be seen in his house, for he vanishes into his private room, where he is hidden from the public, and avoids the theatre, which he leaves to those who run no risk in appearing there.

There are a certain number of young magistrates whom the pleasures of wealth have associated with some of those who are called at Court "*petits-maîtres*," and whom they imitate, behaving in a manner beneath the dignity of the robe, thinking that their age and fortune absolve them from the necessity of observing moderation and discretion. They follow all the bad habits of the Court, and take to vanity, luxury, and intemperance, as if those vices belonged to them, affecting thus a very different character from that which they ought to maintain, and they end as they desire by becoming faithful copies of very wicked originals.

A man of the robe in the city and the same man at Court are two different men. Among his friends he resumes the manners, the gestures, and expressions he left with them : he is neither so perplexed nor so honest.

The *Crispins* club together and collect among the different families so that they may have six horses in their equipage, and with a swarm of men in livery, one from each, they make as much show in the park or at Vincennes as a newly married couple, or as *Jason* whose vanity will be his ruin, or as *Thraso* who is going to marry and has applied for a grand post.

I have heard of the *Sannions*, the elder branch, the younger branch, and the youngest branch of the younger house ; they all bear the same name, have the same coat of arms, only the first bears it plain, the second adds a label, and the third has it indented ; like the Bourbons, they blazon the same colours on the same metal, and like them also they support two and one. They are not fleurs-de-lis, but they console themselves no doubt by thinking in their hearts that their bearings are as noble, and they have them in com-

mon with persons of high rank who are satisfied with
them. Their escutcheons are to be seen in their
chapels, on their houses, and on the pillars of justiciary-
chambers, where they condemn a man to be hanged
who only deserved banishment. Everywhere we see this
coat of arms, on their furniture, on their locks ; their
carriages are emblazoned here and there, and their
liveries do not dishonour their arms. If I were to speak
plainly of the *Sannions*, I would say, "Your folly is premature ; you should have waited till one generation at
least of you had ended. Those who knew your grandfather are old, they cannot live long, and after them
who will be able to say that he kept a shop and sold
his goods very dear ? "

The *Sannions* and the *Crispins* would rather be
thought extravagant than economical ; they tell long,
tiresome stories of feasts and entertainments they
have given ; they talk of the money they have lost at
play, and patronize those who have no money to lose ;
then they indulge in mysterious hints about the ladies
of their acquaintance ; and they have always a hundred
pleasant things to relate to each other, new discoveries
they have made, trying to appear very full of adventure.
One of them goes to bed late in the country, sleeps well
and rises early, dresses in his hunting suit, with all his
accoutrements, ties his hair in a knot, takes up his gun,
and behold a sportsman, if only he could shoot. He
returns at night, wet and muddy, having killed nothing ;
he does the same thing next day, and in this manner
passes his time missing thrushes and partridges.

You say you have seen that man somewhere, but you
cannot remember where, although his face is familiar.
He is well known to others, and if possible I shall
assist your memory. Was it in driving in the boulevard,
walking in the broad walk of the Tuileries, in the balcony

at church, at a ball, at Rambouillet, at the play? In fact
where did you not see him? Where is he not to be
met? If there is an execution or a display of fireworks,
he is sure to appear at a window of the Hôtel de Ville.
If there is a grand review, he has a place on some
platform; a tournament, he is in the amphitheatre. It
the king receives an ambassador, he sees the proces-
sion and assists at the audience, and gets into the
line on the return. His presence is as essential at the
swearing in of the Swiss cantons as that of the Chancellor of the League himself, and his face is present
in all illustrations of the event. He is at every hunt
meeting, every camp-out, and every review. He loves
war, the troops, the militia, understands all the military manœuvres; he is an old sightseer, a spectator by
profession, a man who does nothing he ought, but
boasts he has seen all there is to see, and now will not
regret to die. What a loss that will be to the town !
Who will there be to tell us the park-gates are closed,
and nobody walks there? Who will warn us that
Rochois is suffering from cold, and will not sing for a
week; that Beaumavielle died yesterday; where some enchanting fair is to be held? Who can tell at once who
everybody is by their arms or livery? and lastly, since
there is in this city as elsewhere such a number of dull,
lazy, ignorant fools, who will so exactly suit them all
as he?

Theramenes was rich and talented ; he is now the
heir, and is therefore very rich and very talented. All
the women want to flirt with him, and all their daughters want to marry him. He goes from house to house
to make the mothers think he means to marry. He no
sooner sits down than they retire to give their daughters a chance of charming him, or that he may declare
himself; and he sets himself up against the peaceful

lawyer, he eclipses the cavalier or the gentleman ; a gay,
bright, witty young fellow could not be more passionately desired or better received. They almost snatch
him out of each other's hands, and have hardly time to
smile upon any one else when he is present. How
many suitors has he already defeated, how many good
matches has he spoiled ; he cannot marry all the
heiresses who want him. He is not only the terror of
husbands, but the dread of all who are hoping through
marriage to repair their broken fortunes. Men like
him, so rich and fortunate, ought to be banished from
a well-governed city, and the fair sex ought to be forbidden on the pain of indignity and foolishness to
treat him better than if he had nothing but his merits
to recommend him.

The foolishness of some Parisian ladies in trying
to imitate those of the Court is very vulgar, it is worse
than the coarseness of a lower class or the rude brusque-
ness of villagers.

What a clever invention it is for the bridegroom to
make magnificent wedding presents which cost
nothing, as after marriage they will all be returned in
hard cash !

What a praiseworthy practice it is to spend on the expenses of your wedding a third part of your wife's
dowry. To begin by agreeing to impoverish your-
selves by collecting a heap of superfluities, and to
draw so soon on your capital to pay the upholsterer
and the cabinet-maker !

What troublesome, useless slavery it is for people to
be continually trying to meet each other, quite impatient if they do not meet, to say the most trifling

things, and to tell each other what they are each perfectly acquainted with, and which it would matter little if they did not know. Going into a room simply to come out of it again, going out after dinner and coming in again at night, quite satisfied to have spent five hours in seeing three of your friends' hall-porters, one woman you scarcely know, and another you don't like. If any one will rightly consider the value of time, and how irreparable is the loss of it, he will mourn bitterly over such wretched trifling.

City people pride themselves on their gross ignorance of rural and country affairs. They scarcely know linseed from hemp, wheat from rye, and neither of them from barley. They content themselves with eating and dressing. If you want to be understood, you need not talk to them of fallow ground, staddles, vine-shoots, or after-grass ; they will think you speak another language. To some of them you should speak of weights and scales, to others of petitions and appeals. They know the world, although they are ignorant of nature and her bounties ; their ignorance is often quite voluntary, and founded on the high opinion they hold of their own calling or profession : and the meanest practitioner in the depths of his grimy, smoky chamber, his mind occupied with pettifogging quibbles, prefers his life to that of the labourer who enjoys the free air of heaven, cultivates the earth, sows his seeds in their seasons, and gathers in his rich harvests ; and if at any time he hears of Abel or the Patriarchs and their simply country lives, he wonders how people could have lived in those days without officers or solicitors or presidents or commissioners, and it passes his comprehension to know what they did without registrars and courts of justice and refreshment-rooms.

The Roman emperors never obtained such luxurious service and convenient modes of triumphing over the rain, wind, dust, and sun as the citizens of Paris make use of every day. What an immense distance there is between their comfortable carriages and the mules of their ancestors, who never thought of depriving themselves of necessaries to obtain superfluities, to prefer vain display to solid use. Their rooms were not lighted by wax candles nor heated by stoves ; candles were sacred to the altar or the palace ; they did not rise from a bad dinner to drive in a carriage ; they were persuaded that men's legs were for use, and they walked ; they were dry when the weather was fine, and when it rained they put up with muddy boots, and thought no more of crossing the wet streets and courts than a sportsman thinks of crossing a ploughed field. They had not yet thought of harnessing two men to a chair; there were even magistrates who walked on foot to the law courts with as good a grace as Augustus walked to the Capitol. Pewter in those days shone on the tables and sideboards, and brass and steel in the chimney corners ; silver and gold were stored in their coffers. Women were waited on by women who even served in the kitchens. Such titles as governor and governess were not known to our fathers ; they knew to whom the care of the children of kings and princes was confided, but they shared with their domestics the charge of their own children, content to superintend themselves their regular instruction ; they lived according to their means : their liveries, their equipages, their houses, and their furniture were all appropriate to their incomes and condition. There were, however, outward distinctions among them which prevented any one mistaking the wife of a practitioner for that of a judge, or the plebeian for a gentleman. They were less anxious to spend or to add to their patrimony than to preserve it, and leave it entire to their heirs when they passed from a life of moderation to a peaceful death. There was no complaining of hard times, great poverty, scarcity of money ; they had less than we have, and yet they had enough ; they were richer by their economy and modest wants than by their revenues and estates. To conclude, in olden times people observed this maxim, that what is splendour and magnificence among the great, is extravagance, folly, and dissipation for ordinary people.

THE COURT AND COURTIERS.

IN one sense the most honourable reproach with which you can charge a man is that he is ignorant of Court life. There are no virtues we do not imply by this imputation.

An accomplished courtier is master of his gestures, his eyes, his face; he is deep and impenetrable; he can dissemble when he is doing an ill turn, smile on his enemies, restrain his temper, disguise his passions, act contrary to his feelings, speak against his convictions; and all this polish is only a vice which we call falsehood, and is sometimes of as little use to the courtier as candour, sincerity, and virtue.

Who can define those changing colours, which vary according to the light we see them in. In like manner who can define the Court?

The man who escapes from the Court for a moment renounces it for ever; the courtier who saw it in the morning must see it at night, so that he may recognize it next day, and be known there himself.

A man is of little importance at Court, and however much he may think of himself, he will find it is so; but the evil is universal, and the great are small there.

People in the provinces look upon Court life as something very admirable ; if they approach it, its attractions diminish like a fine perspective when examined too closely.

People have great difficulty in getting used to pass their lives in an ante-chamber, a court-yard, or on a staircase.

Court life does not give a man contentment ; it only hinders him from finding it elsewhere.

It is better that an honourable man should have tried Court life. It will have seemed like an unknown world to him, where vice and politeness have equal dominion, and where good and bad were equally useful to him.

The Court is like a marble edifice ; I mean it is composed of men who are hard, but very polished.

Some go to Court only for the distinction of it, and that, on their return, they may be taken notice of by the nobility and church dignitaries of their province.

The embroiderer and confectioner would be useless and superfluous were we modest and temperate. Courts would be deserted and kings almost desolate, if. we were destitute of vanity and self-interest. Men submit to be slaves in one place, that they may rule elsewhere. The grandees of the Court seem to purchase their airs of hauteur, pride, and authority wholesale, so that they may retail them in the provinces. They do exactly what is done to them—true apes of royalty.

The prince's presence has a strange disfiguring. effect on some courtiers, their faces alter so as to be

I

scarcely recognizable, their expression changes to contemptible servility, and the prouder and haughtier they are, the more marked the change.

He who is modest and honest bears himself best ; he has nothing to amend.

The air of the Court is contagious, it is caught at Versailles, as the Norman accent is caught at Rouen or Falaise.   We perceive it among outriders, grooms, and confectioners.   A man with a little aptitude acquires it easily, but a man of solid worth and culti-vation does not value this kind of talent sufficiently to study it and perfect himself in it, it comes to him intuitively, and he never thinks of throwing it off or eluding it.

N*** arrives with a great bustle, pushes everybody aside, taps, knocks, announces himself, and after a while he is admitted—but with the crowd.

I daresay you know some man who gives you a cold bow as he passes, squares his shoulders, and stretches his neck like a woman, looks the other way when he asks you a question, speaking in a loud tone, as if to indicate that he considers himself above everyone present.   If he stops speaking, the others crowd round him, for, as self-constituted president of the company, he does all the talking, and he persists in this ridiculous affected dignity till some real personage unexpectedly appears, whose presence quickly brings him down from his pedestal to his natural place, which is less mischievous.

Courts could not do without a certain kind of courtier, who can flatter, and insinuate, and pay devoted attention to the ladies, whose amusements he

arranges, while he studies their weaknesses and
smooths over their difficulties. He makes whispered
innuendoes or pleasant little remarks, speaks of
husbands and lovers in suitable terms, guesses at all
troubles and maladies, fixes the fashions, and improves
upon all the niceties of luxury and expense, and teaches
the sex the surest way to consume immense sums of
money in dress, furniture, and equipages. His own
dress shines with splendour, and he does not consider
an old palace fit to live in till it has been restored and
embellished. He eats slowly and delicately, and there
is no self-indulgence he has not tried and can describe. He owes his fortune to himself, and keeps it as
cleverly as he gained it. Proud and disdainful, he
scorns his equals, or no longer recognizes them; he
speaks when others are silent, and pushes in where
the highest nobility would not presume ; not even
those who, through long service, wounds, and honours,
have arrived at the highest dignity, show such an
assured countenance, and display such bold airs. Such
men have the ears of the greatest princes, are par-
takers of all their pleasures and dissipations, and are
quite at home in the Louvre or at Versailles ; they
seem to be everywhere at once, and their faces are
always the first to strike a stranger on arrival at
Court. They embrace, and are embraced. They
laugh, and talk, and jest ; are very agreeable and rich :
and of no importance.

One would suppose that *Cimon* and *Clitander* had sole
charge of the concerns of the state, and that they alone
were responsible, that one of them must be minister of
land, and the other of marine affairs. They are em-
bodiments of restless hurry, activity and curiosity, true
representatives of motion. They never sit, and never
stand, scarcely even walk, you may meet them running

and talking the while, and they will ask you questions but will not wait for your reply. They come from no-where in particular and go nowhere in particular, but are always passing and repassing : do not delay them in their precipitate course, you might put the machinery out of order. Do not ask them any ques-tions or give them time to breathe, or they might remember that they have nothing to do, and might stay with you a long time, go with you even wherever you please to take them. They are not like the satellites of Jupiter, I mean those who gather round the prince, they precede him and announce his coming, and rush so impetuously among the crowd of courtiers that all they meet with are in danger. Their profession is to see and be seen, and they never lie down at night without acquitting themselves of this duty which is so useful and important to the state. They are, besides, thoroughly well posted up in all kinds of gossip, and they know all the little incidents of Court life and intrigue which would be as well ignored. They possess every necessary qualification for their general advancement, being likewise wide awake and on the alert to any thing they think will advantage them, enterprising also and quick-witted: in a word they are carried by the wind, tied to the chariot of fortune though never likely to be seated on it.

A courtier whose name is not good enough for him ought to hide it under a better : but if it is one he may venture to bear, then he ought to insinuate that it is of all names the most illustrious, as his house is of all others the most ancient; he ought to be descended from the princes of Lorraine, from the Rohans, Chatillons, Montmorencies, and, if possible, from the princes of the blood : his conversation should be of Dukes, Cardinals, and prime ministers, with frequent

mention of his paternal and maternal ancestors, for
whom he should find places very near the royal
standard in the Crusades. His hall should be hung
with genealogies and escutcheons of six quarters,
pictures of his ancestors and their kindred by marriage,
he should pride himself on the ancient castle of his
family, its machicolated towers and battlements, take
every opportunity of speaking of " My race, my branch
of the family, my name and my arms." Say of this man,
" He is an upstart ;" of that lady " She is a nobody ;" or
if he is told that *Hyacinthus* has won the great prize, ask
if he is a gentleman? Some men may smile at such
accidents, but he will let them smile ; others may tell
a different tale of him, he will let them talk, maintaining persistently that he takes rank after the reigning
house, and by dint of reiteration he will be believed.

It would be very simple-minded to admit at Court
the slightest strain of plebeian birth ; there all are supposed to be gentlemen. In Court life men lie down
and rise up thinking only of self-interest; morning,
noon, and night, they act on it, think of it, speak of it,
are silent because of it, in this spirit they speak to some
and neglect others, ascend and descend, and by its
rule they note out their cares, attentions, esteem,
indifference, and their suspicions. Even if some of
them advance a little towards virtue, wisdom, and
moderation, the first promptings of ambition carry
them away with the covetous, who are the most
violent in their desires for still higher promotion.
How can one stand still when all are on the move ;
pushing forward, he must go with the tide. Men
think they are responsible to themselves for their
advancement and fortune, he who has not been successful at Court is censured as having been undeserving,
and from this there is no appeal. Whether is it better

to retire without having gathered any fruit or to persist in remaining without favour or reward? This is such a knotty question, so perplexing and difficult to decide, that an infinite number of courtiers grow old between yes and no, and at last die in doubt.

No one is so scorned, so worthless at Court, as the man who can contribute nothing to the making of our fortunes. I am surprised he dares to show himself.

It is too much to expect from a friend, that if he rises to great favour he will still retain our acquaintance.

If he who is in favour knows how to take advantage of it before he loses it, if he can make his way while the wind blows fair for him, keep his eyes open for all vacant posts or church preferments, and has only to ask to obtain, being provided with pensions, commissions and reversions, you complain of his greed and ambition, say he takes or appropriates everything, either for his friends or dependents, and that by the numerous and varied favours which have been heaped upon him, he alone has made the fortunes of many. Yet what would you have had him do? Were I to judge, not by what you say, but by what you would have done yourself in the same circumstances, I should be satisfied he has done right. We blame those who have made large fortunes whilst they had the opportunity, because from the smallness of our own we despair of ever being in a position to draw down a like reproach on ourselves. If we were in the way to follow in their footsteps we should begin to think they were less to blame, and would be more reticent for fear of pronouncing our own condemnation.

We must never exaggerate nor attribute to the Court evil which does not exist there. The worst it does for true merit is to leave it sometimes unrewarded, but it is not always despised when it is discerned, it is only forgotten; though indeed at Courts they understand well the art of doing nothing, or at least very little, for those they esteem much.

It would be strange if of all the instruments a man has used to build up his fortunes at Court, some of them did not fail. One of his friends who has promised to speak for him says nothing; another speaks but with faint praise; a third, by a slip, speaks against his friend's interest and his own intentions. The one lacks good will, the other tact and prudence. To neither would it be such great pleasure to see another happy that they care to exert themselves too much to make him so.

If every one remembered what his own preferment cost him, and the helps which cleared his way to it, we should be ready to make good the services we have ourselves received by rendering them to others in like need, but our first and only care after our fortune is made is to think of ourselves.

Courtiers do not employ their wit, address, and ingenuity to find excuses for helping the friends who implore their interest; but rather to discover specious pretexts for saying that it is an impossibility, and by this they consider themselves discharged from all obligations of duty, friendship, or gratitude.

It is difficult to find a friend at Court who will speak first for you, they all offer to second a proposal; because judging of others by themselves, they hope nobody will propose, and that thus their support will not be required. This is an easy and polite way of refusing to do a kindness to him who has need of it.

How many people who stifle you with their caresses
in private, saying how they love and esteem you, are
yet embarrassed if they meet you in public at a levée
or at mass ; how they avoid meeting your eyes ! There
is only a small proportion of courtiers who are noble-
minded enough of themselves to do honour before the
world to merit alone, devoid of interest.

I see a man surrounded and followed, but he is in
office.   I see another courted by everybody, he is in
favour : this man is embraced and caressed even by
people of rank, but he is rich : that man is regarded
with curiosity and pointed out everywhere, but he is an
eloquent scholar.   I see one whom no one forgets to
bow to, but he is a rogue.   I would like to find a man
who is good and nothing more, who is courted and
sought after.

I think it may be said of an eminent and difficult
position that it is obtained more easily than it is preserved.

We see men fall from great eminence by the very
defects which raised them.   At Court there are two
ways of getting rid of people : get angry with them or
else make them so angry with you that they retire disgusted.

At Court a man is well spoken of for two reasons :
first that he may know people have praised him, and
secondly that he may do the same by them.

It is as dangerous at Court to make advances as it is
embarrassing not to make them.

I am told so many evil things of a man, and I see so

few in him, that I begin to suspect he has some obtru-
sive merit which eclipses that of others.

You are an honest man, and do not trouble about
pleasing or displeasing favourites, are only attached to
your master and your duty; you are a lost man.

None are bold by chance, but by constitution; bold-
ness is born in some, and is natural. He who is not
born so is modest, and cannot easily change from one
extremity to the other. It would be useless to say to
him, "Be bold and you will succeed." A bad imitation
would not profit him, he would soon be stranded.
Nothing less than real naïve impudence is successful
at Court.

We seek, intrigue, busy and torment ourselves,
petition, are refused, ask again and obtain; and then we
say to our friends, without ever having asked for it;
indeed we were thinking of something quite different!"
This was the old style—silly stories which deceived
nobody.

Men are not willing we should discover the prospects
they have of advancement, nor guess that they aim at
a certain dignity, because if they do not obtain it
they are ashamed that they have been refused it; while,
if they attain it, it is greater glory for them to be
thought worthy by him who bestows than to show by
using interest and intrigue that they judge themselves
worthy: they thus find themselves adorned by their
dignity, and at the same time, by their modesty.

Which is the greater shame, to be refused a post we
merit or to be advanced to one we do not deserve?

However great the difficulty may be to get a place at
Court, it is still harder and more difficult to be worthy
of a place.

It is more often said of a man "Why did he obtain that post?" than "Why did he not obtain it?"

Even at the present time the city taxes are contested, and a chair in the French Academy is solicited as if it were a consulship. What reason is there why a man should not work during the early years of his life, to render himself capable of a great post, and ask for it openly without any mystery or intrigue, confident in his ability to serve his country and his prince?

———

I never knew a courtier to whom his prince had presented a good governorship, a large pension, and a high post, who did not, through vanity, or else to show his disinterestedness, assure everybody that he was less pleased with the gift than with the way in which it was given. The only undeniable thing about this is that he says so.

It is churlish to give with a bad grace; the most difficult part is the giving, it costs little to add a smile.

I must confess, however, that there are men who can refuse more courteously than others can give, while some make us ask so, often, and then grant the favour so unwillingly, and impose such disagreeable conditions, that it would be a greater favour still to be excused from receiving anything from them.

———

At Court there are always to be found some so covetous that they will adapt themselves to any conditions so that they may promote their own interest, governor, commander, bishop, it is all the same to them. Their adaptability is such that they are qualified to grace any position; they may be called amphibious, as they can live by the church or the sword, and to these could unite the secrets of the robe. If you ask what do these men do at Court, you might be answered they take all they can get, and envy everybody to whom anything is given.

———

Hundreds of people at Court drag out their days
caressing and congratulating those who receive
favours, and die themselves without having any
bestowed upon them.

———

There is a great and beaten road to honour and
dignity, and there is also a crooked bye-path which
is the shortest.

———

We seek out the unhappy that we may study
their looks ; we stand in a line, or we secure a place
at a window on purpose to examine the countenance
of a man who is condemned to die : a vain, malicious,
cruel curiosity. If men were wise, public places of
execution would be abolished, and it would be considered simply ignominious to gaze at such spectacles.
If you have a curious disposition, exercise it on a
nobler subject. Look at a fortunate man, mark him
on the day of his promotion to a new post, when he
is receiving his congratulations ; read in his eyes
through his studied, calm, and affected modesty, how
pleased and satisfied he is with himself ; observe the
quiet placidity which the accomplishment of his
desires seems to spread over his heart and countenance, as if he had nothing more to think of now
than health and long life ; till, at last, his delight
bursts forth ; it can no longer be restrained : and how
he seems to bend beneath the weight of his own
happiness ; what a serious and reserved manner he
assumes towards those who are no longer his equals !
He seems not to see them, does not reply to their
questions ; and even the attentions of the great, who
are no longer so far above him, begin to weary him.

He is unsettled, pre-occupied, suffering from a kind of mental derangement. You who long for fortune, for favours, sometimes they are things to be shunned.

Knaves are necessary at Court ; the great men and the ministers—even those with the best intentions— have need of them ; but they must be used delicately, and one must know how to work them—sometimes their places could not be filled by others. Honour, virtue, conscience, are always respectable qualities, though often useless : what could one do, on certain occasions, with an honest man ?

The minority of a prince is the source of many fortunes.

How many friends and relatives spring up for a new minister in one night ! Some bring forward old acquaintanceship, school-fellowship, or they claim to be known as neighbours ; others consult their pedigree, and go back to great-great-grandfathers claiming paternal or maternal relationship. Everybody tries to be related to him in some way or other, and they say, over and over again, "He is my friend ; I am very glad of his promotion ; I ought to be greatly interested, for he is my near relative." Vain men, followers of success, empty flatterers, would you have said so a week ago? Has he since then become a more honest man, more worthy of the honour his prince has bestowed upon him ; or, did you have to wait for this circumstance of fortune to know him better ?

What comforts and supports me under the little slights I sometimes sustain from my equals as well as from my superiors is that I say to myself: these men value me by my fortune, and they are right, it is very small, they would doubtless adore me if I were a minister.

If they knew that I was soon to be advanced, had they some foreknowledge of it, how they would salute me, greet me.

I expect it is pleasant for a man of merit to see the place at an assembly or public meeting which has just been refused to him, given to a man who has neither eyes to see nor ears to hear nor sense to understand, who has nothing to recommend him but certain · liveries which he does not even wear himself.

Theodotus has a grave manner, a comical face like a man making his *début* on the stage, his voice, gestures and deportment agree with his face ; he is clever, wily, soft and mysterious, he comes up to you and whispers in your ear, " What fine weather we are having," or " It is a great thaw." If his style is not very lofty, his manners are at least pleasant, if a little finical. Picture to yourself the diligence with which a child builds a card castle or chases a butterfly, and you will have an idea of *Theodotus*, busy about something of so little consequence that it is not worth caring about, although he treats it as seriously as if it were a matter of grave importance. He is in such a hurry, so busy and active about it, that he makes it succeed, and now he is able to rest and breathe, and he is right, for it has given him a great deal of trouble. There are some men whom favour intoxicates, they think of it all day and dream of it at night ; they are continually running up and down the staircases of the minister coming and going to his ante-chamber, having nothing to say, still speaking and speaking again, contented that they have spoken to the man in office. You may press them on any subject, you will squeeze nothing out of them but pride and arrogance and presumption ; you address them, they do not know you, and do not reply ; their eyes have a wild look, their brains seem distracted, their relations ought to see to them and have them confined, for fear their folly should turn to madness, and the world should suffer. *Theodotus* has a quieter mania, he loves favour wildly, but he shows his passion for it less ; he adores it in secret, cultivates it and makes use of it in mysterious ways. He is always on the look out to discover any ·new aspirants, and should they have any claims, he offers them his assistance and intrigues for them, sacrificing in an underhand way those who have more merit and more claim on his friendship or gratitude. If the post of a Cassini were vacant, and the porter or postillion of a favourite took it into his head to ask for it, he would support his pretension, and consider him quite worthy of it, and capable of making astronomical observations and calculations. If you enquire about *Theodotus*, whether he is an original author or a plagiarist, I must give you his works and bid you read and judge ; but to say whether he is a bigot or a courtier, who could decide that from the picture I have drawn of him ? I could more boldly draw his horoscope. Yes, *Theodotus*, I have observed the star under which you were born ; you will be advanced, and soon, you need not trouble yourself and other people any more about it, or print any more of your credentials—the public cries for quarter.

There is a country where the joys are visible but false, and the griefs hidden but real. Who would imagine that the bursts of applause at the comedies of Molière, or the harlequin, the feasts, the hunting matches, balls and banquets covered so many uneasinesses, cares and diverse interests, so many hopes and fears, such ardent passions and serious affairs.

Court life is a grave and melancholy game which requires study. One must range his pieces and his batteries, have a design and pursue it, thwart his adversary, venture sometimes, and at other times play capriciously, and yet after all his considerations and contrivances he may be checkmated. Often when he has manœuvred his men well, the game goes to the queen, and some one more clever or more fortunate gains the game.

The wheels, the springs, the movements of a watch are hidden, nothing is visible but the hands, which insensibly move forward and finish the round : and this image of a courtier is all the more perfect, that after he has gone a long way he returns to the point from which he started.

Two-thirds of my life are already passed, why, then, should I disquiet myself about what is left? The most splendid fortune does not deserve either the torment I put myself to, nor the meannesses I must stoop to, nor the humiliations I am forced to endure. Thirty years will destroy those colossal powers which are so high as to be almost out of sight. We shall disappear, —I who am so little and those to whom I looked so eagerly and from whom I expected all my greatness. The best of all blessings, if there are any blessings, is repose and a quiet retreat of our own. N*** was of this opinion in his disgrace, but forgot it in his prosperity. .

A nobleman who lives at home in his own province is free but unprotected : if he lives at Court he is protected, but he is a slave : so it is balanced.

Xantippus, buried in his province, under an old roof, in a poor bed, dreamt one night that he saw the prince, that he spoke to him, and felt extreme joy.　When he waked he was sad, and told his dream, and said what strange fancies fall into a man's mind when he is asleep.　When *Xantippus* had lived a little longer he came to Court and saw his prince and spoke to him, and went beyond his dream, for he became a favourite.

Nobody is more a slave than an assiduous courtier, unless it be a courtier who is still more assiduous.

A slave has but one master ; an ambitious man has as many as may be useful for his advancement.

Hundreds of men who are nobodies crowd every day to the levée to see and be seen by the prince, who cannot see hundreds at a time, so if he sees only those he saw yesterday, and will see to-morrow, how many will be unhappy.

Of all those who crowd about great men and pay their court to them, a few honour them in their hearts, a great number seek them for ambitious and interested reasons, and the greatest number of all, through a ridiculous vanity or a foolish impatience to be taken notice of.

There are certain families who, according to the ordinary rules of the world and decorum, ought to be irreconcilable, and behold they are good friends ; where religion failed in her attempt to unite, interest succeeded without any trouble.

People tell me of a country where the old men are polite, civil, and gallant, the young men on the contrary, stubborn, wild, without manners or politeness;

free from all sentiment about women, at an age when in other countries they begin to feel it, and prefer feasting and the silliest dalliance. Wine does not elate them, the too frequent use of it has rendered it insipid to them, and they try by brandy and strong liquors to revive their extinguished taste for it; nothing is wanting at their debauches but to drink *aqua fortis*. The women of that country hasten the decay of their beauty by artifices which they think enhance it. It is their custom to paint their lips, their cheeks, their eyelashes, and their shoulders, which, with neck and arms, they imagine they cannot display enough of to please. The physiognomy of the people of that country is not at all clear and distinct, but confused and half hidden by masses of false hair, which they prefer to their natural tresses, and which they dress elaborately and allow to hang loose and long, changing their features, and preventing recognition. This nation has, besides, their own God and their own king. The grandees assemble every day at a certain hour, in a temple which they call a church. At the upper end of this temple there is an altar consecrated to their God, where the priest celebrates some mysteries which they call holy, sacred, and awful; the grandees form a great circle at the foot of this altar, standing with their backs to the priests and the holy mysteries, and their faces raised towards their king, who is to be seen on his knees upon a throne, and to whom they seem to direct all the desires of their hearts. We cannot help seeing in this custom a kind of subordination, the people appearing to adore the prince, and the prince to adore God. The inhabitants of this country call it ——* It is in some forty-eight degrees of latitude, and more than eleven hundred leagues from the Iroquois and the Hurons.

---

* Versailles is meant by this distant country.

K

If you will consider how the whole happiness of a
courtier consists in beholding the face of his king, his
whole life fully occupied in endeavouring to see and to
be seen by him, you may in a measure comprehend that
to behold the face of God must be the fulfilment
of glorious felicity for the saints.

———

Great lords are full of respect for their princes, it is
their employment, and they have their inferiors: less
important courtiers are more lax in this duty; they are
more unconstrained, more free, as men who have no
example to set to any one.

———

What then is wanting in the youth of our day?
They have capacity and knowledge, or at least, if they
do not know as much as they ought to know, they are
no less positive.

———

How weak are men! A great man says of
Timagenes that he is a fool, but he is mistaken. I do
not ask you to reply that he is a man of genius, only be
bold enough to believe that he is not a fool.

He also says that *Iphicrates* is a coward; you have
seen him perform a brave act : keep your mind easy,
I excuse you from publishing it provided that after
what you have heard of him you still remember that
you saw him perform it.

———

How few know how to speak to kings; perhaps this
is one of the things which best determine the prudence
and tact of a courtier. A word escapes and falls on
the prince's ear, lingers in his memory, and sometimes
reaches his heart ; it is impossible to recall it ; all the
care and ingenuity we may use to explain it away will
only serve to engrave it deeper and to strengthen the
effect of it. If it is only against ourselves we have

spoken, although this mistake is not usual, there is a ready remedy; which is, to be taught by our mistake and to endure the consequence of our thoughtlessness. But if our words have been against another, what dejection and repentance we suffer! Could there be a better rule to prevent such harmful uneasiness than always to talk of others to our sovereign, whether it be of their persons, actions, manners, or conduct, with at least as much guarded precaution as we use in talking of ourselves?

An idle jester is a wretched character; if this has not been said already I say it. One who would injure the reputation or the fortune of another for the sake of making a jest deserves an ignominious punishment: I venture to say this which has not been said before.

There are a certain number of ready-made phrases which, as we would do from a magazine, we pick out and use to congratulate each other on the turn of events; they are frequently spoken without any affection and received without acknowledgment: still we must not omit them because they are at least the representatives of the best thing in the world, which is friendship; and since men can scarcely count upon this from each other they seem to agree among themselves to be contented with its semblance.

Having acquired five or six terms of art, and nothing more, we set up as connoisseurs in music, painting, constructing, and junketting; and thinking our powers of enjoyment in hearing, seeing, and eating are greater than ordinary people's, we impose on our fellows and deceive ourselves.

The Court is never destitute of a certain number of

persons in whom fashion, politeness, or fortune take the place of sense, and make up for deficiency of merit: they know how to enter and retire from a room: they evade conversation by never mingling in it: they make themselves agreeable by their silence, and important by the length of time they maintain it, or by speaking at most only a few syllables. A slight inflection of the voice, a smile, or a look is the only return they make to what you say. They have not, I may say, two inches of depth. If you were to try to fathom them you would very soon reach the tufa at the bottom.

———

What shall I call those people who are sharp only towards fools? I know that clever men confuse them with those they impose upon.

He shows a deep cunning who is able to make others think he is but indifferently cunning.

Cunning is neither too good nor too bad a quality ; it floats between vice and virtue ; there is scarcely any occasion on which it might not be, and ought not to be, supplanted by prudence.

Cunning is near neighbour to cheating; the path from one to the other is slippery ; a lie only lies between : if you add that to cunning it is cheating.

Among those who through cunning listen much and talk little do you speak still less, or if you speak much say little.

———

You have some important business which depends on the consent of two persons ; one of them says to you, "I give you my hand upon it provided so and so agrees," and he does agree and desires nothing more than to be assured of the intentions of the other. However, the affair does not advance, months and years roll on unprofitably. "I shall lose it," you say, "and

I do not understand why; there is nothing to do but for them to have an interview and discuss it." Shall I tell you what I see clearly and understand well? They have discussed it.

It seems to me that a man who solicits for others does so with the confidence of one who asks justice; and that in speaking and acting for himself he would be confused and ashamed like one imploring mercy.

There are some occasions in life when truth and simplicity are the best husbandry.

Are you in favour, all you do is good, you can commit no fault, any path you take is right. Otherwise all is at fault, nothing is of use, and any path you take is wrong.

A man who has lived for a certain time in an atmosphere of intrigue cannot do without it; all other modes of life are tiresome.

A man who intrigues must possess talent. He may however have so much talent as to be above intrigue, and above being enthralled by it, finding a more honourable way of making a fortune and a reputation.

With such sublime wit, such universal knowledge, tried fidelity and most accomplished merit, you need not, *Aristides*, be afraid of falling at Court and losing the favour of great men as long as they have need of you.

If we consider many of the people at Court, and attend to their discourse, and follow their conduct, we shall see that they think neither of their grandfathers nor grandchildren: the present is for them, and that they abuse and do not enjoy.

*Straton** was born under two stars, happy and unhappy in the same degree; his life would be a romance but that it lacks probability; he has had no adventures, his dreams have been both good and bad. What am I saying? people do not dream as they live. Nobody has been more favoured by fate than he has been; ordinary and extraordinary things are known to him; he has shone and suffered; he has lived an open life; nothing has escaped him. He made himself valued for the virtues he seriously assured us were in him; he said of himself, " I have wit, I have courage," and everybody echoed, " He has wit, he has courage." In good and in evil fortune he showed the courtier's spirit, and perhaps more good and also more evil was said of him than he deserved. Agreeable, handsome, rare, wonderful, heroic, are the terms used to eulogize him, and quite the contrary to vilify him. His character is equivocal, mixed and mysterious; an enigma, a question at issue.

Favour places a man above his equals, the loss of it below them.

He who knows the proper time resolutely to renounce a great name, great authority, or a great fortune, frees himself at once from many troubles, much sleeplessness and sometimes from many crimes.

In a hundred years the world will still exist as it is now, there will be the same theatre and decorations, though no longer the same actors. All those who

---

* The Duke de Lauzun, the favourite of Louis XIV., afterwards disgraced and sent to the Bastille. Being restored to favour, he again offended the king, and, after five years' imprisonment, he was exiled. He became attached to the Court of James II., and was one of the first to quit the field at the battle of the Boyne.

have rejoiced over a grace received, or who were cast down and afflicted by one refused, all will have disappeared behind the scenes. Already others will have advanced upon the stage who will take the same parts in the same play; they will vanish in their turn, and those who are not yet born will one day be no more, new actors will take their place. How can we depend on the actors in a play?

Whoever has seen the Court has seen the world, and all that is most beautiful, fair and glorious in it; he who despises the Court, having seen it, despises the world

A healthy mind imbibes at Court a taste for solitude and retirement.

THE NOBILITY.

THE great ones of the land have such a fascination for the people, who are so blindly infatuated in favour of their looks, voices, manners, and conduct, that if they would only take it into their heads to be good, they would be idolized.

If you were born vicious, oh, *Theagenes,** I pity you: if you have become so through weakness for those whose interest it is that you should be so, who have sworn among themselves to corrupt you, and who already boast of their success—you must put up with my contempt. But if you are wise, temperate, and modest ; civil, generous, grateful, and industrious ; and moreover, by your rank and birth impelled to set an example rather than take it from others ; to make rules rather than accept them—then agree with those people to follow courteously their irregularities, vices, and follies, when the deference they owe you leads them to exercise all the virtues which you cherish. Bold irony but significant, well calculated to protect your conduct and to ruin all their schemes, and force them to remain what they are, and to leave you as you are.

Great men have an immense advantage over others in one thing. I do not envy them their good living, their furniture, their dogs and horses, monkeys, dwarfs,

---

* It is generally understood that La Bruyère here refers to the grandson of Henri IV., who was Prior and Superior of the Vendome.

fools, and flatterers ; but I envy them the happiness of having in their service men who equal them in heart and intellect, nay, who sometimes surpass them.

The great pride themselves on opening up walks through the forests, making and building up fine wide terraces, gilding their ceilings, making fountains and stocking orangeries ; but to render one sorrowful heart happy, soothe a distracted mind, anticipate and relieve extreme necessity—is farther than their ambition extends.

In comparing the different conditions of men, their advantages and disadvantages, let me ask if you do not remark a kind of balancing of good and bad, which seems to set them on an equality, or, at least, prevents one condition being much more desirable than another. He who is rich and powerful, and who lacks nothing, may ask the question, but the poor man must answer it. Each of these different conditions has, however, a charm of its own, which will abide till misery removes it. For, as the great take pleasure in excess, the poor prefer moderation ; the first like to govern and command, the second have pleasure, and even pride, in obeying. The great are surrounded, saluted, respected ; the humble surround and salute, and both are content. A few words cost the great so little, and from their condition they are not obliged to keep the fine promises they make ; so it is modesty in them not to make them more freely still.

" He is old and used up," says a noble, " he has worn himself out in my service ; what shall we do with him?" Some one younger steps in, dashes his hopes and obtains the post which is refused to this old man only because he deserves it.

I do not understand. You tell me with an injured, indignant air, that *Philanthes* has merit, wit, and pleasant manners, and is punctual over his duties, and faithful in his attachment to his master, but is little liked, valued, or esteemed. Explain yourself; is it *Philanthes* you blame, or the great man he serves?

The great are so fortunate that during all their lives they are not even put to the trouble of lamenting the loss of their best servants, or of persons even moderately illustrious, from whom they have extracted pleasure and useful services, and who can scarcely be replaced. The first thing the flatterers do on the death of such a one, is to discover all his weak points from which they pretend his successor will be exempt, and to boast that the latter, with all the capacity and zeal of him whose place he takes, has none of his defects. And this is sufficient to console princes for the loss of great and worthy servants, and makes them satisfied with indifferent ones. The great scorn men of wit who have nothing but their talents; the men of talent despise the great who have nothing but grandeur; the honest man pities both, if having grandeur and talent, they have not virtue. When I see seated familiarly at the tables of the great some men I know to be bold, intriguing adventurers, both dangerous and disreputable, and on the other hand think of the difficulty some worthy persons find in approaching, I am not always disposed to believe that the wicked are tolerated from interested motives, or that honest men are regarded as serving no purpose; I am only more confirmed in my opinion that greatness and discernment are two different things, and love of virtue and the virtuous a third.

Lucilius prefers to spend his life in making himself endurable to some great people rather than be reduced to live familiarly with his equals. It requires peculiar talents to associate with great people, and is a custom which ought to be restricted.

What is the incurable mania *Theophilus** is afflicted with? He has had it for thirty years and is not cured yet. He was, is, and always will be anxious to govern the great. Death alone will end with his life this thirst for empire and ascendancy over other men's minds. Is it excess of zeal, mere habit, or an over estimate of himself? There is not a palace into which he does not insinuate himself, and he is not contented to pay his visits in the public rooms, he intrudes into private and retiring rooms, and he keeps others waiting for an audience while he speaks long and vehemently. He thrusts himself into family secrets, and concerns himself in everything which happens, fortunate or unfortunate ; but is so obliging and willing in his intermeddling that he cannot be kept out. The care of ten thousand souls for which as well as his own he is accountable to God, is not enough to fill up his time or his ambition; and there are others also of still higher rank and distinction of whom without being called upon to do so he voluntarily takes charge. He is always listening and watching for anything that may possibly feed his spirit of intrigue or interference : a great man has scarcely arrived in town till he lays hold of him; and before we have time to suspect his intentions, we hear that *Theophilus* governs and controls all his actions.

Coldness or incivility from our superiors offends us, but a bow or a smile reconciles us.

---

* The Abbé de Roquette, Bishop of Autun.

Some arrogant men are improved and humbled by the promotion of their rivals ; their mortification has the effect of making them civil, but time, which softens all things, restores them to their natural disposition.

The contempt which the great have for the people makes them indifferent to the praise and flattery they receive from them, and tempers their vanity ; in the same way, princes praised beyond measure by their courtiers and grandees would be more vain if they had more esteem for those who praise them.

The great believe that they alone are perfect, and will scarcely allow to other men the right of judgment, ability, or delicacy ; they consider such gifts due to their high birth. It is, however, a great mistake in them to foster such false prejudices ; the best thoughts, the best sayings, the best writings, and perhaps the most refined behaviour, are not always to be found among them. They possess large estates, and a long line of ancestors—this cannot be denied them.

There are some who, if they could but know their inferiors and themselves, would be ashamed to be above them.

If there are but few excellent orators, are there many people who could understand them? If there are not enough good authors, where are those who could read them? Likewise we are always complaining of the small number of persons qualified to counsel kings and to assist them in the administration of their affairs ; but when such able and intelligent men do appear, if they act according to their light and knowledge, are they beloved or esteemed as much as they deserve? Are they thanked for all they do and think for the country's good ? They are there—that is sufficient ; they are censured if their designs miscarry, and envied if they succeed. Let us then blame those whom it would be absurd to excuse—the people, whose discontent and jealousy the great and powerful look upon as inevitable, and have gradually come to take no notice of ; they rather seem to make it a rule in politics to neglect their suffrages. The common people detest each other when they mutually injure each other ; and the great are odious to them for the ill they do and the good they do not do them; they are to blame for their obscurity, poverty, and misfortune, or, at least, so it appears to them.

It really seems too much condescension for a great man to have the same religion, the same God, as the people. How can they even call themselves Peter, John, James, like the tradesman or the labourer ? Let us avoid having anything in common with the multitude; let us, on the contrary, effect every distinction which can separate them from us. Leave it to the people to appropriate the twelve apostles, the disciples, and martyrs, fit patrons for such people. Let them look forward year by year to the return of particular days which each celebrates as his festival, and let us, the great and noble, resort to profane names, and baptize our children Hannibal, Cæsar, Pompey—these are grand names—or Lucretia, who was an illustrious Roman lady, or Rinaldo, Rogero, Olivero, Tancredo. These were knights errant : and romance cannot point to more heroic names than Hector, Achilles, Hercules, demi-gods, and Phœbus and Diana : and what would prevent our calling ourselves Jupiter or Mercury, Venus or Adonis ?

While the great neglect, I do not say only the interests of princes, but also their own and the public affairs;

whilst they remain ignorant of domestic economy, and
are not masters in their own households, but allow
themselves to be impoverished and ruled over by their
stewards, and are contented to be always eating and
drinking and sitting in their clubs, idly talking of dogs
and horses, and telling tales of all the stages between
Paris and Besançon ; some citizens are instructing
themselves in everything that concerns their country,
studying the art of government, tact, and policy, finding out the strength and the weakness of the state ;
then they think of advancement, are promoted, become
powerful, and ease the prince of part of his public
duties. The great who scorned them end by respecting
them, and are happy if they are accepted as their sons-
in-law.

If I compare the two most opposite conditions of
men, I mean the great and the people, the latter appear
to be contented with necessaries, while the former are
poor, and discontented with superfluities. A man of
lowly condition cannot do much harm, while a great
man does not try to do much good, and is capable of
doing a great deal of evil. The one exerts himself
only for his profit, the other to his injury. Here churlish-
ness and coarseness are ingenuously displayed, there
a corrupt and evil nature is hidden under a surface of politeness ; the people have little wit and the
great have no heart. Those are good at heart with no
external grace, these are all surface, gloss, and no
depth. If I must choose between the two I would not
weigh the matter, but would belong to the people.

However clever the great ones of the Court may be,
and however adroit their art in appearing what
they are not, and not appearing what they are,
they are unable to hide their malice and inclina-

tion to laugh at the expense of others, and to cast
ridicule when it is not deserved. These fine talents
are observable in them from the first, and are no
doubt admirable for misleading the unwary or making
a fool of one who is a fool already, but are
likely to deprive them of the pleasure they might
have derived from a man of wit, who would have
known how to yield himself to their moods in a
thousand amusing ways, if the character of a courtier
did not warn him to be very prudent. He entrenches
himself behind a reserved gravity of demeanour, and
does it so effectively, that the scoffers, much as they
would like to make fun of him, have no opportunity.

An easy life, plenty, and the calm of great prosperity, enable princes to be easily amused ; they laugh
at a monkey, a dwarf, or an imbecile, or a silly tale :
people who are less fortunate only laugh in season.

A great man loves champagne and detests La Brie,
he intoxicates himself with better wine than the poor
man, and this is the sole difference between the
dissipation of the nobleman and that of the footman.

At first sight it seems that there must always enter
into the pleasures of princes a little inconvenience to
others : but this is not so, princes are like other men,
they think of themselves and follow their own tastes,
passions, and convenience ; this is natural.

It seems as if the first care of persons in power or
office is to put as many obstacles as possible in the
way of those who depend on them for the conduct of
their affairs.

If a great man has to a certain extent more happiness

than others, I can only suppose it is because he has it in his power to bestow pleasure, and when such an opportunity arises he ought to take advantage of it. If it is in favour of an honest man, he ought to be afraid to let it slip; and if it is in a just cause, he ought to anticipate solicitation, and not show himself till he has to be thanked ; and if it is an easy thing, he should not set a high value on it ; if he refuses it, I pity both.

There are some men born inaccessible, and they are just the men of whom others have need, and on whom they depend ; they seem always to stand on one foot like Mercury, and are as variable ; continually on the move, flitting here and there brisk and noisy, like the paper fireworks which betoken a public *fête*— they scatter fire and flame, and hiss and sparkle, so that we dare not approach them ; till, being extinguished, they at last fall down, become manageable, but useless.

The porter, the valet, the footman—if they have no more sense than belongs to their condition, never think of themselves according to their birth, but by the rank and fortune of those they serve ; and they consider all who enter their gates and mount their staircases infinitely below themselves and their masters. So true it is that we are destined to suffer from the great and from those belonging to them.

A man in office ought to love his prince, his wife, his children ; and, after them, men of wit and sense. He ought to take them under his protection, always have some about him, never be without them. He cannot reward them too well, I shall not say with pensions and benefits, but with familiarity and attention for all the service he extracts from them without their being aware of it. What idle reports do they not dissipate ; what stories they reduce to mere fiction ! How clearly can they justify ill success by good intentions, prove by the prosperous result the excellence of a scheme, or the justice of measures which may seem extreme ; ward off malice and envy by proving that good enterprises proceed from good motives ; put favourable constructions on bad appearances ; hide little defects, and only allow virtues to be seen, and those in the best light ; sow on all occasions any facts and details which may be advantageous, and turn ridicule against those who dare to doubt or to bring forward adverse facts. I know it is a rule with the great to let people talk, but to continue to act as they choose. But I also know it often happens that allowing people to speak prevents them acting.

To be sensible of merit, and, when once recognized, to treat it well—are two great steps which few men are capable of taking promptly.

You are great and powerful, but that is not enough ; act so that I may esteem you and be sorry either to lose your favour, or not to have been able to gain it.

You say of a great man, or a man in power, that he is very kind and obliging and glad to give pleasure, and you confirm this by detailing what he has done in an affair in which he knew you were taking an interest. This lets me understand that something was done for you ; you were in favour with the ministry, held in esteem by the powers that be ; what else would you have me think?

Some one tells you, " I do not consider I have been used well by such a one; he is proud and disdainful to me since his promotion, scarcely recognizes me." You reply, "I have nothing to say against him, on the contrary, I must speak in his praise, he seems to be very civil," then I understand you also. You wish it to be understood that this man in office has a regard for you, that in the ante-chamber he picks you out from among a crowd of honourable persons, from whom he turns aside for fear he may slip into such an impropriety as returning their smiles and bows. To exalt oneself in praising another, especially some great man, is a delicately conceived topic, for in relating all the good they have done us, or have never thought of doing us, we are praising ourselves. We praise the great to show we are intimate with them, seldom from esteem or gratitude. We often do not know those we praise ; vanity and frivolity even carries us above resentment, for often we are displeased with them, yet praise them.

If it is dangerous to interfere in a suspicious affair, the danger is greater if you find yourself involved with a great man ; he will get out of it and leave you to bear the brunt of it and suffer for both.

A prince's whole fortune would not suffice to recompense a man for a dishonourable service if he judges of it by what it costs the man ; and his power is not great enough to punish him if he measures his vengeance by the wrong done him.

The nobility expose their lives for the safety of the state and the glory of the sovereign, whom the magistrate relieves from the duty of judging the people : both are lofty functions, with noble aims: men are scarcely capable of greater things, and I cannot imagine why the wearers of the gown and of the sword despise each other so cordially.

If it is true that the great yield more in risking their lives destined to gaiety and pleasure than the private man who loses only cheerless days, it must also be confessed that they have a very different recompense in their glory and great renown : the private soldier cannot feel that he will ever be known, he dies obscure in a crowd ; he lived in the same way, it is true, still he lived, and this is one of the causes of want of courage in servile conditions. Those who by birth are exalted above the people are more exposed to praise or censure, and, therefore, if they are not naturally inclined to virtue they are impelled to exert themselves beyond their inclinations, and this constitution of heart and mind which they inherit from their ancestors is that bravery so often recognized in persons of noble birth—perhaps it is nobility itself.

Throw me among the troops as a simple soldier; I am Thersites. Put me at the head of an army for which I am responsible to the whole of Europe, and I am Achilles.

Princes do not require rules of science to aid their intuitive judgment : they are born and brought up in a centre of all that is best and noblest; and they compare all they read and see and hear, and what does not approach such ideals as Lulli, Racine, and Le Brun, they condemn.

It is an unnecessary precaution to talk to young princes of the respect due to their rank, for the whole court consider it their duty and a part of their courtliness to practise respect towards them. They are less apt to be ignorant of the respect due to their birth than to confound persons, and treat indifferently and without distinction all ranks. They have an innate haughtiness which they can assume on any occasion;

they require no lessons except in governing this disposition and to inspire them with good principles, honour, and a spirit of discernment.

———

For a man of a certain degree not to take at once the rank which is his due and which is universally conceded to him, is pure hypocrisy. It costs him nothing to be modest, to mix with the crowd which makes way for him, to take the lowest seat at an entertainment, so that all may see him there and hasten to set him higher. It is more difficult for ordinary men to practise modesty; if they mix in a crowd they get crushed and jostled; if they choose an uncomfortable seat they stay there.

———

The best actions are charged or weakened by the way in which they are performed, and ever leave room to doubt the intentions which prompted them. He who protects or commends virtue for the sake of virtue, who corrects or condemns vice because it is vice, acts simply and naturally, without design, peculiarity, pride or affectation. He neither reproves too gravely nor sententiously, nor makes his reproof a scene of public enjoyment. He does his duty, and sets a good example in doing it, and provides no material for gossip or romance. The good he does is in truth little known, but he has done good, and what can he desire more?

———

The great ought not to love the earlier period of history; it is not all favourable to them. It must be sad for them to see that we are all brothers and sisters; that mankind is but one and the same family; that there is only a greater or lesser degree of relationship.

———

One must have a very bad opinion of men, and yet

know them well, if he believes that he can impose upon them by studied endearments or long and meaningless caresses.

Pamphilus does not converse with the people he meets in the halls and courts, but his grave manner and the way he raises his voice make people think he is formally receiving, giving audience or dismissing one; he has some set terms which are at once civil and haughty, and a kind of imperious courtesy which he employs without distinction; a spurious grandeur which lowers him and embarrasses his friends who do not wish to despise him.

A *Pamphilus* is full of himself, never loses sight of his own merit, his importance and position, his dignity and connections; he musters all his forces, so to speak, surrounds himself with them to add to his consequence; talks of his *order*, his *blue ribbon*, which he either hides or displays ostentatiously. A *Pamphilus*, in short, would be great, believes he is so and is not; he is only a copy of a great man. If at any time he smiles on one of a lower order, a clever man perhaps, he chooses his time so aptly that he is never caught in the act, for he would blush if unfortunately he were surprised in the least familiarity with a person who is neither rich nor powerful, nor the friend of a minister, nor his ally, nor his servant. He is severe and inexorable to him who has not made his fortune. One day he sees you in a gallery, he evades you; the next day he meets you in a less public place, or, though public, if you are in the company of a great man, he takes courage and comes up to you, saying, "Yesterday you pretended not to see me." Sometimes he will leave you brusquely to join a lord or some important man, or if he finds you with one, he will nudge you and carry you off; you meet him another time and he will not stop, you follow him and have to talk so loud that people stare. Thus the *Pamphiluses* live always as if they were in a play; they are bred in falseness, and, disliking nothing so much as to be natural, they are perfect actors in a comedy.

But we are not yet done with the *Pamphiluses;* they are cringing and timid before princes and their ministers; full of arrogance and confidence with those who possess nothing but their virtue; mute and confused before the learned; sharp, forward, and positive before the ignorant. They speak of war to a lawyer, of politics to a banker, of history to a woman, poetry to a doctor, and of geometry among poets. They do not trouble themselves with maxims, and with principles still less; they live at a venture, pushed on by the wind of favour and the attractions of riches; they have no opinions which are really their own, they borrow them just as they require them; and their chosen friends are neither wise, able, nor virtuous, but men of the world.

We feel either fruitless jealousy or impotent hatred towards those who are great or powerful, and this cannot avenge us for their splendour and elevation, but only adds to our own misery the unsupportable burden of another's happiness. What is to be done for such a wide-spread and inveterate disease of the mind? Let us be contented with little, if possible with less, let us learn how to bear losses; this is an unfailing remedy, and I have made up my mind to try it. By this contentment I spare myself the trouble of trying to make another man's porter civil, coaxing a clerk, being pushed and jostled at the gate of a minister's house several times a day, while a crowd of clients and flatterers disgorge themselves. I am saved much weary waiting in the audience-hall to beg of him with

stammering and tremor some just request : I have not
to bear with his gravity or sententious sarcasm now : so
I neither hate nor envy him ; we are equals : the only
difference is that he is not calm and undisturbed, and I
am.

If the great have opportunities of doing us good they
rarely have the will; and if they would do us harm it is
not always in their power ; so we may be mistaken in
the kind of worship we pay them if it is founded on
hope or fear; and a long life often ends without a man
happening to have to depend on the great for any
benefit, or being indebted to them for good or bad
fortune : we must honour them since they are great and
we are humble, and there are others humbler than
ourselves who honour us.

The same passions, the same weaknesses and littlenesses, the same contrasts of disposition, family
quarrels, envyings, and antipathies reign at court and
in the city.   Everywhere there are daughters-in-law,
mothers-in-law, husbands and wives, ruptures,
divorces, misunderstandings, everywhere there are
moods, tempers, likes and dislikes, false reports and
scandals : with eyes to see, you will easily discover the
Rue St. Denis at Versailles or Fontainebleau ; only here
they believe that they hate with greater pride and
dignity, and annoy each other more politely and
cunningly, their rage is more elegant, their abuse
expressed in better terms.   They do not soil the purity
of the language, they only harm men and their
reputations.   All the external aspects of vice here are
plausible, but at the core once more I say, it is the same
as in the most abject conditions, as low, base, weak,
and unworthy.   These men who by birth, favour and
intellect stand so high, these women who are so polite

and witty, these are themselves the people, the people whom they despise. When we say the people, we say many things, it is a wide word and we should be astonished to see all it embraces and how far it extends. There are the people who are opposed to the great, which signifies the mob, the multitude ; and there are the people who are opposed to the wise, learned, and virtuous, and these include the great as well as the humble.

———

The great govern themselves by sentiment. Strong first impressions are formed on idle minds. Something happens, they talk of it too much, soon they speak less, then no more ; action, conduct, performance, event, all is forgotten. Do not ask from them correction, foresight, reflection, gratitude, or reward.

———

Two opinions are expressed about certain persons. After they are dead, criticism is rife among the people, whilst the pulpits resound with their praises. Sometimes they deserve neither criticism nor formal oration, sometimes both.

———

We ought not to talk of the great and powerful, the good we say of them is often flattery. It is dangerous to speak evil of them whilst they live, and cowardly when they are dead.

THE SOVEREIGN AND THE REPUBLIC.

IF, after impartial consideration of all the various forms of government, we cannot decide which is best, finding good and bad in all, it is most reasonable to hold in highest esteem that under which you were born, and to submit to it.

Neither art nor science is necessary in the exercise of political tyranny, which, as it consists only in blood-shed, has narrow limits and no squeamishness; it inspires the destruction of every life which is an obstacle to ambition; and this a naturally cruel man can accomplish without compunction; it is the most horrible and detestable way to wealth and promotion.

A very safe and ancient republican policy is to suffer the people to stupefy themselves with feasting and luxury, and all kinds of vain and foolish spectacles, leaving them to take their fill of empty folly and to enjoy nothing but the meanest trifles: by this indulgence the greatest strides are made towards despotism.

There is no home policy in a despotic country; interest, glory, and the service of the King supply its place.

If changes and innovations are contemplated in a state it is rather the time than the acts which have to be considered: there are certain occasions when we know nothing can be attempted in opposition to the people, and there are other times when anything can be done with them. To-day you may withdraw from that town its franchise, rights and privileges, but to-morrow do not even dream of altering its signboards.

———

When a tumult begins we cannot understand how calm is to be restored; and when all is quiet we cannot imagine how the peace was disturbed.

———

There are certain evils which a government connives at because they delay or prevent greater evils; there are others which are evils only because they are recognized, and which, being originally abuses or malpractices, are less pernicious in their results than a more just and reasonable law would be. There are some wrongs which may be corrected by change and novelty, and this is a very dangerous kind; others are hidden like the refuse in the ground; buried in shame, performed in secrecy and darkness: you cannot examine too closely into them because of the odious poison they exhale; the wisest men sometimes doubt whether it is best to recognize or to appear ignorant of these. The state sometimes tolerates one great evil to avert a number of lesser evils which seem inevitable, and could not be remedied. There are also evils which, although individuals groan under them, tend nevertheless to the public good, although the public is nothing else than a body of those same individuals. There are also personal hardships or evils which turn to the advantage of families; and there are evils which afflict, ruin, and dishonour families, but which contribute to the preservation of the state or government; other evils overthrow governments and raise new ones on their ruins; we have seen that vast empires have been undermined and utterly exterminated to change and renew the face of the universe.

———

What does it matter to the state that *Ergastes* is rich;

that he has a good pack of hounds ; that he leads the
fashions both in dress and equipages, and that he
abounds in superfluities? Where the interest and convenience of the public is concerned the individual
counts for nothing. It is some consolation for the
people, when burdens press on them a little, to know
that they assist the prince and enrich him alone ; they
do not wish to be indebted to *Ergastes* for improving his
fortune.

War has antiquity to plead for it ; it has existed
through all the ages, filling the world with widows and
orphans, and depriving families of heirs, often killing
more than one brother in the same battle.   I mourn
thy loss, young Soyecour ; * such rare wit, lofty virtue,
and wise modesty make me regret the premature death
which has united thee to thy brave brother. War is for
us a deep misfortune, but alas, too common.   From all
time a little spot of earth, more or less, has made men
combine together to destroy, despoil, burn, kill each
other, and to do this the more surely and ingeniously,
they have invented fine laws which they call military
art. The practice of those laws they reward with glory
and the highest honours, and they have from century to
century improved upon this art of self-destruction.
   Injustice among the founders of our race, and the
need which sprang from it of masters who would determine rights and privileges, was the original source of
war.   If, content with their own possessions, they had
not transgressed their neighbours', we might have
enjoyed for ever peace and liberty.
   Those who sit peaceably at home in the midst of
family and friends, in the safety of a large town

---

* The Chevalier de Soyecour, whose brother was killed in the
battle of Fleurus, July, 1690, and who died himself, of wounds
then received, three days after.

enjoying the gifts of fortune, and fearing nothing either
for life or property, are generally those who breathe fire
and sword, and are much occupied in discussing wars,
massacres, and conflagrations, and suffer much impatience of spirit when they hear that the armies which
hold the field have not yet come to an encounter; or,
that having met, there has been no engagement ; or if
they have engaged that the battle has not been more
bloody; that there were less than 10,000 men killed on
the spot.   They sometimes even go so far as to forget
their most cherished interests, repose, and security,
simply through a passionate desire for change and
novelty.   Some of them would even be pleased to see
the enemy at the very gates of their cities, and would
help to build barricades and hang the chains across the
streets for the sole pleasure of hearing and recounting
the news.

Demophilus on my right hand groans and laments
that all is lost, the state is on the brink of ruin ; how
can it stand against such deep and universal plotting?
How can we, I do not say overcome, but hold out
against so many and such powerful enemies?   Such a
state of affairs is unexampled in the history of monarchy.   A hero, an Achilles, would have to succumb to
it !   We have committed, he says, serious faults, and
I know, he adds, what I am saying, for I have seen war
and taken part in it myself, and history has taught me
much more about it.   He thereupon begins to praise
Olivier Le Daim* and Jacques Cœur.†   Those were men,

---

* Olivier Le Daim, a peasant of Flanders, barber to Louis XI.,
who attained the position of Chief Minister to the King, and was
hanged in 1483, at the beginning of the reign of Charles VIII.

† Jacques Cœur, a rich and famous merchant, who became
King's Treasurer.   He rendered valuable services to Charles
VII., who, after loading him with honours, in the end sacrificed
him to a court intrigue.

he says, and ministers, indeed. He invents the most gloomy and prejudicial news, and spreads it everywhere. At one time a part of our army has been drawn into an ambuscade and cut in pieces, then a portion of our troops is confined in an old castle, surrenders at discretion, and is put to the sword ; and if you tell him that the report is false, that there is nothing to confirm it, he will not listen to you, but adds that such and such a general has been killed, and although the truth is that he has received a slight wound, he will not believe your assurances, but insists on deploring his death and pitying his widow and orphans. The state, he sighs, has lost a good friend and a powerful defender. He tells you the German cavalry is invincible, and turns pale if you but name the Imperial Cuirassiers. If we attack that place, he continues, we shall be obliged to raise the siege, for whether we defend or attack we must be defeated; if we are beaten, behold the enemy at the frontier. Yes, according to *Demophilus*, the enemy will immediately be in the heart of the kingdom; he already hears the alarm bells and cries of terror. He thinks of his wealth, his property, and seriously considers where he can place his money and his family in safety, whether he will find a refuge for them and himself in Switzerland or Venice.

But on my left *Basilides* in one moment raises an army of 300,000 men ; not a single brigade will he abate ; he has the list of squadrons, battalions, commanders, and officers, and omits neither artillery nor baggage. He peremptorily disposes of those troops, sends some to Germany, some to Flanders, reserves a certain number for the Alps, a smaller number for the Pyrenees, and transports the rest beyond the seas. He knows every movement of this army, what they have done, and what they have not done ; you might suppose he had the king's ear, or at all events was in all the secrets of his minister. If the enemy is defeated, and loses nine or ten thousand men, he is positive it is thirty thousand, neither more nor less, for his numbers are always exact, as if he were thoroughly well informed. If he hears some morning that we have lost a paltry village, he not only sends to excuse himself to the guests he has invited to dinner, but fasts himself, and if he sups, he has no appetite. If our soldiers besiege a place which, besides. being well fortified is naturally strong, has a good garrison of men commanded by an officer of intrepid courage, and well provided with ammunition and all necessary stores, he tells you that he knows the place has its weak points, is badly fortified and short of powder, while its commanding officer is inexperienced, and that it is sure to capitulate eight days at most after the opening of the trenches. Another time he hurries breathless to inform us of his news. " Listen ! " he exclaims, after he recovers a little : " I have news, great news : they are defeated, totally routed, the general, the principal officers, or at least most of them killed, a terrible slaughter indeed, and we have had a glorious victory." Then he sits down to rest after having published his news, which is complete but for one circumstance, namely that it is quite certain there has not been a battle at all. But he goes on to assure us that a certain prince* has repudiated the league and quitted the confederacy, that a second† shows signs of following him, and that a third, according to popular belief, is dead‡, and he names the place of his interment ; and even when the whole town is undeceived, he persists in the truth of his report. He has the most reliable authority for saying that Tékéli, the Hungarian general, has risen against the Emperor, that the Sultan

* Duke of Savoy. † Charles II. of Spain. ‡ Charles II. of England.

will not hear of peace, and that his Vizier will once more appear at the gates of Venice. He claps his hands, and seems greatly excited about this event, as if he had no doubt of it. The triple alliance is to him a Cerberus, and enemies so many monsters to be overpowered ; he can talk of nothing but laurels, triumphs, and trophies. His favourite expressions are, " Our august hero, our great potentate," or, " Our invincible monarch." He cannot say simply, " The King has many enemies ; they are powerful, united, and incensed ; he has vanquished them, and I hope will always be able to vanquish them." This style is too bold and decisive for *Demophilus,* and is not pompous and exaggerated enough for *Basilides,* whose head is full of grand flights of fancy ; he is thinking of inscriptions for triumphal arches and pyramids, which will adorn the capital on the day of the victorious entry, and as soon as he hears that the armies have met, or a town is invested, he airs his grandest robes that they may be ready for the thanksgiving service in the cathedral.

The main point of the affair which is to be discussed by the ambassadors of kingdoms and republics, must be very intricate and important, if it takes longer to conclude, than has already been taken to settle the preliminaries, and all the ceremonious rules of precedence and rank. A public minister or an ambassador is a chameleon, a Proteus ; sometimes like a clever gambler he has to disguise his mood or temper, it may be as much to avoid discriminating surmises, as to prevent the risk of anything escaping him through weakness or passion. He knows how to assume the character most in keeping with his views, and, as necessity arises, he appears to be what it is to his interest that others should believe him to be. Therefore, if the matter is very formidable, he is resolute and inflexible, so that people may not attempt to obtain much from him; but if he feels his position rather weak, he unbends, so that by giving others the chance of asking, he may have the same liberty. At another time, either he is profound and subtle to conceal a truth while he pretends to publish it, because it is important that he should have told it, but that it should not be believed: or else he is frank and open, so that when he does dissemble and conceal what must not be known, no one will suspect him of being hypocritical, but will believe he told all he knew. He can adroitly inspire others to talk, and at the same time prevent them talking to him of things he does not wish to talk about or to tell. He talks of so many different things, that meanings get confused, modified, or destroyed, and as he inspires as much fear as confidence, in people's minds, he is able to recover at once a lost opportunity, and at the same moment to gain another. Or he is cool and silent, and having set others talking, he will listen patiently for a long time; so that when he desires to speak he may obtain the same attention; for his discourse is generally full of power, and has great influence when it contains promises or threats, which are either moving or disturbing to those at whom they are directed. At one time he will open the discussion, speaking first that he may discover what contradictions, intrigues, or cabals are to be brought forward (by foreign ministers) to oppose his proposition, take measures accordingly, and have a reply; at another time he waits till the last so that he may not say a word too much, but to the point, having discovered exactly what it is necessary to make important for his master, or his allies; what to ask; and also what he is likely to obtain. He knows how to speak in clear and formal terms, and also how to use ambiguous, equivocal language which will hide his true meaning, using words which he can twist to suit himself or his interests.

He asks little when he does not wish to yield much, and he asks much so that he may be sure of a little. His first exactions are unimportant, so that later he may declare that as they were valueless to him he ought not now to be denied something greater. He will avoid gaining an important point, if it is likely to prevent him gaining several which though of less consequence separately, yet together exceed the first. He asks something extravagant so that he may be denied, his object being to give himself the precedent for refusing something he knows will be asked, and which he does not wish to grant, and he is as careful to exaggerate the unreasonableness of the request, and to explain the reasons why he cannot listen, as to weaken the reasons advanced by those who did not agree to his solicitation. He is equally anxious to exalt and magnify the little he offers, as to despise openly the little which is granted to him. He feigns extraordinary concessions which breed distrust, and oblige his opponents to reject, what if accepted, would be useless; this, however, gives him the excuse to make exorbitant demands, and to put in the wrong those who refuse to agree to them. Sometimes he grants more than is asked, so that he may obtain more than he ought to have, or he requires much solicitation for some trifling request, to extinguish hope, and prevent any idea of larger demands, and when at last he is persuaded to grant it, he attaches such conditions to his assent as will make it as advantageous to him as to those who receive the favour. He directly or indirectly embraces the interests of an ally, if he finds it will be useful for the advancement of his own party. His conversation is entirely of alliances, peace, public tranquillity, and public interests; in fact, he thinks of nothing but

M

the interest of his master and the republic. Now and
then he reconciles those who were antagonistic, and at
other times he divides those he finds united ; he
intimidates the strong and powerful, and encourages
the weak, or he unites several feeble interests against
a more powerful one, to render the balance equal ; then
he joins with the former that they may lean on him, and
he makes them pay dearly for his alliance and
protection. He knows how to interest those with whom
he treats, and by delicate address and cunning subter-
fuge, he makes them aware of private advantages,
wealth, and honours, which they may hope for through
a certain laxity which will not clash with their duty,
nor with the wishes of their masters. And so that he
may not be thought altogether invincible on this point,
he displays on his own account a little concern as to his
own future, and by this means he draws proposals from
them which discover their secret intentions, their most
profound designs, and the extent of their resources ;
from this he profits. If at some time he is wronged in
any particular which is afterwards rectified, he is loud
in his remonstrances, but if it is the other way he is
louder still, and throws the injured back on their
justification and defence.

Everything he does is examined and ordered by the
court, every step is regulated, every advance directed
and limited ; nevertheless he acts even in difficult and
contested points, as if he were yielding of his own
accord quite readily and simply. Through his obliging
disposition he ventures to say that he will make the
proposition meet with approval : he is sure it will not
be denied them. He has false reports bruited about
concerning the business he is secretly charged with,
but reserves his own particular powers and instructions,
which he never discloses till some extremity arises,
when it would be hurtful not to put them in operation.

His intrigues aim above everything at what is solid and essential, and he is always ready to sacrifice for them all minutiæ and trifling points of honour. He is phlegmatic and armed with plenty of patience and courage ; he fatigues and discourages others, but is never wearied himself, is forewarned and hardened to bear all delays and affronts, reproaches, suspicions, difficulties, obstacles, and defiance; fully persuaded that time and circumstances will arrange matters and influence people's minds as he desires. He will even pretend that he would rather break off the negociation, when all the time he is most ardently hoping it will go on: but if on the contrary he has strict orders to try to break it off, he thinks the best way to succeed is to press the conclusion of it. If some great emergency occurs, he either gives way or is inflexible according as it will be to his advantage or prejudice: and if by great tact he can prevent it, he will temporise and urge according to the hopes and fears of the state for which he acts, and he regulates his conditions by his needs. He takes great heed of time, place, and occasion, of any power or weakness, and of the genius of the nation with whom he treats, and the temper and character of the persons with whom he negociates. All his schemes and sayings and subtle policy have but one aim, which is never to be imposed upon himself, but always to deceive others.

The character of the French nation requires gravity in the sovereign.

One of the misfortunes of a prince is that he is obliged to bear the burden of his secrets, because it is dangerous to discover them ; he is fortunate if he finds a faithful confidant.

A prince wants nothing but the pleasures of a private life to complete his happiness; and only the charms of friendship and the faithfulness of his friends can console him for this loss.

A king who is worthy of his throne finds pleasure in sometimes laying aside his greatness and state, and enjoying the unconstrained intimacy of his friends.

Nothing does more honour to a prince than the modesty of his favourite.

No doubt a favourite who possesses strength of mind and good principle, must often be annoyed and disconcerted by the mean and petty flatteries, and silly and persevering attentions of those who pay their court to him, and follow him about like dogs. He probably laughs at them in private for all the trouble their slavish attentions give him.

A favourite should have no followers, no ties or relationships. He may be surrounded by friends and dependants, and take no heed of them. He is severed, isolated from them all.

Men in office, ministers, favourites, allow me to advise you. Do not trust to your descendants to preserve your memory and continue your name; titles pass away, favour vanishes, honours are forgotten, riches melt away, and merit degenerates. It is true you have children, who seem worthy of you, and capable, I may even add, of upholding your character, but who can vouch as much for your grandchildren? If you do not believe me, look for once at certain men whom you never notice but with scorn and disdain. They had ancestors whom, great as you are, you can only

endeavour to resemble. Be virtuous and humane, and
if you ask me what more is necessary, I would reply
benevolence and virtue. You will then be master of
the future, independent of posterity, and your name
will live as long as monarchy itself endures ; and when
future generations are shown the ruins of your castle,
or it may be only the site whereon it stood, the remembrance of your great and noble acts will still be fresh
in the minds of the people, who will eagerly examine
your portraits and medals, and will say—"That man*
always spoke to the prince with force and freedom ;
he was more afraid of injuring than displeasing him ;
he encouraged him in all acts of kindness and generosity, and taught him to say, 'My good city!' 'My
own people !'" That other picture † on which you look
is remarkable for the strength of character the face
displays, and its air of grave austerity and majesty.
As the years passed they only added splendour to his
reputation; the greatest politicians suffered from comparison with him; his great aim was to establish the
authority of the prince and the security of the people
by humbling the nobility : and from this aim neither
opposition, conspiracy, treason, terror of death, or his
own infirmities had any power to turn him. Besides
this he found time to set in operation an undertaking
afterwards continued and finished by one of the greatest
and best princes‡ the world has ever seen, namely
the extinction of heresy.

The most plausible and cunning snare which was
ever laid for nobles by their treasurers, or for kings by
their ministers, is the means they advise them to take
to pay off their debts and enrich themselves. It is

---

admirable counsel they give, most fruitful, worth indeed a mine of gold, Peru itself, for those who are clever enough to instil it into their masters.

That is a fortunate nation whose king admits into his counsel and chooses for his ministers those very persons whom the people would have chosen for him if they had been his advisers.

Knowledge of details, and diligent attention to the smallest needs of the republic, is an essential part of good government, which in truth was formerly too much neglected both by kings and ministers, and is a quality which cannot be too earnestly desired in a sovereign who does not cultivate it, nor overestimated in him who possesses it. For how does it really affect the prosperity of the people, or their ease and comfort, that their king extends the bounds of his dominions beyond those of his enemies ; that he makes their states provinces of his kingdom; that he is as superior to them in sieges as in battles, so that they cannot resist him either on the field or behind the strongest fortress; that neighbouring nations have to call on each other to enter into leagues to defend themselves and put a stop to his conquests ; that all this is in vain, for he is always advancing, always victorious; and the last hopes of his enemies are dashed to the ground by the re-establishment of such health in this great monarch, as gives him the prospect of seeing his grandsons able to support and augment his good fortune by leading his victorious armies to the conquest of new states, and able to command old and experienced officers, less by their right of rank and birth, than by merit and wisdom, following in the footsteps of their victorious father, imitating his goodness, justice and mildness, as well as his vigilance and bravery.

How, I repeat, does it affect me, or the people, that

the sovereign and his children are covered with glory, wealth, and honour, and that our country is great and powerful, if we have to exist under the dismal burden of poverty and oppression ; if while protected against the inroads of the enemy, we are exposed within the walls of the city to the violence and cruelty of a tyrant? How much better would I and my fellow-subjects be, if security, order, and cleanliness had not rendered life in our cities so delightful, and if plenty and prosperity did not include for us the pleasures of society, or if being feeble and defenceless we were subject to attacks from every neighbouring great man, if no provision had been made to protect us against his injustice? If I had not at hand so many excellent teachers to train my children in those arts and sciences which will one day raise their fortunes; if the facilities of trade had not brought good clothing within my reach, and health-sustaining, nourishing food, which I can buy cheap? If, in short, the solicitude of my sovereign had not given me as much reason to be contented with my fortune, as his virtues must make him with his?

Eight or ten thousand men are to a sovereign like money, with which he buys a town or a victory. The more he can spare his men, the cheaper is his purchase like a merchant who gets the best value for his money.

All things prosper in a kingdom in which the interests of the sovereign and the state are one.

To say that a king is the father of his people, is no more praising him than calling him by his name and title.

There is a sort of commerce or reciprocal rendering of duty between a sovereign and his subjects. Which finds these duties the greatest tie or the most troublesome to perform? I will not decide, for this

would involve judging between the strict requirements
of reverence, obedience, and dependence on the one
side, and the supreme obligation to kindness, justice,
and protection on the other. To say that the king is
the arbitrator of the people's destinies, is only to tell
us that the crimes of mankind have naturally placed
them in subjection to laws of justice, of which the
king is the guardian, but to add that he is absolute
master of his subjects' wealth, without discussion, consideration, or question, is the language of flattery, or
the opinion of a favourite who will retract his words
only at the point of death.

A lovely day is fading into evening and you may see
a large flock of sheep dotted over the hillside, quietly
feeding on the sweet wild thyme, or in the meadow
nibbling the young and tender grass which has escaped
the reaper's scythe. The careful watching shepherd is
not far from his flock, he keeps his sheep always in
sight, and leads them and follows them to new pasture
ground. If they wander he gathers them together
again; if a hungry wolf appears, he sets his dog to
hound him off; he nourishes and protects them; day-
break finds him already in the field, which he only left
with the sun. What care! What watchfulness!
What servitude is this! Which condition appears to
you the most free and delightful, that of the shepherd
or his sheep? Is the flock made for the shepherd or
the shepherd for the flock? This pastoral imagery
represents the people and the prince who governs
them, if he is a good prince.

A proud, luxurious king is like a shepherd adorned
with gold and precious stones; a golden crook is in his
hands, a collar of gold round his dog's neck, and he
has a cord of gold and silk to lead him by. But how
will all this gold protect the flock from the wolf?

What a delightful post is that which gives frequent

opportunities of doing good to thousands: what a miserable one is that which at any moment exposes a man to the necessity of injuring millions.

___

If there is in this world no happiness for men greater, more natural, and more sublime, than the knowledge of being beloved; and if kings are men; can they ever purchase the hearts of their people too dearly?

___

There are few general rules or proved measures for good government. Times and circumstances have to be considered which mingle prudence and caution with the aims of those who reign. Therefore perfect government shows a master mind; though perhaps it would be impossible to attain, if the people did not contribute towards it by their habits of dependence and submission.

Those who hold the highest posts under a great monarch have very easy places, and fill them with little trouble. Everything flows from the fountain head. The authority and genius of the prince makes the way plain, smooths all difficulties and makes things prosper beyond expectation. They have only the merit of subalterns.

If the care of one family is such a burden, if it is enough for a man to have to answer for himself, what a weight, what a load is the charge of a whole kingdom? Is the sovereign recompensed for all his anxiety by the humble reverence of his courtiers, or the pleasures an absolute power seem to give? I reflect on the painful, and dubious, and dangerous paths he is sometimes forced to follow in order to establish public tranquillity. I think over the extreme though necessary measures he is often obliged to use for a good end, and knowing that he is accountable to God, even for the felicity of his people, that good and

evil are in his hands, and that he has no excuse of
ignorance ; I ask myself, Would you wish to reign?
Would a man who is moderately happy in a private
condition of life quit it for a throne? Is it not enough
for him who is born a king to discharge his hereditary
duties.

How many gifts from heaven are required to help a
prince to reign well*? An august birth, a royal and
commanding air, a face which will satisfy the curiosity
of those who crowd to see him, and which will inspire
respect in his courtiers, a perfectly even temper, an
aversion to ill-natured jesting, or good sense enough to
suppress it. He must never threaten, reproach, or give
way to his passion, and yet exact obedience. His disposition must be pliant and engaging, his heart sincere
and open, so that all may think they understand him.
This will help him to make friends, dependants, and
allies. He must be always reserved, deep, and impenetrable as to his motives and designs, be very grave
and serious in public ; dignity, justice, and brevity must
all unite in his replies to foreign ambassadors and in
his council chamber. In bestowing favours his manner
must have such grace as will seem to double the benefit ;
and in his choice of persons to be thus gratified he must
show great discernment, discriminating between the
qualifications, talents, and dispositions of those who are
chosen as ministers and generals, or to hold office. He
must have such a firm and decided judgment that in
all affairs he will at once see what is best and most
just; and his understanding must be so righteous and
sincere as to make him sometimes declare against himself in favour of the people, his allies, or his enemies.
He must possess such a happy memory that he recalls

---

* In answering this question, La Bruyère gives an ideal
portrait of Louis XIV.

at once the needs of a subject, and even names, faces, and petitions; a wide intelligence, which extends not only to foreign affairs, commerce, state policy, and political views, new conquests, and the defence of them by impregnable fortresses, but he must know also how to confine himself to home concerns and be acquainted with all the details of the realm, knowing when to abolish all false worship which might be prejudicial to sovereignty, to put down all cruel or reprobate customs, to reform laws if they are full of abuse, to make his cities secure and convenient, noble and magnificent; punishing severely all scandalous vices, and and by his authority and example advancing the honour of religion and virtue. He must protect the church and the clergy, their rights and liberties; treat his people as kindly as a father treats his children, always planning for their comfort, trying to lighten their taxes and other burdens that they be not impoverished. He must have great talent for war, be vigilant, diligent, and unwearied, able to command in person his numerous armies, be calm and fearless in the midst of danger, sparing himself only for the good of the state, caring for its welfare and for its glory more than for his life. His power must be so absolute that there will be no opportunity for intrigue, and he will try to lessen the great distance between the nobility and the people by drawing nearer them himself, so that all may be equally submissive. His knowledge must be so extensive that everything will be under his own eyes, and all acts will proceed directly from him; his generals, however distant, must be but his lieutenants, and his ministers his ministers only. His wisdom must be so profound that he knows when to declare war, when to vanquish, and how to make the best use of victory; knows how to make peace and when to break it, and how to constrain his enemies as diverse interests arise, to set bounds to ambition, and how far to extend his conquests. Even in the midst of enemies, secret or open, he must find leisure for plays, feasts, and spectacles, cultivate the arts and sciences, design and erect magnificent edifices. His genius must be so vigorous and universal that he is beloved and revered by his own people and feared by strangers. His court, and indeed his whole kingdom, is like a single family, perfectly united under one chief, a union which renders them formidable to the rest of the world. All these admirable virtues seem to be comprised in my idea of a sovereign. True, we rarely meet with them in one person ; too many things have to contribute. at once, mind, heart, temperament, and external circumstances : but it appears to me that a prince who unites all these in his person is very worthy of the name of " Great."

Do not let us be angry with man when we find him stubborn, unjust, proud, and selfish ; men are made so, it is their nature; we might as soon remonstrate with the stone for falling, or the sparks for flying upward.

In one sense men are not fickle except in trifles. They change their clothes, their language, their habits, and sometimes their tastes, but they always preserve their evil inclinations, are firm and constant in wrongdoing, and in their indifference to virtue.

Stoicism is an idle fancy, an idea something like the republic of Plato. Stoics pretend that a man may laugh at poverty, be insensible to injury, ingratitude, the loss of wealth, relations, friends; look coldly on death as a thing of no consequence, which ought neither to make him merry nor sad ; that neither pleasure nor pain ought to overcome him, and that he ought to undergo the torments of fire or sword without uttering the faintest cry or shedding a single tear ; and this imaginary phantom of virtuous endurance they are pleased to call a wise man. But, after all, mankind is left in possession of every defect those stoics found in him; they have not cured him of a single weakness. Instead of depicting vice in its most hideous or ridiculous forms to disgust him with it, they have indicated an idea of heroism and perfection of which man is not capable, and exhorted him to strive after the impossible. Thus this imaginary wise man is to find himself naturally and by his own strength above regarding any circumstance or ill; neither the most agonizing attack of gout, nor the sharpest twinge of pain, is to have power to draw from him the least complaint.   Heaven and earth may be turned upside down, but it is no concern of his; and he would be supposed to stand firm on the ruins of the universe, while another man nearly loses his senses, cries and bewails, and flashes fire from his eyes and loses his breath for the sake of a lost dog or a piece of broken china.

Restlessness of mind, irregularity of temper, inconstancy of heart, and uncertainty of conduct, are all mental defects, but all different, and, notwithstanding the relation they all appear to bear to each other, they are not necessarily found in the same person.

A changeable man is several men in one, he multiplies himself every time he acquires a new title or puts on a different manner.   He is not this minute what he was the last, and he will be the next what he never was before, he is always succeeding himself.   Do not ask what his disposition is, but what his dispositions are; nor what his humour, but how many varieties of humour he has.   Are you not mistaken, was it not *Euthycrates* you met to-day?   How stiff he was to you. Yesterday he sought you out and made so much of you that all his friends were jealous of you; do you think he knows you? tell him your name.

*Menalcas** goes down stairs, opens his door to go out, shuts it.   He then perceives that he is still in his night-cap, and examining himself a little closer he discovers that only half his face is shaved; that he wears

---

* Said to be the Duke de Brancas, the most absent-minded man of his time.

his sword at his right side and his stockings hanging over his heels. If he walks into the street he feels something strike him on the face, he cannot imagine what it can be, till waking up he opens his eyes and finds that he has run into a carriage shaft, or hit against a plank on a carpenter's shoulder. He was once seen to run up against a blind man with such force that both fell backward. He often happens to come up forehead to forehead with the prince, and has scarcely time to squeeze himself close to the wall to prevent a collision, with difficulty making room for him to pass. He is seeking for something, gets confused, calls out that he cannot find it, gets into a heat, calls his servants one after the other, tells them they lose everything, put everything out of the way, and demands his gloves which are in his hands, like the woman who asked for her mask when it was on her face. He enters a room and passes under a lustre to which his wig gets hooked and remains hanging. The courtiers look at it and laugh, *Menalcas* looks also and laughs louder than the others; he looks all round the company to discover who shows his ears and has lost his wig. If he goes into the city, he has gone only a short distance when he believes he has lost his way, makes a great disturbance, and asks the passers by to tell him where he is. They tell him the name of the street he lives in, so near is he to his own house which he enters, but quickly runs out again thinking he has made a mistake. On coming out of the palace he finds a carriage at the foot of the grand staircase; he mistakes it for his own and gets in, the coachman touches up the horses and believes he is taking his master home. *Menalcas* jumps out, crosses the court, mounts the stairs, walks through the ante-chamber, chamber, and closet, everything is familiar—nothing new, he sits down, rests, and feels at home. Presently the master comes in, he rises up to receive him, treats him very politely, begs him to be seated and does the honours of the place. He talks, reflects, and talks again, the master of the house is tired and astonished, and *Menalcas* is no less so, but does not say what he thinks, he sees he has to do with some troublesome, idle fellow, who will take himself off sometime, no doubt; he must just have patience. Night comes on, when with some difficulty he is undeceived. Another time he pays a visit to a lady, and, being persuaded that she is visiting him, sits down in her arm-chair and never thinks of giving it up. He begins to think the lady pays very long visits, and expects every moment she will get up and leave him at liberty, but the time drags on, he is hungry, and as night comes on he invites her to sup with him. She laughs, and laughs so loudly that he wakes up. He gets married one morning, but forgets all about it by evening and goes to the country. Some years after he loses his wife, who dies in his arms; he is present at the obsequies, and next day when his servants come and tell him dinner is served, he asks if his wife is ready, if they have told her.

It was he also who, going into a church, took the blind man sitting at the door for a pillar, and his dish for the holy water basin, plunged in his hand and crossed his forehead, when suddenly he hears the pillar speak and ask for alms. He walks up the nave, and thinks he sees a kneeling cushion, kneels heavily on it, and lo! the machine bends, sinks, and tries to cry out. *Menalcas* is surprised to find himself on the legs of a very little man, leaning on his back, with his two arms over his shoulders, while his clasped hands are stretched across his nose and mouth. He retires confused, and goes and kneels elsewhere; he draws out his prayer-book, as he supposes, and behold it is his slipper which he has put in his pocket instead.

He is scarcely outside the church, when a man in livery runs after him, and asks him, smiling, if he has not got my lord's slipper. *Menalcas* shows him his own, and says—"This is the only slipper I have about me." He searches, however, and finds he has also the Bishop of ——'s slipper, whom he has been visiting, and found sitting by the fire, a little indisposed, and whose slipper he had picked up on leaving, instead of one of his own gloves he had let fall. He goes by water one day, and asks what o'clock it is ; they hand him a watch ; he has no sooner looked at it than he forgets both the hour and the watch, and throws the latter into the river as a thing which was in his way. First he writes a long letter, and, having sanded it, throws the sand into the inkstand, then a second, and having closed both, makes a mistake in addressing them, and the Duke, to whom he wrote first, reads, " Mr. Oliver, do not fail to send me, immediately you receive this, my usual supply of hay." His factor receives the other, and when he opens it, reads, "My Lord, I receive with a blind submission the orders which it has pleased your Grace —etc." He writes another letter at night, and after having sealed it, he blows out his candle, and is surprised to find himself in the dark ; can scarcely understand how it happens. Coming downstairs from the Louvre he meets some one coming up, takes him by the hand, saying, " You are the very man I want to see ; " and drags him along with him, crosses several courts, goes in and out of several halls, and then, as they retrace their steps, *Menalcas* looks at the man he has been dragging after him for the last quarter of an hour, and wonders who he is, and what he wants ; he has nothing to say to him, lets him go, and turns the other way. He will often stop to ask you a question, but is already a long way off before you can answer him, or he will ask you how your father is, and when you tell him he is very ill, he exclaims cheerfully—how glad he is !

N

One morning he orders dinner to be got ready early, as he has important business to attend to; he rises before the fruit is served, and takes leave of the company, but he may be seen that day in all the chief parts of the city, except where he has made the appointment which interfered with his dinner, and obliged him to go out on foot, as he was in too much haste to wait for his carriage. You may hear him violently railing against one of his servants, "Where is he? what can he be doing? he is always out of the way when he is wanted ! He need not come near me again : I shall give him warning from this day.". While he is speaking the servant comes in; he asks him in a passion where he has come from, and is answered, "From the place you sent me to," and he gives a faithful account of his errand. You very often take him to be what he is not ; for a stupid, because he hears little and speaks less; for a fool, because he talks to himself, and has a habit of making grimaces and absurd motions with his head ; for a proud, uncivil man, because when you bow to him he passes without looking, or looks at you without returning your salute; for a thoughtless man, because he talks of bankruptcy in a family which has a bankrupt relative, of executions and scaffolds to a person whose father was beheaded, of low birth to a man who has become rich and wishes to be thought noble. In fact, he thinks and speaks at the same time, but what he speaks of is rarely what he is thinking of, therefore there is very little coherence in what he says. He usually replies yes instead of no, and when he says yes you may suppose he means to say no; he may answer you with his eyes attentively fixed on yours, but he does not see you, he is not thinking of you or of any one or anything in the world; all you can draw from him, even in his most attentive mood, is something like this—"Yes, indeed, truly good, all the better, certainly I believe so," or something quite as inappropriate. His mind is never with those he appears . among, he quite seriously calls his footman "Sir" and his friend "Thomas," he says "Your Reverence" to a prince of the blood, and " Your Highness" to a Jesuit. When he attends mass, if the priest sneezes, he cries out "God bless you." A grave and venerable judge asks him if such a thing happened, he replies "Yes, miss." On one occasion, as he was returning from the country, his servants undertook to rob him, and succeeded; they jumped down from behind the carriage and held a lighted torch in his face, demanding his purse, which he delivered to them. When he arrived at home he recounted his adventure to his friends, who kept plying him with questions about it; he told them to ask the servants, saying they were there !

Impoliteness is not a vice of itself, but is caused by several mental defects : foolish vanity, ignorance of duty, idleness, stupidity, contempt of others, jealousy. If it is displayed by outward manner, it is even more objectionable, being then a visible and manifest defect. It is true, however, that it offends us more or less according to the original cause of it.

If we say of a bad-tempered, unequal, quarrelsome, peevish, formal, capricious person, "It is only his disposition," that does not excuse him, as people seem to think, but is an unconscious confession that such great defects are incurable.

Temper, as we call it, is too little kept in check among men. They ought to understand that it is not enough to be good : they must also show it, at least if they wish to be sociable and fit for kindly intercourse ; in other words, if they would be men. We do not expect of malignant minds that they should be agreeable and kind; they can be so when such qualities are required to ensnare the simple or to turn their own cunning to account. But we desire that those who are good at heart should be always affable, obliging, and courteous, so that it may no longer be said that the wicked do us harm and the good make us suffer.

It is generally the case that if a man is angry with you his next step is to injure you ; some, however, act quite differently; they first offend and then get angry, and we are so surprised at this proceeding that no room is left for resentment.

Some men do not apply themselves enough to looking for opportunities of giving pleasure to others. They seem only to wish to be obliging, and they are not. The thing we do most promptly is to refuse; that we do at once, but we grant only after reflection.

Know exactly what you are to expect from mankind in general, and also from individuals, and then venture into the world.

If poverty is the mother of crime, want of sense is the father of it.

It is difficult to understand how a dishonest man can have sense. A penetrating, straightforward nature goes with order, truth, and virtue. It is want of sense and penetration which makes a man obstinate in wickedness and falsehood. We seek in vain to correct these faults by caricaturing them in others, but he does not recognize the sarcasm, it is like railing at a deaf man. It would be better for the benefit of honest men and for public satisfaction if a rogue were not so devoid of feeling.

There are some vices we owe to nobody, they were born with us, and are strengthened by habit ; there are others which are quite foreign to us, these we contract. Some men are born with easy manners, complaisance, and a desire to please; but from the treatment they receive from those with whom they live, or on whom they depend, they are soon forced to change their ways, and even their dispositions; they become fretful and melancholy, they see the change in themselves, and at last are astonished to find that they are hard and sharp.

Some ask why mankind in general do not compose one nation, and are not contented to speak one language, to live under the same laws, and agree among themselves to have the same customs and the same worship; whilst I, seeing how contrary are their minds, their tastes, and sentiments, wonder to see even seven or eight persons living between the same walls under one roof and making a single famiiy.

There are some strange fathers who seem during the whole course of their lives to be chiefly occupied in preparing reasons for their children to console themselves on their death.

The morals, the manners, and the humours of most men are unnatural. During all his life one man has lived bad-tempered, passionate, greedy, and selfish; he was born gay, peaceful, generous, noble-minded, and far above all meanness; but the necessities of life, circumstances, situations, and the law of necessity force nature and cause such great changes. Thus a man can scarcely understand himself; so many things beyond his control spoil his character, upset and unsettle him, that he is really neither exactly what he thinks he is, nor what he appears to be.

Life is short and wearisome; it is spent in vain longings; and we put off to the future our rest and enjoyment, often delaying till an age when our best blessings, health and youth, have already disappeared. The time comes and surprises us still in the midst of new desires, and we are still busy with them when a fever seizes us and extinguishes us. If we are cured, it is only to desire more.

When we wish a thing, we surrender at discretion to the wish of him from whom we hope. If we are sure of a thing, we temporize, parley, and then surrender.

It is such a general thing for a man not to be happy, and so essential that every good thing must be acquired with difficulty, that when something comes easily we are suspicious, and can hardly understand how that which costs us so little can be much to our advantage, or that we could so easily, and by using only honest measures, reach the end we proposed. We think we deserve success, but ought seldom to rely on that.

The man who says he was not born fortunate might at least become so by the kindness of his friends and relations. Envy robs him of this last resource.

Although, perhaps, I may have said elsewhere that the afflicted have themselves to blame, men seem to be born for misfortune, grief, and poverty. Few escape it, and since any calamity may befall them, they ought to be prepared for all adversity.

What difficulty there is in arranging business affairs ! Men are so keen over the least advantage, and bustle

up at every obstacle, so willing to deceive and so un-
willing to be deceived, setting such high value on what
belongs to them and so small a price on what belongs
to others, that I confess I do not know how or when
they are able to conclude marriage contracts, purchases,
peace treaties, truces, or alliances.

With some, arrogance supplies the place of greatness;
cruelty, obstinacy, and deceit the place of wit. Cheats
easily believe others to be as bad as themselves ; they
are hard to deceive, but neither can they deceive
long.

I would rather be considered stupid than a cheat.

No blessing attends cheating, for malice and falsehood go with it.

We hear nothing in the streets of great cities but
such words as writs and executions, and the passers
by talk only of bonds and pleadings. Is there not the
smallest amount of equity left in the world? Is it on
the contrary full of people who demand what is not
due to them, and who boldly refuse to pay what they
owe?

Parchments were invented to remind men of their
word and to persuade them to keep it. What a disgrace to mankind!

If you were to take away passion, self-interest, and
injustice, what a great calm would fall upon our cities!
The necessaries of life do not make a third part of the
turmoil.

Nothing so much helps a reasonable mind to support
quietly the injuries he receives from relations and
friends, as reflection on the vices of humanity, and

the difficulty men have in being constant, generous, and faithful, or of being sensible of any affection greater than their own interests. If he reflects, he will understand the range of their capacity, and will not expect them to penetrate solid bodies, fly in the air, or possess rectitude. He may hate mankind in general for having so little virtue, but he excuses individuals, he even loves from some higher motive, and tries as much as possible not to require similar indulgence.

There are certain benefits we passionately desire ; the mere idea of them excites and moves us, and if we happen to obtain them, we accept them with greater tranquillity than we thought possible, and are less engaged enjoying them than in aspiring after still greater things.

There exist such frightful evils, such horrible misfortunes, that we dare not think of them, the very prospect of them makes us tremble. But if they happen to fall on us, we find that we have more resources than we imagined, we brace ourselves to bear misfortune, and endure it better than we expected.

Sometimes very little is required to mitigate a great grief ; we interest ourselves in a pleasant house, or find ourselves the possessors of a fine horse or a good dog, even a new carpet or a new clock will help to make us feel a great loss less.

I first try to imagine to myself that men are to live for ever on this earth, and then I meditate as to whether they could do better for themselves in these circumstances than they do now.

If life is miserable, it is painful to endure it, if it is happy, it is terrible to lose it; both come to the same thing.

There is nothing man is so anxious to preserve, yet takes less care of, than life.

Irene* goes at great expense to Epidaurus, she visits the temple of Æsculapius, and consults him about all her ailments. First she complains that she is weary and worn out with fatigue; the god pronounces this the effect of her long journey. She says she has no appetite for supper; the oracle orders her to eat less dinner; she adds that she is troubled with sleeplessness; he tells her never to lie in bed by day. She asks how she can become thin; the oracle replies that she must rise before noon and sometimes use her legs to walk on. She declares that wine disagrees with her; the oracle bids her drink water: she suffers from indigestion, she must diet herself. "My sight," complains *Irene,* "begins to fail me." "Use spectacles," is the reply. "I am getting so weak," she continues; "I am not nearly so strong as I was." "You are getting old," said the god. "But how am I to cure this languishing feeling?" "The shortest way, *Irene,* is to die, as your grandfather and grandmother did before you." "Son of Apollo," exclaims *Irene,* "is this the wondrous skill men rave about? You have told me nothing new or mysterious; did I not know all that you have told me before?" "Why did you not put your knowledge into practice, then," is the answer, "without coming so far to seek me, shortening your days by a long and tedious journey?"

Death only comes once, but we feel it every moment of our lives: it is harder to apprehend than to suffer it.

---

* Madame de Montespan, a *malade imaginaire.*

Uneasiness, fear, and dejection cannot keep death from us, yet I doubt if much laughter suits mortal men.

The certainty of death is mitigated by its uncertainty; in its indefiniteness there is something of infinitude, or what we call eternity.

We are sighing now for the loss of our vanished youth; let us remember that decay will come, and then we shall regret this, our age of maturity, which we do not appreciate.

We fear old age, yet we cannot be sure of attaining it. We hope to grow old, and still we fear old age; that is to say, we love life and long to escape death.

It is better to give way to nature and fear death than to be always fighting against it, arming ourselves with reasons and arguments why we should not fear it.

If some died and others did not, death would be a terrible affliction.

A long illness is placed between life and death, so that when death comes it may be a relief both to those who die and those who are left.

Humanly speaking, death is a good thing, it puts an end to old age. The death which prevents dotage is more opportune than that which ends it.

The regrets men suffer for mis-spent time do not always lead them to make a better use of what remains to them.

Life is a sleep. To the old the sleep has been longest; they only begin to awake as death approaches. If they could then pass in review all the years of their lives, they would not find in many of them either virtues or praiseworthy actions to distinguish one from the other; the different stages of life are blended and confused, and nothing stands out to measure life by. It seems an incoherent dream, and the dying feel like those who awake, that they have slept long.

There are but three events which happen to mankind, birth, life, and death. Of birth they know nothing, in death they suffer, and forget to live.

Children are proud, hasty, envious, inquisitive, selfish, idle, frivolous, timid, ungovernable, false, and deceitful; they laugh or cry in a moment, are extravagantly happy or in great grief over trifles; they would not suffer evil but love to do mischief. They are men in miniature.

Children think neither of the past nor future; they enjoy what we rarely do, the present.

Children seem to be all the same; it is only by very careful and minute attention we can distinguish differences; these increase, however, as reason comes, because with it the passions and vices of nature grow, and these alone make men so unlike each other, so complex to themselves.

Children possess two faculties which old people lose, imagination and memory; and they make marvellous use of them in their games and amusements, for by their aid they repeat things they hear, and imitate what they see done; they try everything and occupy themselves with all kinds of inventions, even copying the movements and gestures of different artizans by way of amusement, or transporting themselves into imaginary palaces or enchanted castles, where they have grand equipages and trains of followers, lead their armies into battle, and enjoy all the pleasures of victory, talk with kings and princes, or are themselves kings with numerous subjects and vast treasures, which are only leaves or pebbles; they are what during the rest of their lives they cannot be, the arbitrators of their own fortunes, and masters of their happiness.

There are no exterior vices or defects which children do not perceive at once, and they can indicate them in fitting words; we could not ourselves express them so happily. But when they become men they are loaded in their turn with the same imperfections, and are themselves mocked.

The chief endeavour of children is to find out their master's weak points and the weaknesses of all to whom they are in subjection; and as soon as the discovery is made they get the upper hand, and never give up their advantage ; for what made us forfeit our advantage in their eyes will prevent our ever recovering it.

Idleness and laziness, which are so natural to children, disappear in their games, where they are quick, lively, and exact, great advocates of rule and order, which they insist on for their companions, and they will themselves begin a thing many times if they fail, certain sign that though they may one day neglect their duty, they will never forget their pleasures.

In children's eyes everything is great, gardens, buildings, furniture, men, and animals. To us, worldly affairs seem great, and I daresay for the same reason, because we are little.

. Who doubts that children do not originate, judge, and reason correctly?—and if only in little things, that is because they are only children and have not much experience, and if they use wrong words it is less their fault than that of their parents and masters.

Children lose confidence in you, and you are useless to them, if you punish them for faults they never committed, or speak severely to them about trifling things; they know exactly what they deserve, better than any-one else indeed, and they seldom deserve more than they dread. When they are chastised, they know if it is rightly or wrongly; and undeserved punishment does them more harm than indulgence.

We do not live long enough to profit from our mis-takes; we are committing them during the whole course of our lives, and all that we can do without failure is to die corrected.

It is hard to confess our faults; we would rather hide them or lay them on some one else; and this is what gives a director an advantage over a confessor.

The faults of fools are sometimes so awkward and so difficult to foresee that they put wise men in the wrong, and only serve those who commit them.

Party-spirit lowers the greatest man to an equality with the rabble.

Vanity and decorum lead us to do the same things and in the same way as if we were prompted by inclination or duty. A great man* has died in Paris of a fever caught nursing his wife, whom he did not love.

All men desire at heart to be esteemed; yet they are careful that no one shall discover how much they covet esteem: because, if men wish to possess a certain virtue and yet to reap some merit from it, that is to say esteem or praise, that is no longer being virtuous but loving esteem and praise, or being vain. Men are very vain, yet they dislike nothing so much as being thought so.

A vain man likes to speak of himself either good or ill; a modest man never speaks of himself. ·
Vanity is ashamed to show itself, and often hides under a semblance of modesty, and in this is its absurdity very plainly to be seen. False modesty is the most cunning kind of vanity; it makes a man assume a virtue he does not possess, and gives him a character opposed to his merits, and this is a lie. False glory is the temptation of vanity, it leads men to try to gain esteem by qualities which, though indeed they possess, are too insignificant to exalt them.

Men speak of themselves in such a way that if they confess to small faults they at the same time imply that they have great talents and fine qualifications. Thus, though they complain of a bad memory, they are at the same time well contented with their good sense and judgment, and if they are reproached for absent-mindedness, they seem to think it is a sign of wit; they acknowledge that they are awkward, can do nothing with their hands, but are quite consoled for the loss of such talents by their mental gifts and spiritual powers which

---

* The Prince of Conti.

everybody admits. They talk of their idleness in terms which show their indifference and their want of ambition. They are not ashamed of slovenliness, which marks only a carelesness in little things, and makes it appear that they are diligent only over solid and essential things. A soldier is fond of saying that it was foolhardiness or curiosity which placed him in danger in the trenches, or some other perilous position whither he had not been ordered, and adds that his General reprimanded him.

In the same way a great genius, born with all the prudence which others vainly endeavour to acquire, who has had the natural bent of his mind strengthened by wide experience, to whom the number, weight, variety, difficulty, and importance of affairs is an employment, not an oppression; who, by his deep insight and penetration makes himself master of all events; who, far from being biassed by all the reflections which are thrown on the government and the political situation, is perhaps one of those lofty souls born to rule others, and by whom some of the laws were suggested, is prevented by the great things he does from having the enjoyment of the pleasant things he might read, but he loses nothing if he turns over the leaves of his own life and actions. A man thus endowed may say safely that he knows nothing of books, and never reads.

Men would sometimes hide their weaknesses, or make them less important by confessing them freely. "I know nothing," says one, who is really very ignorant. "I am quite old," says another, who is past sixty; "I am not rich," confesses a man who is miserably poor.

The world is full of people, who, making superficial comparisons between themselves and others, always decide in favour of their own merits, and act accord-ingly.

———

You say modesty is a necessary virtue, and people of good birth say the same: then you ought to prevent those who yield through modesty being tyrannized over, and those who bend being crushed. Some also say people should be modest in their dress, and those who know their own value desire nothing more, but the world cries for ornament and gets it ; it covets super-fluities and receives them. Some esteem others only for their fine linen or rich stuffs, and we cannot always refuse to be impressed by such things. There are certain places we would like to be seen in, but our admittance depends on the width of a gold strip.

———

As we ought not to indulge in that vanity which makes us imagine that others are regarding us with curiosity or esteem, and converse only to entertain each other with our praises, so ought we also to have as much confidence in ourselves as will prevent us thinking that our friends only whisper to speak ill of us, and that they never laugh but to ridicule us.

———

How is it that *Alcippus* salutes me to-day, smiles to me, and almost throws himself out of the carriage in his eagerness to catch my eye? I am not rich, and I am on foot; it would have been more fashionable not to see me. Can it be that he wished me to see him driving with a great man?

———

Most people are so full of themselves that they show it in everything they do, they love to be seen, pointed out, saluted even by those they do not know. If they are not recognized they are angry ; they think people should know intuitively who they are:

We look beyond ourselves for our happiness, and seek to find it in the opinion of men whom we know to be flatterers, insincere, unjust, full of envy, caprice and prejudice. What folly!

———

We expect people to laugh at what is ridiculous only, but we see them laughing quite as much at what there is no absurdity in. If you are a fool and thoughtless, and some silly thing escapes you, they laugh; if you are wise, and only say sensible things in a proper manner, they laugh all the same.

———

If we find it so easy and pleasant to make fun of and despise others it is very unfair that we should feel angry with those who laugh at or despise us.

———

Health and wealth, by depriving men of all experience of misfortune, harden them towards their fellow-creatures: whilst those who are bowed down by their own misery enter compassionately into the sorrows of others.

———

It would seem that the effect of music and feasting on a truly good heart is to make the calamities of friends and relatives more keenly felt and realized.

———

A great mind is above injury, injustice, grief, or mockery, and would be invulnerable if it did not suffer through compassion.

———

There are some miseries which, to see, make us feel ashamed of being happy.

———

Men are quick to be aware of their smallest advantages, and slow to recognize their defects. They are not ignorant of their fine eyebrows and well-shaped nails, but they would rather forget that they are blind in one eye, and do not know that they are devoid of sense.

Argyra pulls off her glove to show her beautiful hand, and does not neglect to allow her little shoe to be seen that her small feet may be imagined. She laughs at everything, grave and gay, to display her fine teeth, and if she shows her ears it is because they are well-shaped. If she does not dance it means that she is not quite satisfied about her figure, which is broadening. She understands very well all her own interests except one thing—she speaks too much and has no sense.

Men reckon as almost valueless all the virtues of the heart, and idolize their wit and personal gifts. He can say coolly of himself, without any thought of boasting, that he is good, constant, faithful, sincere, just, and grateful, but would not dare to say that he is smart, has fine teeth, and a soft skin; that would be going too far.

It is true that there are two virtues which men admire, courage and liberality; because these are two things which they esteem much; and while these virtues make them neglect life and money, yet nobody boasts of himself that he is brave and liberal.

Nobody says of himself, especially without reason, that he is handsome, generous, high-souled; those qualities are so rare, and are valued so highly, that people content themselves with thinking they possess them.

Although there appears to be some resemblance between jealousy and emulation, there is in truth as much difference between them as between vice and virtue.

Jealousy and emulation are directed towards the same object, which is either the wealth or the attainments of another, with this difference, that the latter is a free, outspoken, sincere sentiment, which produces intellectual fruit, and profits by great examples, so as often to excel what it admires ; whilst the former is a violent effort, and enforced confession of merit greater than its own, which will even go so far as to deny virtue where it undoubtedly exists, or if forced to recognize it, refuses all praise and envies all reward; a fruitless passion, which leaves a man in the condition it found him, fills him with conceit and self importance, makes him a hard and cold judge of another man's acts or exertions, and even makes him feel only astonished that there exist in the world talents other than his own, or other men who possess the very talents he prides himself in.

This is a mean defect, which, if allowed to go to excess, becomes vanity and presumption, and does not so much convince the person who is affected with it that he has more talent and more merit than others, as it makes him believe that he alone possesses talent and merit.

It is persons of the same art or condition, or who possess the same talents, who are jealous of, or emulate each other. The worst craftsmen are the most apt to be jealous ; those who profess the liberal arts or polite literature, painters, musicians, orators, and poets, ought not to be capable of more than emulation.

Jealousy is never free from some degree of envy, and the two passions are often confounded. Envy, however, sometimes exists apart from jealousy, as, for instance, when it makes us long in our hearts for benefits much above our condition, as fortune, favour, or some high appointment.

Envy and hatred are always united, and strengthen

each other with the same object ; they are scarcely distinguishable from each other, but in this, that one fixes on the person, the other on his state or condition.

A sensible man is not jealous of an armourer who has wrought a fine sword, or of a sculptor who has made a fine statue ; he knows that in these arts there are rules and methods which he does not understand, that there are tools to be wielded of which he does not know the use or name or form, and it is enough for him to know that he has not learned a trade to be contented that he is not the master of it. He may, however, be quite susceptible to envy and even jealousy towards the government or some special minister. But reason and sound sense which he possesses in common with them are not the only means employed in ruling a nation and presiding over public affairs ; they cannot supply the place of rules, precepts, and experience.

We meet with few entirely dull or stupid minds, fewer sublime or supremely excellent ; men, in general, float between these two extremes, and the intermediate space is filled up by numerous ordinary geniuses who are very helpful, and serve their country ; including in their ranks the useful and agreeable, such as mercantile and financial affairs, the details of war and navigation, arts and professions, as well as memory and wit, which are necessary in society and conversation.

All the sense in the world is useless to him who has none ; he has no aims, and cannot profit by another man's.

The next step to reason would be to feel the want of it. A fool is not capable of such perception. So also, the next best thing to sense is to know that we are devoid of it, we would then be able without sense to do right and not to be a fool, a coxcomb, or impertinent.

A man who has but little sense is serious and equable ; he never laughs or jokes, nor makes fun of trifles, and is as incapable of rising to anything great as of accommodating himself even by way of relaxation to trifling things ; he can hardly play even with his children.

Every one says of a coxcomb that he is a coxcomb, but no one does so to his face ; he dies unknown and unregretted.

What a strange want of apprehension there is between the heart and the mind. The philosopher lives wickedly, in spite of his precepts; and the politician, with all his farsightedness, cannot govern himself.

Wit decays like other things : science is its food, and nourishes while it consumes it.

Those who have no need for them, often possess a thousand virtues which they do not know how to profit by.

We meet with men who lightly support the weight of favour and authority, who are quite accustomed to their deserved greatness, and whose heads are not turned by the high posts they are raised to. But, on the other hand, there are those whom fortune, without either choice or discernment, has blindly overwhelmed with blessings, and they enjoy them proudly and im- moderately. Their eyes, their conduct, their voice, declare openly the admiration they feel for the

eminence they have reached, and at last they become
so rampant that disaster alone can tame them.

A tall, robust man with a full chest and broad shoulders carries a heavy burden lightly and gracefully, and
still has one hand free; a dwarf would be crushed
with half the weight ; in the same way eminent posts
make great men greater still and small men even
less.

One would expect of a man who has once been
capable of a noble, heroic action known to the whole
world that, without appearing to be spent by this one
great effort, his conduct during the rest of his life
would at least be as wise and judicious as that of
ordinary men ; that he would not be guilty of any
meanness unworthy the high reputation he has acquired; that mixing less with the people, and not giving
them time to see too much of him, their curiosity and
admiration would not be allowed to grow into indifference, and perhaps contempt.

It is easier for certain men* to cultivate a thousand
virtues than to correct a single fault.   They are even
so unfortunate that this one fault is often one quite un-
suited to their condition, and it makes them appear
ridiculous in the eyes of the world.   It weakens the
effect of their great qualities, hinders them from being
perfect, and leaves their reputation not unstained.   We
do not ask that they should be more enlightened or
more incorruptible, fonder of order and discipline,
more faithful to their duty, more zealous for the public

---

*Harlay de Chauvallon, Archbishop of Paris, who was not
devoid of virtue and talent, but who very badly fulfilled one of
his duties.   It will easily be guessed which.

good, more grave; we ask only that they should not be
amorous.

Some men in the course of their lives change so
much in heart and mind that we should quite mis-
understand them if we were to judge them only by
what they appeared to be in their youth. Some were
pious, wise, and learned, who through that weakness
which is inseparable from much basking in fortune's
smiles, are so no longer. We know others who in the
early part of their lives applied all their energies to the
pursuit of pleasure; and who, as the result of misfortune, have become religious, wise, and temperate. The
latter are generally great men on whom we may rely,
their sincerity has been proved by patience and adversity; they are deeply imbued with the courtesy which
misfortune and home association has given them, and
to which they owe their well-regulated minds, powers
of reflection, and capacity.

Great evils spring from our dislike to be alone—
gambling, luxury, extravagance, wine, women, ignorance, scoffing, envy, and forgetfulness of God and ourselves.

The generality of men employ the best part of their
lives to make the last part miserable.

Hatred is so enduring and so obstinate that a true
symptom of approaching death is a desire for recon-
ciliation.

We gain the affection of others either by flattering
their passions or pitying their bodily infirmities: these
are the only ways in which we can be attentive to them:
therefore it is that the rich and fortunate are the most
difficult to control.

An old man in love is one of the greatest anomalies in nature.

The niggardliness of old men does not proceed from the fear that they will one day want money, for some of them have such immense wealth that they can scarcely have any such uneasiness. Besides, how can they fear that in their dotage they may lack necessaries when they voluntarily deny themselves to satisfy their avarice? Neither is it a desire to leave great riches to their children, for they naturally love nothing so much as themselves, and moreover there are many misers who have no heirs. This vice is more the effect of age and constitution ; old men abandon themselves to it just as naturally as they devoted themselves to pleasure in their youth, or to ambition in maturer years. Neither youth, vigour, nor health is required to be a a miser : a man does not require to take any trouble to save his income : he need only lock up all his wealth in his coffers, and deny himself everything. This suits old men, who must have one passion, because they are men.

The remembrance of youth is pleasant to old men : they love the places where they spent it ; the people they knew in that distant time are very dear to them ; they affect in their speech many of the words they used when they were young ; they keep to the old ways of singing and dancing, boast of the fashions of long ago, in clothes, furniture, and equipages ; they can never disapprove of things which ministered to their passions, or which added to their pleasures, and which remind them of them. How can they be expected to prefer new customs and recent modes in which they have no part, and from which they have nothing to hope, which young people have invented, and in their turn will store up similar memories against old age.

Too much negligence has the same effect on old men as too much adornment, both increase wrinkles and make old age more apparent.

An old man is proud, disdainful, and difficult to manage if he has not a great deal of sense.

An old man who has lived at Court, and has good sense and a faithful memory, is an inestimable treasure ; he is full of facts and maxims ; he can tell the history of the century, adorned with many curious details, which are to be found in no books ; he can give us rules of conduct and manners which are always trustworthy, because they are founded on experience.

Young men, because of their passions, which beguile them, are more fit for solitude than old men.

We see certain sullen animals scattered over the country; they are male and female, dark and leaden-hued, tanned by the sun, and bound to the earth which they are always digging and turning over with unconquerable obstinacy ; they have voices almost articulate, and when they raise themselves on their feet they show human faces, and in truth they are men. They retire at night into their dens, where they live on black bread, water, and roots ; they save other men the trouble of sowing, labouring, and reaping for their livelihood; and thus do not deserve to lack the bread which they themselves have sown.

Don Fernando in his province is idle, ignorant, slanderous, quarrelsome, deceitful, intemperate, impertinent ; but he draws his sword against his neighbours, exposes his life for trifles, and as he has killed men for little reason so he will himself be killed.

The provincial noble, useless to his country, his family, or himself, often without a home or clothes, or any merit, repeats ten times a day that he is a nobleman; despises the wealth of the city, and occupies all his time with his parchments and titles, which he would not change for the mace of a chancellor.

In all men there may be found infinite combinations of power, favour, genius, riches, dignity, nobility, strength, industry, capacity, virtue, vice, weakness, stupidity, poverty, obscurity of birth and vulgarity. All these qualities blending together in a thousand different ways, and balancing each other in various persons, make all the diverse states and conditions of men. When men, moreover, know each other's strength and weakness, they act reciprocally, as they believe it their duty to act, recognizing their equals, and understanding the respect due to their superiors, and what they have a right to expect from others : from this proceeds either familiarity or deference, pride or contempt; and from the same cause it happens that in public places we find ourselves continually meeting those we wish to be intimate with and those we would rather avoid ; we are honoured by knowing one and ashamed to know the other; or it happens that the man you wish to speak to does not wish to be troubled with you, leaves you for another who is ashamed to be seen speaking to him, and so on in this strange intercourse one despises here, and is despised there ; and what we gain on one side we lose on the other. Would it not be better to renounce for ever haughtiness and pride, which are so unbecoming for weak men, and to arrange to treat each other with mutual kindness, which would ensure the advantage of never being mortified ourselves, giving us also the satisfaction of never mortifying any one else.

Instead of being afraid or blushing at the very name of philosopher, there is no one born into this world who does not owe it to himself to acquire a slight knowledge of philosophy. It is suitable for every body, and is useful for every age, sex, and condition; it consoles us in other people's good fortune, when the unworthy have the preference over us, and in unsuccessful efforts and in decline of strength or beauty; it arms us against poverty, old age, sickness, and death, against fools, and evil scoffers, enables us to live without a wife, or helps us to endure the one we have.

In one day a man will open his heart to the enjoyment of trifles, and allow himself to be overcome by small annoyances ; nothing is more unequal and less coherent than the changes which pass so rapidly over men's hearts and minds. The only remedy for this evil is to estimate the things of this world at what they are worth.

It is as difficult to find a vain man who considers himself appreciated as it is to find a modest man who thinks himself undervalued.

The poverty of the vine dresser, the soldier, or the stone-cutter, prevents me thinking myself poor when I see the wealth possessed by princes and ministers, and which I lack.

Only one real misfortune can befall a man, and that is to feel himself in fault, and to have cause for self-reproach.

Most men are more capable of one great effort to attain their ends than of long perseverance. Laziness or fickleness robs them of the fruit of a good beginning, and they often allow themselves to be outstripped by others who started after them, and who proceed slowly but surely.

I venture almost to assert that men know better how to propose measures than how to follow them, or to resolve what to do or say, rather than do or say what they ought. In some matter of business we firmly determine to be silent about a certain thing, and then either through passion, or in the excitement of conversation, it is the first thing to escape us.

Men act feebly in things which are their duty; while they make it a merit or even a conceit to be eager about those things which neither belong to them nor suit their character and position.

When a man assumes a character foreign to his nature, there is as much difference between what he seems to be and what he is as between a mask and a face.

The greatest wits are unequal, brilliant one day, and dull another. If then a wit is wise, he speaks little and writes nothing when he is out of humour, does not try to amuse. Do we sing if we have a cold? Must we not wait till the voice returns.

The fool is automatic, a machine, a spring, moved by weights, always in the same way, and with the same regularity. He is equable, never in a bustle. If you have seen him once, you have seen him as he always is. He is like the bull who bellows, or the blackbird who whistles, his nature is quite settled;

what seems the least evident in him is his soul, that
has no life, no action ; it sleeps.

The fool never dies, or, if according to our way of speaking, he dies, we may truly say that he gains by it, and
that in the moment when others die he begins to live ;
his soul then thinks, reasons, infers, concludes, judges,
foresees, and does everything it never did before. It
finds itself freed from a mass of flesh, where it was
buried without any function or movement or any
worthy exercise ; I merely said that it blushed to have
been bound for so long to such a coarse and imperfect
body, of which it had only been able to make a fool or
an idiot. It is now equal to the greatest souls, those
which have animated the bodies of the greatest and
wisest of men. There is now no difference between
the soul of *Alain* and that of the great Condé,
Richelieu, or Pascal.

False delicacy in common things, such as manner
and behaviour, is not called so because it is feigned,
but because it is exercised on familiar occasions when
it is not necessary. False delicacy in taste or constitution, on the contrary, is real because it is feigned or
affected, like *Eliza*, who screams out with all her
strength in some small danger of which she is not at
all afraid, or *Nina*, who turns pale at the sight of a
mouse, or *Georgette*, who is fond of violets, and faints
at the sight of a tuberose.

Who will venture to hope that he can satisfy mankind ? A prince, however good and powerful he may be,
need not undertake it. Let him make men's pleasures
his chief concern ; let his courtiers have the freedom
of his palace, even of his private rooms, and of those
places the very sight of which is an entertainment ; let

him provide them with many other sights, games, concerts, and splendid feasts, and perfect liberty to enjoy them all; let him even enter into all their amusements himself; the great man may be affable, the hero kind and familiar, still he would not have done enough. Men end by wearying of the very things which charmed at first. They would forsake the table of the gods, nectar would in time become insipid; they do not scruple to criticise perfection; in this lies their vanity and affectation : their taste, if we are to believe them, is superior to all our attempts to satisfy it, even after the most royal expense has been lavished to try to succeed, and malice will even prompt them to try to lessen the pleasure experienced in trying to content them. These same people who are generally so fawning and civil can belie themselves so that we scarcely recognize them; we see the man even in the courtier.

Affectation in gesture, speech, or manners, is often a result of idleness or indifference, and it is observed that some serious attachment or important business forces a man to be natural.

How does it happen that the same individuals who can receive tidings of the greatest disaster with phlegmatic indifference are beside themselves with anger over the most trifling inconvenience? Such conduct is not wisdom; for virtue is equable, never noisy and excited : it is therefore a vice and nothing less than vanity which never rouses itself except over events which make people talk, and most about self, taking no interest in anything else.

We seldom repent of talking too little, but very often of talking too much. This is a common and trivial maxim which everybody knows and nobody practises.

If men could blush at their own actions how many sins, public and private, would they be spared.

If certain men are not so upright as they might be, it is through some defect in their education.

Some men have just sense enough to be prudent.

Timon, the misanthrope, may be at heart stern and reserved, but outwardly he is civil and polite, although he does not belie his nature and become sociable with others ; on the contrary, he treats them gravely and courteously, acting so as to hold them at a distance. He does not wish to be familiar with them, to make friends of them ; and in this he resembles a woman visiting another woman.

After having maturely reflected on mankind, and discovered the falsity of their thoughts, sentiments, tastes, and affections, we are forced to admit that they lose less through inconstancy of disposition than through obstinacy.

How many weak, effeminate, ordinary people there are with no great defects, and who yet are objects of ridicule ? And how many varieties of ridiculous persons are scattered among men attracting no attention by their peculiarity, and equally useless for instruction or to point a moral. Their weaknesses are unique, are not infectious, and are more personal than general.

NOTHING is more like firm conviction than great obstinacy. Plots, parties, and heresies proceed from it.

We are not always constant to our opinions : disgust follows close on infatuation.

Great things startle us ; small things are tedious ; custom familiarizes us with both.

There are two extremes of contrariety, both of which equally attract us—custom and novelty.

There is nothing more mean and underbred than to talk much in praise of those very persons of whom we thought little before they were promoted.

A prince's favour neither includes nor excludes merit.

It is strange that with all our puffed-up pride, and the high opinion we have of our own good judgment, we neglect to make use of it to speak in praise of others. Fashion, princely or popular favour, rouses our enthusiasm. We commend what is praised much more than what is worthy of praise.

I do not know that there is anything in the world which has more difficulty in obtaining praise than that which is most worthy of approbation; or that virtue, merit, beauty, and good actions, or good work of any kind, do not rouse stronger antipathy than envy

and jealousy.   It is not of a saint that a devotee*
speaks well, but of another devotee.   If a beautiful
woman praises another's beauty, we may conclude she
possesses more than she praises.   If a poet praises
another's verses we may wager they are very poor.

It is not natural for men to like one another; they
have only a weak inclination to approve of each
other's actions, conduct, thoughts, expressions; nothing
satisfies or even pleases.   They are always substituting
for what others read, or write, or speak, what they
themselves would have done in similar circumstances,
what they have thought or written on such and such a
subject; and they are so full of their own ideas that
they have no room for those of others.

The generality of men are so inclined to irregularity
and trifling, and the world is so full of pernicious or
ridiculous examples, that I almost think singularity, if
kept within bounds, would come nearest to sound
reason and regular conduct.

We must do as others do: a dangerous maxim which
nearly always means we must do ill; at least when we
carry it beyond purely exterior and immaterial things
which have no influence, and are only matters of
custom, fashion, or convenience.   •

If men were not so like bears and panthers, if they
were equitable and just to themselves and others,
there would be no plaintiffs or defendants, and what
would become of the laws and text-books, the pro-
digious accumulation of commentaries, and the whole
science of jurisprudence?   To what would you reduce

---

* Note by La Bruyère.—False devotee (hypocrite).

P

those who swell their wealth by the pickings they are authorized to make in maintaining those laws? If men were honest and straightforward, and free from prejudice, whither would the disputes of the schools and the law-courts vanish? If they were temperate, chaste, and moderate, what need would there be for the mysterious jargon of medicine, which is a mine of gold for those who practise it. Lawyers, physicians, doctors, what a fall you would have, could we all discover the way to wisdom!

How many great men in the different spheres of peace and war could we have done without! To what point of refinement and perfection have we not brought those arts and sciences which ought never to have been necessary, and which exist in the world only as remedies for all the evils of which our wickedness is the source!

Since the time when Varro lived how much is known of which he was ignorant? Would even the wisdom of Plato or Socrates suffice us?

We listen to a sermon or a piece of music; we look at a gallery of pictures, and we hear on our right and left precisely opposite opinions expressed. This makes me say freely that of every kind of talent it is safe to risk good and bad together; the good pleases some, the bad others, and even the worst has its admirers.

The phœnix of song rose from his own ashes, and in one day saw his reputation die and revive again. The public, that stern and infallible judge, was change·able for once on his account, and was either mistaken or is now deceived. He who would now say that Quinault* is a poor poet would speak almost as foolishly as he who formerly said he is a good poet.

---

* French dramatic poet, born 1535. His popular operas excited the envy of Boileau.

Chapelain was rich, Corneille was poor. "La Pucelle" and "Rodogune" each merited the other's fate: and it is thus in certain professions, one man has made a fortune and another has missed it: and men must seek the reason of this in their own caprice, which in the most important conjunctures of their affairs, their pleasures, their health, or their life, often leads them to leave the best and take the worst.

The profession of an actor was infamous among the Romans and honourable among the Greeks. How is it with us? We think of them as the Romans did, and live with them as the Greeks did.

It was enough for Batyllus to be a clown to be run after by the Roman ladies, for Rhoé to be a ballet-dancer, and for Roscia and Nerina to sing in the chorus, to attract a crowd of admirers. Self-conceit and bold-ness, the result of too much power, had deprived the Romans of all taste for secrecy and mystery; they enjoyed making the theatre the scene of their love-making: they had no jealousy of the amphitheatre, nor of sharing the charms of their mistress with the multitude; their pleasure lay in showing they loved not a beauty, or even an excellent actress, but an actress.

Nothing shows better the appreciation men have for the sciences and literature, and their sense of their value to the republic, than the price set upon them, and the repute in which they, whose profession it is to culti-vate them, stand. There is no trade, however mechanical and mean, which has not more certain, prompt, and solid advantages. The comedian, lounging in his carriage, bespatters the very face of Corneille walking on foot. To many, the names of scholar and pedant are synonymous. Often when the rich man speaks, and speaks of learning, the scholar must be silent, listen and applaud, at least if he wishes to be credited with learning.

———

There is a kind of courage required in the presence of certain people to support the disgrace of being learned. They are prejudiced against scholars, to whom they deny any knowledge of the world, how to live in it, or how to behave in society; and having thus despoiled them, they dismiss them to their study and their books. As ignorance is a peaceful state which costs little trouble, most people adopt it; and form such a numerous company, both in Court and city, that they overwhelm the scholars; and even if the latter cite in their favour such names as Estrée, Harlay, Bossuet, Seguier, Montausier, Vardes, Chevreuse, Novion, Lamoignon, Scudéry, Pelisson, and many other personages equally learned and polite, nay, if they even dare to mention such great names as Chartres, Condé, Conti, Bourbon, and Vendome, as princes, who combined the highest knowledge of the Greeks with the smooth politeness of the Romans, they will be told without any scruple that these are singular examples; and if they then try to reason from an intelligent view, they are not powerful enough to stand against the voice of the public. It seems, however, that the public should be more cautious in deciding on this; and should at least take the trouble to question whether the mind which has made such great progress in knowledge as to be capable of thinking, judging, speaking, and writing well, could not also be polite. Very little depth is required to improve a man's manners, but much to polish his mind.

"He is a scholar," says a politician, "therefore incapable of business; I would not trust him with

the care of my wardrobe," and there is reason
in this. Ossat, Ximenes, and Richelieu were
learned; were they excellent in business? Did they
act even as good ministers? "He understands
Greek," says the statesman ; he is a scribbler, a philosopher, and, at this rate, an Athenian fruiterer must
have been a philosopher. Languages are but the
keys of science, no more ; neglect of one includes the
other, and it is of no importance whether languages
are ancient or modern, dead or living, but whether
they are uncivilized or polite, whether their literature
is in good or bad taste. Suppose that our language
should one day share the fate of the Greek and Latin
tongues, should we be thought pedantic if some centuries after this, when French is no longer spoken, we
should read Molière or La Fontaine ?

If I name *Euripilus*, and you say he is a wit, you
say also of him who works on a plank, he is a carpenter ; and of him who builds up a wall, he is a mason. I
ask you where is the workshop in which this wit follows
his trade ? what signboard has he ? how shall I know
him ? what are his tools ? a wedge, a hatchet, or a chisel ?
Where does he cleave his wood and hammer it, and
expose it for sale ? A workman boasts that he is a
workman, does *Euripilus* boast that he is a wit ? If
he does, he is a coxcomb, a mere sordid machine, to
whom the description witty or talented could not be
seriously applied; but if it is true that he boasts of
nothing, I tell you I will accept him as a wise and
talented man. Do you not also call a prig a clever
fellow, and say the same of an indifferent poet ? And
do you consider that you yourself have no talent ? No
doubt what you have is of a fit and proper kind, therefore you are a wit. But if it happens that you take
the name as an insult, do so. I consent to give it to

Euripilus, and to speak ironically as fools do who have no discrimination, or judgment; or as ignorant people who console themselves with it for the culture they neither possess themselves nor see in others.

I wish never again to hear of pens, ink, or paper; or of style, printer or printing; let no one ever again say to me, "You write so well, *Antisthenes!* * go on writing; are we never to see your work in a folio volume? never to see all the virtues and all the vices treated of in one large book, connected, methodical, and without an end?" they might add without sale, too. I renounce for ever all which was, or will be a book. The sight of a cat sends *Beryllus* into a fit, the sight of a book sends me into one. Am I better fed or clad, or have I a more luxurious room after being on sale for twenty long years? You say, I have a great name, much renown : say rather that I have plenty of empty praise which does me no good. Have I a single grain of that metal which procures everything? The pettifogger swells his bill and reimburses himself the expenses he never paid, and has a count or a judge for a son-in-law. A lackey becomes a commissioner, and is soon richer than his master ; the livery is buried in oblivion, and with his money he buys a title. Benoit has amassed a fortune by a puppet-show, Barbareau by selling bottles of water ; another charlatan comes over the mountains, and has scarcely unpacked his box when he is ready to return whence he came, with waggon loads of rich spoil. Mercury is Mercury and nothing more ; and gold not being enough to pay his mediations and intrigues, favours and distinctions are added.

And now let us speak of legitimate remunerations.

---

* Supposed to mean the Author himself.

You pay a tile-maker for his tiles, a workman for his time or labour, but do you pay an author for his thoughts or writing? Is he enriched or ennobled by doing his work well? Men must be clothed and shaved, and when they retire to their houses they must have doors which shut close, but is it necessary to be well informed? It is folly, simplicity, imbecility, continues *Antisthenes*, to set up as an author or philosopher. Have, if possible, a lucrative appointment which will make life agreeable, and enable you to lend to your friends, give to those who cannot repay, write for amusement, or to pass the time as *Tityrus* played or whistled on his flute. That or nothing ; and I write on these conditions, and thus submit to the violence of those who would take me by the throat and declare "You shall write." Well, they will read as the title of my new book " Some ideas of the good, the beautiful, and the true, with primary causes," by *Antisthenes* the Fishmonger.

If the Ambassadors* of foreign princes were educated monkeys, who had learned to walk on their hind feet, and to make themselves understood by interpreters, we could not be more struck with astonishment than we are by the propriety of their replies and the good sense which they evince in all their discourse. Prejudice and pride in our own nation makes us forget that reason belongs to every climate, and that there are wise thoughts wherever there are men. We do not like to be so treated by those we call barbarians; and if there is any barbarity among us, it consists in being surprised to see people of other countries able to reason like ourselves. All foreigners are not barbarians ; and all our countrymen are not

* Those of Siam, who came to Paris at this time.

civilized; and just as all the country people are not ill-
bred, so all citizens are not polite.   In a corner of a
maritime province in a certain kingdom in Europe,
the villagers are affable and gentle-mannered, and the
citizens and magistrates coarse through hereditary
rusticity.

———

With such purity of language, fine clothes, and
cultivated manners, good laws and white complexions,
we are still in the eyes of some people barbarians.

———

Should we be told of the Orientals that their
ordinary beverage is a liquor which flies to their heads
and makes them mad and sick, we would say "How
extremely barbarous."

———

That prelate seldom goes to Court or into society, is
never seen with ladies, does not play or assist at *fêtes*
and shows, is not a man of intrigue or of any party
spirit, but is always to be found in his diocese, where he
constantly resides.   He thinks of nothing but edifying
his people by instructive words and his own good
example.   He consumes his wealth in charity and his
body in penance, and imitates in every way the zeal
and piety of the Apostles.   Time changes things, and
in this reign he is threatened with a more eminent
title.

———

May we not try to make persons of a certain
character, and of what we may call a serious profession,
understand that they are not obliged to make the world
talk of them, and say that they play and sing and make
jokes like other men, and that to see them so pleasant
and agreeable, one would not believe that they could
elsewhere be so regular and severe?   May we not
venture to suggest to them that such manners detract

from the polished refinement on which they pride themselves; that outward appearances ought to agree with that refinement instead of contrasting with it, and showing the same man in such different lights, making him indeed a whimsical oddity.

We ought not to judge of men as of a picture or a statue, at first sight; we must search the heart and mind; the veil of modesty hides merit, and the mask of hypocrisy disguises malignity. Few people are discerning and correct judges; it is only by degrees and through time and circumstances that perfect virtue or consummate wickedness shows itself.

A FRAGMENT.*

Wit in that lovely woman was like an exquisitely set diamond; good sense and graceful elegance are so blended in her that she captivates heart and mind of all who speak to her; they know not if they admire or love; there is that in her which will make either a perfect friend or will force you to go beyond friendship. Too young and beautiful not to please, but too modest to think of pleasing, she esteems men only as they merit, and thinks of them only as friends. Full of vivacity, and capable of deep feeling, she surprises as much as she interests; and, without forgetting the most refined delicacy in her conversation, she yet introduces such humorous sallies that besides the pleasure they give they require no reply. She talks to you as one

---

* This is a portrait of Madame Catherine Turgot; she was beloved by the poet Chaulieu, whose portrait La Bruyère gives us under the name of *Artenice.* He addressed several poems to her under the name of *Iris.* "She was," said he, "the loveliest woman I ever knew, and she possessed, besides beauty, sweetness of temper and brilliant wit. No one ever wrote better than she did, and few as well."

who is unlearned, doubtful, anxious to be enlightened ;
and she listens to you like one who knows a great
deal, and is perfectly aware of the importance of all
you are telling her, and on whom your conversation
will not be lost. Far from laying herself out to
contradict you in a witty way, like *Elvira*, who prefers
to be considered sharp, rather than a woman of good
sense and propriety, she adapts your sentiments till
they become her own, and enlarges and beautifies
them so that you have the pleasant feeling that your
ideas have been better and more happily expressed
than you had thought. She is even above vanity, and
in speaking or writing she never sacrifices truth to
brilliancy, for she understands that true eloquence is
simple. If it is a matter of helping some one, and
you wish her interest, *Artenice* will not approach her
as he would *Elvira*, with flattery and pretty phrases, but
with sincerity, ardour, and earnestness. Her greatest
pleasure is in reading and conversing with persons of
fame and talent ; less for the pleasure of being known
than for that of knowing them. We may safely
predict that she will attain to great wisdom ; and praise
her for the merit she is storing up for future years :
since, added to a good disposition, she has the best
intentions and the highest principles, of infinite use to
those who like her are exposed to flattery and
attention. She is reserved without being rude, is even
a little inclined to solitude, and requires only opportunities for her virtue to dazzle all beholders.

The more natural a beautiful woman is, the more
lovely ; she loses nothing by being simple and un-
adorned, except by the charms of her own youth.
Innocent grace shines in her face and animates every
movement ; so that there is less danger in seeing her
decked with all the finery and ornament of fashion

than in her simplicity. In the same way an honest
man is respected for himself, and is not dependent on
external aids to render his person more esteemed and
his virtue more apparent. An invalid air, an affected
modesty, or a singularity in dress, adds nothing to
probity nor heightens merit : they burden it and
probably make it appear less pure and ingenuous.

Studied gravity becomes comical if carried to excess ;
for extremes meet, and dignity is found between, and
he who apes gravity will never attain it. A man is
either naturally grave or he is not so ; it is less difficult
to lay gravity aside than to assume it.

A renowned and talented man, if he is strict and
stern, frightens young people, gives them a wrong impression of virtue, and makes them shy of reformation
as too troublesome to practise. If, on the contrary,
he is kind and sociable, virtue becomes an easy lesson
to them ; and he teaches them that it is possible to live
happily and industriously, and to have serious aims
without renouncing honest pleasures ; he becomes an
example they may follow.

Physiognomy has no rule by which we may judge
man ; it serves only as a means of conjecture.

An air of intelligence is to men what regular features
are to women. It is a kind of beauty the vainest may
aspire to.

A man who is known to have much merit and great
talent is not ugly if he has the most deformed features ;
or if the deformity is noticed it makes no impression.

How much art is employed to imitate nature ! how
much time, what rules and attention and labour to be
able to dance with the same freedom and grace you

walk with, to sing as you speak, and to speak or express yourself as you think; to put as much force and spirit and passion into a studied public speech as we sometimes quite naturally entertain our friends with !

Those who, not knowing us well, think ill of us, do us no wrong. It is not us they attack, but a phantom of their own imagination.

There are some little rules, duties, kindnesses which belong to certain times, places, or persons. We do not know them intuitively, but custom teaches us with little trouble. To judge of men by their neglect of such things before they are instructed, is like judging of them by their nails or by the set of their hair, forming a decision which will one day be changed.

I do not know if it is permissible to judge of a man by a single fault; allowance should be made for extreme necessity, violent passion, or first impulse.

Truth is often found to be contrary to the current reports of persons or things.

Unless we keep a bridle on our tongue, and pay particular attention to all our words, we are liable every hour to say "Yes" and "No" on the same subject or of the same person. It depends only on the spirit of the society and conversation which naturally inclines us not to contradict this one or that one, although they talk differently of the same things.

A man who has partialities is exposed to frequen: mortifications, for it is as impossible that his favourites can be always gracious and wise as that those he declares himself against can be always to blame. From this cause he is often put out of countenance in public, either by the misfortunes of those he upholds, or by new glories acquired by those he condemns.

A prejudiced man who accepts a dignity, either secular or ecclesiastic, may be compared to a blind man who would paint, or a deaf man who would judge of a symphony; and this is but weak imagery in which to express the misery of prejudice.

We must add that it is a terrible malady, incurable, and apt to infect all who come in contact with the sick man. It makes us desert our equals, inferiors, relations, and friends, even our physicians; and the patient is far from being cured if he can neither be made to acknowledge the malady nor to understand the remedy; which is first to doubt, then to inform and enlighten himself. Flatterers, cheats, and backbiters, those who never unloose their tongues but to lie in their own interest, these are the knaves in whom he confides, and they make him swallow anything they please ; they also poison him, and then kill.

The rule of Descartes, never to decide on the least truth till it is clearly and distinctly understood, is so good and just that it ought to be extended to the judgment we form of persons.

Nothing better avenges the evil judgment men form of our talents, our morals, and our manners than the unworthy, wicked characters of those of whom they approve. With the same faculties with which we neglect a man of merit we admire a fool.

A fool is one who has not even the necessary wit to be a coxcomb.

A coxcomb is one whom fools believe to be a man of merit.

An impertinent fellow is an absurd fool; the coxcomb wearies, disgusts, repels; the impertinent fellow is repulsive, underbred, irritating, offensive : he begins where the other ends.

The coxcomb is between the fool and the impertinent fellow; he is made up of both.

Vices have their origin in a depraved heart; the effects of vice are in the constitution; absurdity comes from want of sense. If a man makes himself ridiculous he has the appearance of a fool. The fool is never free from absurdity, it is his character. Another pretends to be so, but not for long. An error may put a wise man in an absurd position. A fool is foolish, a coxcomb vain, and impertinence is rudeness. Absurdity is sometimes in the imagination of those who believe they see it where it does not exist and never can.

Rudeness, roughness, and brutality, may be vices of a man of wit.

A stupid man is a fool who never speaks; in this he is more endurable than the fool who speaks.

A jest or a simple remark from the lips of a wise man would be foolishness in a fool.

If a coxcomb could believe in his silliness he would lose his character.

One sign of indifferent sense is to be always telling stories.

The fool is embarrassed in himself; the coxcomb has an air of freedom and assurance; the impertinent fellow carries it off with impudence; merit is always modest.

The self-sufficient man is one in whom the management of a few details which he dignifies by the name of business is united with indifferent sense. A grain more sense and an ounce more business would make of him an important man.

The honest man is between a clever man and a good man, although equally distant from these two extremes.

The distance between an honest man and a clever man grows less every day, and is on the point of disappearing.

The clever man hides his passions, understands his interests, and sacrifices many things to it; has acquired wealth and knows how to keep it.

The honest man is one who neither robs nor kills, whose vices are not scandalous.

We know that a good man is an honest man, but it is amusing to think that every honest man is not a good man.

The good man is neither a saint nor a hypocrite, but confines himself to being virtuous.

Genius, judgment, talent, and good sense are very different things, though not incompatible.

There is as much difference between good sense and sound judgment as between cause and effect.

Talent is to genius as the whole to a part.

Shall I call him a man of talent who is limited and confined to one art, or even to one particular science, which he cultivates to perfection, and beyond that shows neither judgment, memory, quickness, practical principles, nor management; who does not listen, never thinks, and expresses himself badly? A musician, for example, who, after he has enchanted me with his harmony, seems to shut himself up with his lute in its case, and who, without his instrument, is like a machine out of working order, from which we need expect nothing more.

What shall I say now of gambling? Can any one define that to me? Is no foresight, cunning, or skill required to play at ombre or chess? If so, how is it that we see imbeciles excel in these games, while very clever people are unable even to attain mediocrity, and are quite put out of countenance if they take a piece or a card into their hands.

There is something which, if possible, is even more incomprehensible : a man* who, to outward appearance, is coarse, heavy, and stupid, knowing neither how to converse or to describe things he has just seen ; but who, if he sits down to write, is the model of a good story-teller. He makes animals speak, and trees, and stones ; everything which does not speak. His works are light and graceful, full of beauty and natural elegance.

Another† is simple, timid, and tiresome in conversation, uses inappropriate words often, and judges of the merit of his writing only by the money it brings him in. He can neither recite nor read his own writing : but leave him to his lofty compositions, and he is not inferior to Augustus, Pompey, Nicomedes, Heraclius; he is a king, a great, a glorious king, a politician, a philosopher. He creates heroes, and, when

---

. .. ..   * La Fontaine.   † Pierre Corneille.

he describes the Romans, they are greater and grander, and more Roman in his verses than in their own history.

Shall I give you another prodigy? Imagine a man who is easy, soft, kind, compliant; in a moment he becomes outrageously violent and capricious. Imagine a simple, ingenuous, credulous, giddy trifler, a grey-haired child; but stay till he pulls himself together, or rather gives himself up to the genius which works within him; I may almost say without effort or even knowledge on his part. What life and spirit and imagination, and what a Latin scholar!

You ask me do I speak of one man? Yes, of one —*Theodas**, and of him only. In his excitement he cries and rolls on the ground, then rises up, thunders and gesticulates, and from the midst of this storm comes a light which dazzles and delights us. Let us speak plainly. He talks like a fool, and thinks like a philosopher; tells us truths in a ridiculous way, and in his foolishness shows sense and reason. He seems to possess two souls, having no connection with each other, each having its distinct work and action. This portrait would be wanting in one important characteristic, if I were to forget to say that he is insatiably greedy of praise, always ready for criticism, and, on the whole, willing enough to profit by censure. I begin myself to think that I have drawn the portraits of two different people; and it would not be impossible to find even a third in *Theodas*, for he is a good, agreeable, and excellent man.

Next to a faculty of discernment, diamonds and pearls are the rarest things in the world.

---

* Santeul, who wrote Latin verses of great beauty. He became a devotee towards the end of his life, and was both eccentric and capricious. Died in 1697.

Q

One man is well known in the world for his superior talents, and is honoured and cherished wherever he goes ; but in his domestic circle and among his relations he is unable to gain esteem.

Another man, on the contrary, is a prophet in his own country, enjoys the popularity he has among his own people, which, however, is confined to the walls of his own house. His family praise his rare and singular merit ; he is their idol. But when he goes abroad his fame never accompanies him, he leaves that at home.

―――――

The world rises against a man who begins to gain a reputation. Even his friends can scarcely forgive him his growing merit, or the just report which seems to associate him with the glory they were already in possession of. They hold out to the last, and not till the prince has acknowledged him by rewards do they congratulate him ; only from that day does he take his place among men of merit.

―――――

We often affect to praise excessively some who are very ordinary men. We would elevate them if we could as high as those who truly excel; because we grow weary of always admiring the same persons; or because their glory thus shared becomes less offensive in our eyes, more endurable, and soothing to us.

―――――

We meet with men who in the beginning of their career are carried away full sail on the wind of favour. They lose sight of land in a moment, and go on their course ; everything smiles on them, everything succeeds with them ; all their actions, all their words are received with praise and loaded with rewards. They never show themselves without being complimented and made much of. Through it all they are as firm as a rock on a sea-shore, though the waves dash and break at its feet. All the winds of power, riches, violence, flattery, authority, favour, do not move them; but the public is the rock upon which they run aground and are shipwrecked.

It is a common and natural thing to judge of the labour of others by the bearing it has on the work we are occupied with ourselves. Thus the poet, full of grand and sublime ideas, puts little value on the discourse of the orator, which is often directed to simple facts; and the historian cannot understand how a reasoning mind can be employed in imagining fictions or in finding a rhyme. And the student, deep in the study of the early centuries, thinks all other knowledge dull, vain, and useless, whilst he is likely despised in his turn by the geometrician.

One may have enough sense to excel in a particular study, and be able to instruct in it and yet not have sense enough to see that he ought to be silent on another subject of which he has only a slight knowledge. He shines within the limits of his own genius; but beyond it he makes a clever man talk like a fool.

Whether *Herillus* talks, harangues, or writes, he must always quote. He calls up the prince of philosophers, to tell us that wine will make us drunk, the Roman orator, to tell us that water qualifies it. If he gets on the subject of morality, it is not he, but the divine Plato, who assures us that virtue is good and vice odious, or that both may grow into habit; the most common and trivial things he is capable of thinking himself he must owe to the ancients, to the Latins and Greeks, and it is not to give greater authority to what he says, nor to gain honour for what he knows; it is simply that he must quote.

It is often hazarding or even throwing away a good jest to give it as your own; it falls flat on men of wit, or on those who think themselves witty, though they could not have said it themselves. But if the jest is told as another's, it is more thought of, being something they were not obliged to know; it is told more insinuatingly, and received with less jealousy; no one feels outdone; they laugh if it is laughable, and admire if it is admirable.

It has been said of Socrates that he was like a fool delirious with wit; but those Greeks who spoke thus of that wise man were more like fools themselves. "What odd and whimsical portraits does the philosopher give us," said they. " What strange and peculiar manners he describes. How did he dream of such extraordinary ideas? What kind of a pencil or what colours did he use? They are all idle fancies he paints." But they were wrong. He did, indeed, depict monsters of· vice, but he drew them from nature, so that they were afraid to look at them. Socrates was far from a cynic; he spared persons, but condemned morals which were wicked.

One who has become rich through his knowledge of the world knows a philosopher, his precepts, morality, and discipline; and, never imagining that men have any other aim in their actions than that which he has aimed at all his life, says in his heart: I pity him, I look on him as a failure; his censure is too strict, he is misled, gone far out of the way. This is not how we take the wind which carries us to the delicious port of fortune. He argues according to his principles.

" I pardon those I have praised in my works," says *Antisthius;* "although they forget me, what have I done for them? They deserve praise. I shall not, however, so easily pardon forgetfulness in those whose vices 1 have attacked without touching their persons. They may owe to me the great advantage of improvement; but, as this is an issue rarely seen, it follows that neither the one nor the other is obliged to thank me."

"They may," adds this philosopher, "envy or deny my writings their reward, but they cannot diminish their reputation, and if they could what would prevent me despising it?"

It is a good thing to be a philosopher, and of little use to pass for one. We are not allowed to call some philosophers; they would consider it an affront until men are pleased to restore to such a great name its proper and suitable meaning, and give it all the esteem it merits.

There is a philosophy which raises us above ambition and fortune; makes us equal to it; nay, what do I say? Raises us above the rich, great, and powerful; makes us despise preferment and those who can procure it; exempts us from the need of begging for it, and saves us from excessive transports of joy over success.

There is another kind of philosophy which disposes us to submit to all these things for the sake of our friends and relations. This is the best kind.

It will save us much time and discussion to think of certain persons as incapable of speaking justly; and therefore to condemn all they say, have said, or will say.

We approve of others only for the resemblance we think they bear to ourselves, and in esteeming them we seem to put them on a par with ourselves.

The same defects which we find insupportable in others seem quite proper in ourselves; they are no burden, we do not feel them. A man draws a frightful portrait of another man, never seeing that he is depicting himself. Nothing would so quickly correct us of our faults as the capability of admitting them to ourselves, and seeing them in others. At such a distance they would appear as they are, and we should hate them as they deserve.

Wise conduct turns on two pivots, the past and the future; he who has a faithful memory and great foresight is in no danger of censuring in others what he may have been guilty of himself; or of condemning an action, which, were he one day placed in similar circumstances, would be equally unavoidable.

Neither the soldier, the politician, nor the clever gamester makes his chance; they prepare it, induce it, seem almost to determine it; they not only know what the fool and the coward ignore, but they take advantage of chance when it comes. They even know how to profit by their precautionary measures on such and such a chance, or on several at once; and if in the nick of time the expected turn comes, they gain; if the other turn, they still gain; or the same turn may make them gain in several ways. These wise men may be commended for their good fortune as well as for their wise conduct, and chance ought to be rewarded in them as if it were virtue.

The only person I would set above a great politician is the man who despises to become such, and is more and more persuaded that the world does not deserve that he should occupy his attention with it.

In the best advice there is something to displease us; it is not our own thought, and therefore our presumption or caprice rejects it, and we receive it only when necessity or reflection forces us to do so.

What surprising success has accompanied that favourite during the whole course of his life. Who has been so fortunate? No interruption, no disgrace, high posts, the prince's ear, vast treasures, perfect health, and a peaceful death.

But what a strange account he will have to render of a life passed in favour! Of counsel given and not followed, and of counsel he has neglected to give, good deeds not done and evil deeds done, either by himself or others—in a word, for all his prosperity.

By our death we gain the praises of our survivors, and frequently our only merit is that we are no more. The same praise serves for *Cato* and *Piso*.

It is rumoured that *Piso* is dead. It is a great loss. He was a good man, and deserved a longer life; he was talented and agreeable, resolute and courageous, faithful and generous! Add, provided he is dead.

The way in which we run down some people who distinguish themselves for their trustworthiness, disinterestedness and honesty, does not redound so much to their praise as to the discredit of mankind.

One relieves the poor and neglects his own family, and leaves his son in poverty. Another builds a new house, who has not yet paid for the lead of that which was finished ten years ago. A third makes presents and donations, and ruins his creditors. I wish to know whether pity, liberality, or magnificence can be virtue in an unjust man; or whether oddity and vanity are not rather the cause of his injustice.

Promptitude is an essential part of the justice we owe to others : to keep anyone waiting is unjust.

Those do well or do their duty who do what they ought. He does badly whose conduct is such that it is said of him, " He will in time do well."

It is said of a great man who sits down to table twice a day, and whose time is spent in digestion, that he is dying of hunger; meaning he is not rich, that his affairs are in a bad state. This is a figure of speech which might more literally be used of his creditors.

The kindness, consideration, and politeness of people advanced in years, to each other of either sex, give me a good opinion of what we call the olden times.

Parents are too hopeful if they expect everything from the education of their children : but it is a great error to expect nothing and neglect their education.

Were it true, what many say, that education does not change the heart or disposition, or make any important difference to a man, being merely connected with superfluities, I would still affirm that it is not unprofitable.

He who speaks little has the advantage : the presumption is that he possesses wit; and if indeed he is not without it, it is presumed that he has exceeding great wit.

To think only of ourselves and the present is a source of error in political affairs.

Next to being convicted of a crime, the greatest misfortune is often that of having had to justify ourselves. We may be discharged and absolutely acquitted by all except the voice of the people.

———

A man is faithful to certain practices of religion ; we see him perform them punctually, no one commends or disapproves of him, he is not heeded. Another follows his example after ten years of neglect, and he is lauded and praised ; for my part I blame his long forgetfulness of duty, and think him fortunate in returning to it.

———

Some are forgotten in the distribution of favours, and this makes us ask why they were forgotten. And if they had been remembered we should have asked why they were distinguished. Whence proceeds this contrariety ? Is it the character of these persons, or the uncertainty of our judgments, or both ?

———

We begin to predict who will be chancellor after such a one; who will be archbishop or pope; or we go further, and each according to his wishes or caprice settles the promotion, often giving it to persons more aged and feeble than those at the time holding the post; and as there is no reason why the dignity should kill the persons who are at the time invested with it, as it ought rather to rejuvenize them, and give them new mental as well as bodily resources, it is not a rare event that the man holding office buries his successor.

———

Disgrace extinguishes hatred and jealousy, and it may well do so since the man in disgrace does not irritate us by being in favour. There is no merit or virtue he will not be pardoned, he may even be a hero with impunity. Nothing is of any importance in a disgraced man or a man out of favour ; his virtue, his merit, both are unworthy, misunderstood, or imputed to vice. He may have great courage, be afraid of neither fire nor sword, or he may possess the chivalry of a Bayard ; it is nothing but bravado, people say scornfully, "He is no hero." I contradict myself, it is true; but blame for this mankind of whom I only relate my judgment ; I do not speak of different men, but of the same men who judge so differently.

We do not require to wait twenty years to see men change their opinions on the most serious things, or on those which have appeared to them the most sure and true. I shall not attempt to advance a theory that fire in itself, independently of our sensations, has no heat, that is to say nothing approaching the sensations we feel when it comes near us, for fear that some day it should become hotter than it has ever been. It would be as far from me to assert that one right line falling on another makes two right angles, or equals two right angles, for fear that men should discover something more or less, and I should be laughed at for my proposition. And also, on another subject, I would not agree with all France that Vauban is infallible, that there is no appeal from this. But who will guarantee that, in a short time some one will not insinuate that even on sieges, upon which his decision has been held supreme, he errs sometimes, and is liable to make mistakes, like *Antiphilus.*

If you believe what people say when they are irritated against each other, till passion masters them, the scholar is a prig, the magistrate a boor, the banker an aggressor, the gentleman an upstart; but it is strange that these names, which anger and hatred have invented, have become so familiar to us, that disdain, cold and quiet as it is, ventures to use them.

You hurry and rush about, especially when the enemy begins to fly, and the victory is no longer doubtful. You do the same before a town which has capitulated. During a battle or a siege you pretend to be in a hundred places at once, and are nowhere. You foresee the General's orders, so that you may not follow them, and seek opportunities rather than wait for them. Is it possible that this is false courage?

Place men to guard a post where they might be killed and are not killed; they love both honour and life.

To see how men love life can it be supposed that they can love anything else more than life; or that glory which they prefer to life is often an opinion of themselves established in the minds of a thousand people whom they neither know nor esteem?

Some who are neither soldiers nor courtiers go to war or follow the Court; they do not make the siege, but they assist, and have soon satisfied their curiosity about a battlefield as well as about the trenches and the effect of bombs and cannon and sudden dashes, and about the order and success of an attack which they just got a glimpse of. Resistance is maintained; the rainy weather comes on and fatigues increase; mud has to be waded through, and both the weather and the enemy have to be encountered; the lines may be forced, and thus shut up between a town and the army, what an extremity; courage flags, and they begin to grumble and say, "Is it such a difficult thing to raise a siege?" Does the safety of the state depend on a citadel more or less? "Ought we not," they add, "to submit to the decrees of heaven, which is against us, and delay the campaign till another time?" They are no longer

brave, and if they dared they would say what they
think to the General, who is only hardened by obstacles,
and cheered and excited by the difficulty of the undertaking ; watching by night, and exposing himself by
day to carry it through to the end.   Should the enemy
capitulate, these   same   poor-spirited   creatures   will
extol the importance of the conquest, predicting the
results, and exaggerating the necessity there was for it,
the peril and the disgrace which would have been
theirs had they abandoned it ; and demonstrating that
the army which covered us from the enemy was invincible.   They return with the Court ; and as they
pass through towns and villages are proud to be gazed
at by the people who crowd the windows ; they triumph
by the way, and when they reach home they deafen
you with their right, left, and their talk of forts, ram-
parts, flanks and bastions ; and weary you with their
tales of the danger their curiosity led them into, leading you to believe that they ran a great risk of being
captured or killed by the enemy.   The only point on
which they are silent is that they were afraid.

It is a little inconvenient to come to a full stop in a
sermon or oration, but it leaves the orator free to
exercise all the wit, sense and imagination, morality and
doctrine he possesses, and robs him of nothing ; but we
cannot help being surprised that men, having once
affixed a kind of disgrace to such a failure, should
expose themselves, by long and often useless discourses, to the risk of it.

Those who make the worst use of their time are the
first to complain of its shortness ; as they consume it
in eating and sleeping, in foolish talk, arranging what
they ought to do, and oftenest in doing nothing, so they
want more of it for their business or their pleasures.

Those, on the contrary, who make good use of it, have some to spare.

There is no minister, however busy, who does not manage to waste at least two hours every day; which makes a great deal of time in a long life : and if the evil is much greater among all conditions of men, what an infinite waste goes on in the world of this precious thing which you complain you have not enough of.

There are creatures of God called men. They have souls which are spiritual, yet their whole lives are employed in, and their whole attention concentrated on, the sawing of marble. This is very simple and trifling ; but there are others who seem much astonished at them, though they are entirely useless. They pass their days in doing nothing at all, which is still more trifling than sawing marble.

The greater part of mankind so far forget that they have souls, that they engage in many things in which the soul is of no use; so much so that we consider we speak very favourably of a man when we say of him, " He thinks." This has become quite an ordinary way of eulogizing a man, and yet it only raises him above a dog or a horse.

" How do you amuse yourself? How do you pass your time?" is asked both by fools and sensible people. If I reply, "In opening my eyes and seeing, in giving ear and hearing, in enjoying health, repose, and freedom," that is saying nothing ; the greatest and only advantage is not mentioned or taken into account. " Do you gamble or dance?"

Is liberty such a great boon for man, since it can be so great and so free that at last it prompts him to desire something more, which means that he has less liberty.

Liberty is not idleness, it is a free use of time. It means choosing our labour, our exercise. To be free does not mean to do nothing, it is to have the sole control of our actions, what we shall do and what we shall not do. In this sense what a blessing liberty is.

Cæsar was not too old to think of the conquest of the universe. He had no other bliss to strive after but to live a brave life and have a great name after his death. Born proud and ambitious and strong, he could not better employ his time than in conquering the world.

Alexander was very young for so serious a design. It is astonishing that at his age women or wine did not frustrate his enterprise.

A young prince* of an august race, the hope and joy of his people, a gift from heaven to prolong liberty upon earth, greater than his forefathers, son of a hero who is his model, has already convinced the universe by his divine qualities and promising virtues that the sons of heroes are nearer being heroes than other men.†

If the world is to last a hundred million years, it is still in its pristine freshness. It has scarcely begun, and we ourselves are not far removed from the first men and the patriarchs, and who will distinguish us from them in the distant ages?

But if we may judge of the future by the past, how

---

* The Dauphin, son of Louis XIV.

† Note by La Bruyère.—Contrary to the trivial Latin maxim, "Heroum filii noxæ," which means that the sons of heroes degenerate from their fathers.

much is still unknown to us in art, science, and nature, and I may even say in history. What discourses will be made, what diverse revolutions may not happen over the whole face of the earth in states and empires, what ignorance we live in, and how small our experience of six or seven thousand years?

There is no way too long for him who walks gently and without hurry; and there are no advantages too distant for those who patiently prepare themselves for them.

To court no one, neither to expect courtship, is a happy condition, a golden age, and the most natural state of man.

The world is for those who follow Courts and people cities, but nature is for those who dwell in the country. They alone live, or at least they alone know that they live.

Why do you treat me coldly, and complain of what I have said of some of our young courtiers? You are not vicious, O *Thrasyllus;* at least, I did not know it, though you say so. What I do know is that you are not young, and that you are possibly offended at what I said of some great people. But do not cry out at the wound of another.

Are you haughty, malicious, sarcastic, a flatterer or a hypocrite? If you are I did not know it; I spoke of some great people.

A spirit of moderation and a medium amount of prudence leave men in obscurity; to be famous they must have great virtues or else, perhaps, great vices.

Men are prejudiced, charmed, or infatuated by the

conduct of great and obscure persons, according to the success achieved by them ; very little will prevent a fortunate crime being commended as a virtue, or wealth supplying the place of every virtue : this is outrageous, mean, and odious, a thing which no success can justifiy.

Men are led astray by fine appearances and plausible pretexts, and are easily induced to regard with favour the ambitious project of some great man ; they speak of it with much interest ; are even pleased with the novelty or boldness of his scheme, soon get accustomed to it, and confidently expect it to succeed ; if on the contrary it miscarries, they say with equal confidence, and with no idea of deceiving, that it was too rash, and could not have been successful.

Some schemes* are so brilliant, have such important issues depending on them, are talked of so long, and are the subject of so many hopes and fears, according to different interests, besides compromising the whole future glory and honour and fortune of one man, that having made so great a display, he finds it impossible to retire from action ; however great the disaster he begins to foresee as the end of his enterprise, he must encounter it, and his least misfortune will be defeat.

In a wicked man there is nothing to make a great man. Commend his views and projects, admire his conduct, exaggerate his ability in making use of the shortest and most fitting means to attain his ends, if his ends are bad, prudence has had no share in them ; and, where prudence is wanting, find greatness if you can.

---

* An illusion to William, Prince of Orange, taking the throne of England from James II.

" O this age and its customs!" exclaims *Heraclitus.* 'O unhappy century, full of bad examples, a time when virtue suffers and crime rules triumphantly! I would be a Lycaon, an Ægisthus. There could not be a better opportunity, more favourable circumstances, at least if I desire to prosper."

A man said* " I shall cross the sea; I shall rob my sire of his patrimony; I shall drive him and his wife and his heir from his own possessions;" and as he said so he has done. All he had to fear was the resentment of, many kings, outraged in this king's person. But they supported him, encouraged him, all but said to him, "Cross the sea and rob your sire ; show the whole world that it is possible to drive a king out of his own kingdom as easily as a petty noble from his castle or a farmer from his farm. Show that there is little difference between obscure individuals and us ; that we are tired of these distinctions ; teach the world that the subjects God has given us can abandon and betray us, surrender us and themselves to a stranger, and that they have less to fear from us than we from them and their strength."

Who can regard events so sad and gloomy unmoved? All responsibilities have their privileges, and every rightful holder of these privileges will, by word and act, exert himself to defend them. Royal dignity alone no longer has such rights and privileges, for have not kings themselves repudiated them? One only, ever good and magnanimous,† received an unfortunate family with open arms. The others leagued themselves to avenge themselves on him for the support he was extending to a cause which was common to them all. Pique and jealousy were roused among them to the prejudice of political interest, honour, and

---

* The Prince of Orange.

† Louis XIV., who received James II. and all his family when they were forced to leave England.

religion. Was it as much for their personal and
domestic interest ? It is a vital point, concerning, I do
not say their election, but their succession, and their
hereditary rights.   Thus, as in everything, the man has
the advantage of the sovereign. A Prince* who might
deliver Europe and himself from a fatal enemy, who
might possess the glory of having destroyed a great
empire,† neglects all for a doubtful war. Those who
are born umpires‡ and mediators temporise, and when
they might have already usefully interposed their
mediation they only promise it. "O herdsmen," continues *Heraclitus*, "ye boors who dwell in cabins roofed
with thatch ! If the dire events which are happening
in the world do not reach you, if your hearts are not
broken by the malice of men, if men are no longer
spoken of where you live, only foxes and lynx-eyed
wolves, let me come among you, to live with you,
and eat of your black bread and drink of the water
from your wells."

---

* Leopold I., Emperor of the West.
† Turkey.   ‡ Innocent XI.

WE only betray our foolishness and weakness if we allow fashion to interfere with what concerns our food, our manner of living, our health or conscience. Venison is out of fashion, therefore insipid. It would be sinning against fashion to cure a fever by bleeding ; for this same reason it has for a long time been unusual for the dying to have *Theotimus* to soothe their last moments ; his tender exhortations can no longer save the rich, only the people hear him now ; he has lived to see his successor.

Curiosity is not a taste for what is good and beautiful, but for what is rare and unique, a longing to possess what others have not discovered. It is not an attachment to what is perfect, but to what is much sought after or fashionable. It is not an amusement but a passion, and is often so violent that it yields neither to love nor ambition except in the meanness of its object. It is not a general passion for things which are rare and much sought after, but for a certain thing which, besides being rare, is in the fashion.

A florist has a suburban garden ; he spends all his time there from sunrise to sunset ; one might say he is planted there, has taken root among his tulips, beside his *"Solitaire;"* he rubs his hands and gazes at it, stoops to examine it closely, for he never saw anything so beautiful, his heart expands with the delight he feels in it ; he leaves it to look at his *"Orientale,"* and from it he goes to the *"Veuve;"* then to the *"Drap d'or,"* then to the *"Agate,"* from which he returns to the

" *Solitaire*," where he stands tired till he sinks down beside it and forgets his dinner ; beholding and admiring its perfect vase-like flower, its calyx, and the lovely shaded, shining petals of the gracefully opening flower. God is in everything in nature, though our florist admires nothing beyond his bulb ; his tulips he would not part with for a thousand crowns, although he will give them away for nothing when tulips are out of fashion and carnations are in ! This reasoning being who has a soul, a creed, and a religion, returns home tired and hungry, but highly pleased with his day, for he has seen his tulips.

Now try to speak to that other man of the beauty of the crops, the plentiful harvest or the rich vintage ; he is interested only in fruit, so you cannot make him understand you ; speak to him of figs and melons, tell him that the pear trees are bending under their weight of fruit this year, that the peach trees also are laden, it is all an unknown language to him ; he is interested only in plum trees, and does not answer you ; will not even converse with you about them, for he cares for only a single kind ; at the mention of any others he only smiles sarcastically ; he leads you up to the trees, and in a scientific way plucks an exquisite plum, which he divides, giving you the half and keeping the other : " What exquisite fruit," he says, " Just taste it, is it not divine ! I am convinced it is matchless ; " and his nostrils dilate with pride as he tries to hide his pleasure and conceit under a veil of modesty.

O man ! divine indeed, man whom we cannot praise and admire enough, man who will be spoken of during all the ages ; I ponder on his face and figure, I remember the features of him who alone among mortals possessed such a plum !

You visit another man, and his conversation is of the curious people he knows, especially *Diognetus*. " I admire him," he says, "and I understand him less than ever." Do you suppose he is seeking knowledge through medals, that he looks on them as the existing proofs of certain facts, fixed and indubitable monuments of ancient history? No less than that; you believe, perhaps, that all the trouble he gives himself to recover a certain head is because of the pleasure it gives him to see an uninterrupted suite of emperors. No! it is even less important still. *Diognetus* is a connoisseur in medals. He can tell at once if one is genuine, he understands every stamp. He has a case in which every space is full except one: this empty space is an eyesore to him: it is literally and truly to fill up this empty space that he spends his fortune and his life.

"Will you look at my prints?" says *Democedes*. And presently he spreads them out before you. You pick out one which is neither well printed, well engraved, nor well drawn, and much more suitable to decorate the new bridge on a *fête* day than to be carefully preserved in a cabinet. *Democedes* admits that it is badly engraved and badly designed, but he assures you that it was executed by an Italian whose works are very scarce; that this is the only one in France of his productions; that he paid a high price for it, and would not exchange it for a much better one. "But I have," he continues, "a great grief, one which will force me to renounce engravings for the rest of my life. I possess the whole series of Callot's* pictures except one which, although it is not one of his best, indeed it is one of his worst; still it spoils my set, and it is very hard, for I have been trying for twenty years to discover that print to complete my Callots; and now I despair."

---

* An eminent French engraver (1593—1633).

I meet another man who is satirical when he speaks of people who, either from restlessness or curiosity, travel much and yet keep no journal to make a memoir of afterwards : who go to see and see nothing, or else forget what they have seen ; who seem simply to have wished to visit some new towns and churches, and to sail on rivers which are called neither the Seine nor the Loire ; they leave their own country only to return again with the prestige of having returned from afar. This criticism is not unjust, and might be listened to.

But when he adds that books are more instructive than travelling, and makes me understand from his conversation that he has a library, I desire to see it, and I pay him a visit. He receives me in his house, and even on the staircase, indeed. I feel faint with the scent of the morocco with which all his books are covered ; in vain he tries to reassure me, shouting that they are all gilt-edged and first editions ; and he names the best of his collection one after the other ; telling me that his room is full, except one or two places which are painted to represent books arranged in cases, and so well done that the deception is not observed ; then he adds that he never reads or even sets foot in this room. He comes there now only to give me pleasure. I thank him for his kindness, and have no more wish than he has to revisit his tannery, which he calls a library.

Some people have such an eager thirst for knowledge that they cannot bear to be ignorant of anything. They dip into everything and master nothing ; they prefer to learn much rather than learn well, to be superficial and weak in many sciences rather than to be deeply versed in one. Thus they find that on every subject there is someone who excels them and can correct them ; they are mere dupes of their own vain curiosity, and can only after long and painful efforts overcome their gross ignorance.

Others possess the keys of all learning. yet never use them. They spend their lives in puzzling out all the known languages, and even would discover that which is spoken in the moon. The most useless idioms, the most ridiculous and mystical characters, are precisely those which awake their passion for languages and excite their industry. They pity those who are contented to know their own language, or at most, Greek and Latin. Such people read all books of history and yet know nothing at all of history; they skim through so many books that they profit by none ; they could not well be more barren of facts and principles, but they certainly have the best collection of words and phrases which can be imagined; their memories are oppressed and loaded with them, while their minds remain empty.

A citizen has a mania for building, so he builds himself a house so grand, and beautiful, and richly decorated, that it is uninhabitable. He is ashamed to live in it himself, and yet he cannot resolve to let it to a prince or to a rich merchant; so he retires to the garret, where he lives whilst his house is overrun by English and German tourists. There are incessant knocks at the door and demands to see the house, but not its master.

We know another man who has unmarried daughters to whom he cannot give dowries; or worse still, he can scarcely give them food and clothing; he is so poor that he has to deny himself a bed and a change of linen. The secret of this poverty is not far to seek; it lies in a lumber-room full to obstruction of rare sculptures, already covered with dust and dirt, the sale of which would free him ; but he cannot make up his mind to part with them.

*Dephilus** is a bird fancier; he had only one to begin with, and ends with a thousand. His house is not improved by them; they fly about all over the sitting-room, the hall, the staircase, bedrooms, study; birds are everywhere. It is no longer a sweet warbling sound they make, but a noisy discord. The winds and floods of autumn do not cause such a shrill and piercing noise. People cannot hear themselves speaking even in the rooms they wait in till they are announced, for there they are annoyed with little yelping dogs. *Dephilus* finds his craze no longer an agreeable amusement; it has become a tiresome business which he can with difficulty overtake; and he spends his days, those days which pass never to return again, scattering grain and cleaning bird-cages. He pays a large salary to a man whose only service is to whistle on a bird-organ and breed canaries. True, what he spends in one way he saves in another, for his children have neither teachers nor education. In the evening, tired out with what he calls pleasure, he shuts himself up and is not able to enjoy the least repose till his birds are at roost, till the small creatures which he loves only for their singing, cease to sing; he thinks of them all night in his sleep, or is himself a little tufted canary, and chirps, and perches, and dreams that he is moulting or brooding.

Who can, indeed, describe all the different varieties of curiosity? Would you imagine, to hear a man talk of his *léopard* and his *plume,* boasting of them as the most wonderful and marvellous things in the world, that he wants to dispose of his collection of shells? And why should he not boast since he bought them for their weight in gold?

Another admires insects; every day he adds to his

---

* The whimsical Santeul, already referred to.   .

collection ; he is the greatest authority on butterflies in Europe; he has them of all shapes and colours. What an unfortunate time to pay him a visit ; he is plunged in bitter grief, and is very irritable, to the discomfort of his whole family ; for he has had an irreparable loss. Go nearer and look at what he shows you on his finger— a lifeless thing, it has just expired. A caterpillar, and such a caterpillar !

Duelling is one of the triumphs of fashion, and the thing in which her tyranny has been exercised with the most brilliant results. It is a custom which has not left the coward liberty of life, for it forces him to allow himself to be killed by a braver man than himself, and even to seem a man of courage. It attaches honour and glory to a foolish and extravagant action. Kings have approved of it by their presence, and it has sometimes been practised as a religious duty. It has established a man's innocence, and in capital crimes has been exercised to decide whether an accusation were true or false ; and, at least, it became so deeply rooted in the opinion of the world, and got so firm a hold of the hearts and minds of men, that it has been one of the finest points in the life of a great king to cure his people of this folly.

A man of fashion is not long so, for fashions change. If by chance he is a man of merit he will not be put down, extinguished ; something of him will always remain, and be worthy of esteem, although less valued.

Virtue has this comfort, it is self-sufficing, and can exist without admirers, partizans, or protectors. The want of support and admiration not only does not harm a virtuous man ; it preserves, purifies, and renders him more perfect : for whether virtue be in the fashion or not, it is always virtue.

If you tell people, and especially the great, that such a one is virtuous, they will say, "Let him keep his virtue;" and if you tell them he has a great deal of pleasant and amusing wit, they will answer, "So much the better for him." You say, "His mind is well cultivated, he knows many things:" they ask you what o'clock it is, or what kind of weather. But if you tell them that he is a juggler who can perform marvellous tricks, then they cry, "Where is he? Bring him here to-morrow, this evening; will you bring him at once?" He is taken to them, and this fellow, who is only fit to amuse people at a fair, is admitted into their intimacy.

There is nothing which brings a man more suddenly into fashion than playing high. It is equal to any debauchery. I would like to see any man, were he as polished, playful, free and witty as Catullus, try to compare with him who loses eight hundred pistoles at a sitting.

A fashionable man is like a certain blue flower which, growing wild in the fields, chokes the corn, spoils the crops, and takes up the place of something better. It is a thing of little beauty and no value, except what it borrows from a light caprice, which is born and gone almost in the same instant; to-day it is in fashion, and all the women adorn themselves with it; to-morrow it will be neglected and left to the people.

An estimable person, on the other hand, is a flower which we do not describe by its colour, but which we call by its name; and cultivate for its beauty and perfume. It is one of the graces of nature, one of the things which beautify the world; it is for all time, and its fashion is both ancient and popular. Our fathers esteemed it, and we esteem it after them, and neither the disgust nor the antipathy of any one can harm—a lily or a rose.

We see *Eustrates* sitting in his boat enjoying the pure air and the beautiful calm sky. He sails on with a fair wind which, to all appearance, will not change; but all of a sudden the sky is overcast, the storm rises, and the boat is dashed about among the waves, till at last it sinks. *Eustrates* is seen to rise to the surface and tries to swim ; we hope that he will at least be able to reach the shore in safety, but another wave seizes him, and we think he is lost; he appears once more, and our hopes revive, when a great billow overcomes him, and he sinks, and is never seen again, he is drowned.

Voiture and Sarrazin were born for the age they lived in; they came just when they were wanted. If they had appeared later I doubt if they would have been as much esteemed as they were.

The light and airy style of conversation, reunions, charming familiar letters, delicate jesting, and the select parties where wit only was allowed to enter ; all have disappeared, and there seems little chance of their being revived. All I can hope for is that the spirit of the same genius may revive in another way. But the women of the present day are either saints or coquettes ; and the men devote their time to gambling or ambition, and some are all these things at once. Self-interest, play, gallants, and confessors, are the fashion, and hold their place against men of wit.

A ridiculous coxcomb wears a broad hat, a doublet with flying shoulder-knots and long boots ; he wonders by night where and how he can make himself remarkable the following day. A philosopher leaves his tailor to make his clothes ; there is as much weakness in evading the fashion as in affecting it.

———

We dislike a fashion which divides a man's height into two equal parts, one half being the head and shoulders, and the other all the rest of the body ; we condemn those who make a woman's head like the base of an edifice of several stories, the order and structure of which change according to caprice ; who drag the hair away from the part of the face it is meant to shade, and raise it after the manner of a Bacchante ; seeming only anxious that women should change the sweet and modest expression of their faces to one which is proud and bold ; and lastly we exclaim against such and such a fashion, which, however, odd as it may be, improves and adorns while the fashion lasts, and from which we gather all the advantages we required of it, namely, to please. It seems to me that we ought rather to admire the inconstancy and frivolity of men who approve of and admire such opposite things in succession, and use for fun and frolic the same adornments which formerly served more grave and serious purposes ; how short a time it takes to mark so wide a difference.

———

N * * * is rich, she eats well and sleeps well ; but head-dresses change when she expects it least and feels happy ; now hers is old-fashioned.

———

Iphis sees at church a new-fashioned shoe, he looks at his own and blushes for it, he no longer feels dressed ; he used to attend mass that he might be seen there, and now he hides ; and is held by the foot in his room all the rest of the day. He has a soft hand, and he preserves it with perfumed paste ; he takes care to laugh that he may show his teeth ; he

wears a set smile, admires his legs, looks at himself in
the mirror ; none can be so pleased with another as
he is with himself; he has acquired a delicate and clear
voice, and luckily he speaks with a burr ; there is an
expressive turn of his head and an inexpressible sweetness in his eyes which he does not forget to make
use of; he walks slowly and holds himself as gracefully as possible ; he uses rouge, but only now and
then, he does not make a custom of it'; it is true,
however, that he wears shoulder knots and a hat, and
has neither ear-rings nor a necklace ; therefore I have
not put him in the chapter about women.

The very same fashions which men follow so willingly in their persons they will not have copied in their
portraits, as if they felt and foresaw how ridiculous
they will appear when they have lost what we call the
fascination and charm of novelty. In their portraits men
allow themselves to be adorned very indifferently,
according to the arbitrary fancy of the painter, and in
a way which suits neither their character nor their face,
which recalls neither their manner nor their person.
They choose a constrained or immodest attitude, and a
hardened, rough, unnatural manner, which makes a
young abbé into a captain, and changes a judge into a
harlequin ; makes Diana of a city dame; an Amazon
or a Pallas of a simple, timid woman; a Laïs of an
honest woman ; a Scythian or Attila of a prince who is
good and magnanimous.

One fashion has hardly destroyed another when it is
abolished by a newer one, which itself gives way to the
next, which will not be the last. Such is our frivolity ;
during these revolutions a century flows on and puts all
finery among past things which are no more. The
fashion, then, which is most curious, most uncommon,
and most agreeable to our eyes, is the most ancient.

Time and years make it appear as charming in portraits as the sagum or Roman costume on the stage, or the Oriental mantle, tiara, and veil in our tapestries and pictures.

Our fathers have transmitted to us, together with some knowledge of their persons, an idea of the dress, arms, and ornaments which they preferred during their life. We cannot better extend this benefit to our posterity than by accommodating them in the same way.

Formerly the courtier wore his own hair, doublets and large breeches, and was a libertine; this is so no longer: now he has a full wig, a close suit, plain stockings, and he is devout; all is the result of fashion.

He who has studied life at Court understands the difference between virtue and false devotion; he can no longer be deceived.

To neglect vespers as an obsolete and unfashionable custom, to keep our own place for the benediction, and to know all the best parts of the chapel where we can be seen, and where we are not seen; to think in the house of God of our own business, to receive visits there, and give orders and instructions, and wait for the replies; to have a confessor who is listened to rather than the Gospel; to derive all our holiness and credit from the reputation of our director, despising and hardly admitting the possibility of salvation for those who attend the ministrations of one less fashionable; to love only as much of the Word of God as is preached in our own church by our special director; to prefer his mass to other masses, and the Sacraments from his hand rather than from any other; to feast only on mystical books as if there were neither Gospels, Apostolic Epistles, nor the spiritual writings of the

fathers ; to read and speak a religious jargon unknown
in the early ages ; to be very careful at confession ; to
detail the faults of others and to palliate our own ; to
underrate our suffering and patience, to deprecate our
feeble progress in heroism ; to have private leagues
with certain persons against certain others, consider-
ing only ourselves, and our own clique, and suspecting
even virtue itself ; longing only for the selfish enjoyment of prosperity and favour ; never assisting merit,
and making piety subservient to ambition ; even seeking after salvation by means of fortune and honour—
this, at present, is the finest effort of the devotion of
our time.

A *(false)* devotee is one who, under an atheist king,
would be an atheist.

Onuphrius has only a rug of grey serge for his bed,
still he lies on cotton and down ; his dress is likewise
simple and comfortable, I mean it is of light material
in Summer, and of something soft and warm in Winter ;
he wears very fine linen, but is most careful to hide it.
He does not speak of his coarse clothing, or of his self-
discipline ; on the contrary, he looks what he is, a hypocrite, though he intends to pass for a devout man ; it is
true he leads us to believe without saying it, that he
wears a hair shirt and exercises a severe discipline. *
He has many books lying carelessly about his room ;
if we examine them we find the " *Spiritual Combat,*"
" *Christian Life,*" the " *Sacred Year,*" etc. ; his other
books are under lock and key. If he walks along the
street and sees in the distance a man to whom he
would appear devout, he plays his part with downcast
eyes, slow and modest gait, and a thoughtful air of con-
templation. If he enters a church he first takes heed

---

* A parody on Molière's Tartuffe.

whose eyes are on him, and according to the discovery
made he falls on his knees and prays, or else he neither
thinks of kneeling or praying. If a man of wealth
and authority comes beside him and observes, perhaps
would hear him, he not only prays, but deeply ponders,
sighs, and groans ; but as soon as the rich man retires
he utters no more sounds. Another time he goes into
a holy place, crushes through the crowd, chooses a
place for his devotion where everybody can see how
he humbles himself; if he sees any courtiers who
laugh and talk, making more noise in the chapel than
they would make in the antechamber, he makes still
more noise in order to silence them ; and resumes his
meditations that he may be favourably compared with
them. He avoids deserted and solitary churches where
he may hear two masses in succession, the sermon,
vespers, and compline, and all between God and himself without anyone to give him credit ; he likes the
parish church, or frequents crowded temples, for thus
his aim is gained, and he is seen of the congregation.
He chooses two or three days in the year on which to
fast, not special fast days ; but about the end of winter
he has a cough, a weak chest, indigestion, or a feverish
attack ; his friends beg and pray and earnestly implore
him to break his lenten fast as soon as it is begun, and
he complacently yields. If *Onuphrius* is named umpire
in a quarrel among relations, or in any family disagree-
ment, he is on the side of the strongest, that is to say,
the richest, for he cannot be persuaded that he who has
much wealth can ever be wrong. If he happens to find a
rich man on whom he can impose and take advantage
of, he becomes his parasite ; he does not wheedle his
wife, or make the least advance or declaration to her ;
he will evade her unless he is as sure of her as he is
of himself. Still further would it be from him to employ the jargon of false devotion to flatter her and

lead her astray. He does not usually talk that language; only as it is useful to him, and never when it might chance to make him appear ridiculous. He knows where to find women more sociable and easy than his friend's wife, and from them he does not absent himself for long, unless it be to have it said of him in public that he has taken a vow of retreat. Who indeed could doubt it when they see him reappear with the worn face of a man who does not take care of himself.

The women whose intrigues prosper under the shade of devotion suit him, with only this little difference, that he slights those who have grown old, and cultivates the young, and among them only the most beautiful attract him. They come and go as he does, and he has the pleasure of seeing them at all hours, in all places ; and who in his position but would be edified ? They are devout, and he is devout. He does not forget to take advantage of his friend's blind prepossession in his favour ; sometimes he borrows money from him, and at times he manages so well that his friend offers him some, and even reproaches him for not making use of him when he has need. He will not accept a mite without giving an acceptance for it, which, however, he is very sure will never be redeemed. At another time he says, in a certain tone, that he is in need of nothing. This is when he wants only a small sum. Another day he publicly praises the generosity of this man in order to pique him into bestowing some liberal gift on him. He does not expect to succeed to all his property, nor to receive a deed of gift of all his personal estate, especially if there is a son or lawful heir. A devout man is neither covetous, violent, unjust, nor self-interested.

Onuphrius is not devout, but he wishes to be thought so, and by a perfect, though false, imitation of piety

he silently takes care of his own interests. Thus he does
not aim his designs at the direct line of a family, and
never insinuates himself where there are daughters to
provide for, or a son to establish. These are claims so
strong and unquestionable that they cannot be set
aside without causing some stir, which might, perhaps,
come to the ears of the prince, from whom he conceals
such aims for fear of being discovered to be what he
is. He chooses the collateral line which he can attack
with impunity. He is the terror of male and female
cousins, nephews and nieces ; the flatterer and open
friend of all the uncles who have made a fortune. He
gives himself out as the lawful heir of all the old men
who die childless and rich, and they must disinherit
him if they wish their relations to benefit from their
estates. If *Onuphrius* does not find means to defraud
them altogether, he will at least take a large portion
from them. A small calumny, less than that, a slight
slander, is enough for his pious design, and this is a
talent he possesses to a high degree of perfection, so
much so that he makes a point of not allowing it to
lie useless. There are, according to him, people one is
obliged in conscience to slander, and these people are
those he does not like, whom he desires to injure and
ruin. He gains his ends without ever giving himself
the trouble of opening his mouth. You talk to him of
Eudoxus; he smiles, and sighs. You question him,
you even insist ; but he makes no answer, and he is
right ; he has said enough of him.

When a courtier shall be humble, cured of pride and
ambition, when he ceases to establish his own fortune
on the ruin of his rivals, when he becomes just to his
dependants, pays his creditors, is neither knavish nor
slanderous, renounces luxury and unlawful love, prays
even when not in the presence of the prince, and not

with his lips only; when I find that he is not austere and forbidding, and difficult to approach, is not idle and dreamy, knowing how to give scrupulous attention to diverse but congruous employments, when he can and will turn his mind to great and laborious affairs, especially those which involve far-reaching, extended results for the people and for the whole state, when his noble qualities make me afraid to name him in this place, and his modesty stops me even though I do not name him plainly, I shall say of this personage* " He is truly devout," or rather, " He is a man given to his age as the model of genuine virtue, and for comparison with hypocrites."

During the present century arts and sciences have been advanced to the highest degree of refinement. Even the plan of salvation has been reduced to rule and method, and augmented by all the finest and most sublime ideas which the mind of man could conceive. Devotion (false) and geometry have their own forms of expression, and are called, " art terms ;" he who knows them not is neither a devotee nor a geometrician. The early Christians, even those who were instructed by the Apostles, were ignorant of such terms ; those simple people had only faith and works, and confined themselves to believing and living a good life.

It is a delicate thing for a religious prince to reform the Court and make it pious ; aware how much the courtier desires to please him, and what sacrifices he has to make in order to advance his fortune, the prince treats him with prudence, and humours and tolerates him even if he dislikes him, for fear of plunging him into hypocrisy or sacrilege ; he expects more from God and time than from his own zeal and industry.

* The Duc de Beauvilliers.

In Courts there is an old custom of giving pensions and distributing favours to a musician, a dancing-master, a comic actor, a flute player, a flatterer; they possess certain merits and certain acknowledged talents which amuse the great people and provide them with relaxation. One knows that Favier is a fine dancer, and that Lorenzani composes beautiful sacred music; but who knows if the devout man has any virtue? There is nothing for him in the privy purse or in the treasury, and with good reason, for his is a profession easily counterfeited, which if it were rewarded would often expose the prince to the mistake of honouring dissimulation and knavery, and allowing pensions to hypocrisy.

We must hope that the piety of the Court will not prevent its devotees remaining there.

I do not doubt that true devotion is the source of repose; it enables one to endure life and makes death sweet; we cannot derive as much comfort from hypocrisy.

Each hour in itself, so far as regards us, is unique; when once it has glided away it has perished for ever, millions of ages will not bring it back; days, months, years, fly past and are lost in the abyss of time. Time itself shall be destroyed; it is only a point in the immense span of eternity, and it shall be blotted out. There are some light and trifling circumstances of time which are unstable and which pass away. I call these circumstances fashions, greatness, riches, power, authority, independence, pleasure, joys, superfluity. What shall become of these fashions when time itself shall have disappeared? Virtue alone, though least in fashion, will survive time.

SOME CUSTOMS.

THERE are some people who require wealth to make them gentlemen. There are others who would have been gentlemen could they have obtained six months' longer delay from their creditors.

Others lie down plebeians and rise up gentlemen.

How many gentlemen are there whose fathers and brothers are plebeians !

A certain man disowns his father, who is known to have a farm and a shop ; he goes back to his ancestor who has been dead a long time, and is unknown and forgotten, and boasts of him ; now he has a large income and a great estate ; his children marry well, and he requires only a title to be a gentleman.

To rehabilitate, is the expression commonly used in law, and letters of nobility, formerly necessary in France, are now obsolete : to be rehabilitated is to suppose that a man who originally held the patent which entitled him to be called gentleman, has become rich, and he is reinstated in his gentility ; this means that he may honestly bear the title, although his father may have degraded himself by ploughing, digging, wearing a livery, or carrying a pedlar's box ; still the son is only restored to the original privileges of his ancestors, and of continuing the arms of his house, even although he has invented new ones quite different to those engraved on his pewter.

In a word, letters of nobility would not be suitable

for him ; they honour only a plebeian, that is, a man who is still longing to discover the secret of how to grow rich.

An uneducated man asserts that he has seen some prodigy, and ends by believing he has really seen it. Another conceals his age, and even persuades himself that he is as young as he would like others to believe he is : and in the same way the man of humble parentage, by continually talking of his descent from some ancient baron or great nobleman, has the pleasure of persuading himself that he has a noble pedigree.

Is there a man of low degree, who, having made some money, lacks a coat of arms, and to the arms, supporters, and a motto, and perhaps a war-cry?

Helmets are an obsolete distinction ; it is a matter of no importance now, whether they are borne in front or sidewise, close or open, and with few or more bars ; no one takes any heed of such minutiæ: so our rich plebeian aims direct at coronets, which is the simplest way ; he considers himself quite worthy of one, and it is bestowed on him. Among the better citizens, however, there is a little modesty left, which deters them from adorning themselves with a marquis's coronet, and leaves them satisfied with an earl's ; and some of them do not go very far for it ; they take it from their signboards to put on their carriage.

You may have been born in a thatched cottage far away in the country, or in a damp, broken-down ruin in a marshy swamp, a place you grandly call a castle ; if you have only not been born in town you will, on your own word, be credited with noble birth.

Some men have three names in case one should be

forfeited ; they use one at their country place, another in the town, and the other in their public life. Others have one name of two syllables, which they distinguish, as soon as their fortunes improve, by the particles *du* or *de*. Another by the suppression of a syllable makes an illustrious name of one which is obscure. Another changes one letter only, and makes a parody; from Syrus he becomes Cyrus. Some suppress names they might have borne honourably in order to adopt grander ones ; and in this way they lose by the comparisons made between the name they bear and the great men who once bore it. Lastly, there are some people, who, born within the walls of Paris, would like to pass for Flemish or Italian : so they lengthen their names by some foreign termination, forgetting that plebeians are of every country, they seem to think that to come from afar is to be grand.

Need of money has drawn nobles and plebeians nearer each other, and has made the evidence of greatness disappear.

How many would gain by a law which decides that good birth must come from the mother's side, but how many more would lose by it !

There are few families who are not related at one end of their pedigree to the greatest princes, and at the other to the humblest of the people.

I declare frankly, so that all may be prepared and none surprised ; if it one day happen that some great man thinks me worthy of his notice, or if I ever make my fortune ; there is one Geoffroy de La Bruyère, whom all the records place in the ranks of the greatest nobles of France ; he followed Godefroy de Bouillon to the conquest of the Holy Land : take notice therefore from whom I am descended in direct line.

If nobility be a virtue, it is lost by that which is not virtuous ; and if it be not a virtue, it is a trifle.

If we search into the principles and first institutions of some things, they are very wonderful and incomprehensible. Who could imagine, for instance, that a certain abbé, whose dress is in perfect taste, and who is as effeminate and vain as it is possible for any person of either sex or condition to be ; who is as much a favourite with ladies as the marquis or the rich banker; who would think, I say, that he was originally, as the spelling of his name proves—one of the fathers of a society of monks, humble men, devoted to solitude, to whom he ought to be an example. What an abuse of power that is, not to speak of greater evils. Have we not cause to dread the day, should it ever come, when this simple abbé will be arrayed in the figured velvet of a cardinal, and in patches and rouge like a woman !

Beautiful things are less beautiful out of their proper place ; fitness makes perfection, and reason employs fitness. Thus, we could not listen to a jig in church, nor to a sermon declaimed like a stage oration. Temples are not adorned with profane images ; a Crucifix and the Judgment of Paris were never seen in the same sanctuary ; nor is the retinue and equipage of a cavalier appropriate for one whose service is sacred to the church.

People do not make vows or pilgrimages to obtain from any saint a more loving spirit, or a more grateful heart ; to be made more just and less wicked ; to be cured of vanity, restlessness, and discontent.

Can you think of anything more extraordinary than a crowd of professing Christians of both sexes meeting together in a place of entertainment, for the purpose of applauding a band of excommunicated persons who are placed under the ban of the church solely on account of the pleasure they have been paid to give them. It seems to me that either theatres should be closed, or the players should be treated less severely.

The fees for a baptism are less than for a marriage and more than for a confession. We might suppose that this tax is put on the sacraments to make them more valued; but it is only a custom, and those who receive for those holy things do not think they sell, nor do those who give think they buy. Such appearances of evil might well be avoided for the sake of the simple and devout.

A youthful, ruddy, priest in fine linen and point lace has his place during the service near the dignitaries and grandees; he digests his dinner comfortably, whilst the monk or friar leaves his cell or his retreat to which propriety and his vows bind him, to come and preach the sermon for the priest and his flock, receiving payment for it as if for a piece of mercery. You interrupt me, saying, "What an unheard of and disrespectful kind of criticism; would you like to prevent the priest and his flock hearing the Gospel preached, and deprive them of the bread of life?" Quite the contrary, I would only have the priest officiate himself, morning and evening, in public and in private, on the housetops, in the churches. I would have none pretend to such a great and glorious office unless they were capable and fully purposed to perform all the duties, and deserving of the large offerings and rich contributions attached to it. I cannot; it is true, blame a young priest for continuing a usual and established practice, which he will have to leave to his successor : but I cannot approve of a custom so extraordinarily un· reasoning and unnecessary : it is even more objectionable than his being paid four times for the same obsequies, his private fee, his clerical fee, a third for his presence and a fourth for his assistance.

* * *

Titus has been twenty years in the second rank of priests, and yet when a vacancy occurs in the first rank he is not considered worthy of it. Neither his talents, his doctrine, his exemplary life, nor the wishes of his parishioners, can give it to him; some cleric starts up from underground, as it were, to fill the vacancy, and *Titus* is pushed back or dismissed ; he does not complain, it is the custom.

* * *

"Who shall force me to go to matins, am I not the Dean, the master of the choir? My predecessor never attended, and am I a less important man than he was ? Ought I to consent to lower my dignity, or even to leave it as I found it?" "It is not," says the Canon, "my own interest I look to ; I regard the interest of the Prebendary : it would indeed be hard that I should be obliged to listen to the service, whilst the Treasurer, the Archdeacon and the Vicar hold themselves exempt." "I have a good precedent," declares the Provost, "for demanding my dues without the formality of attending prayers ; for twenty long years I have been allowed to sleep undisturbed, and I shall end as I began ; no one will ever see me do anything derogatory to my title ; I know what is due to me as the head of a Chapter, and my example cannot be of any consequence."

In this way do they all vie with each other as to who will not praise God, and who will show best reason why from long custom he is not obliged to do it ; there could not be a more fervent emulation as to who shall absent themselves most frequently from divine service. The bells ring through the still night air, and their melody which awakes the choir men and the child choristers, only lulls the canons to a peaceful slumber and gives them pleasant dreams ; they rise late, go to church, and receive a salary for having had a good night's sleep.

If experience did not force us to observe it, could we imagine that it is difficult for men to resolve to enjoy their rightful happiness ? that it is even necessary to have an order of men who by preparing tender and pathetic speeches, by appeals made eloquent by tears and gestures, by violent and exhausting action, succeed after long effort in persuading a reasoning Christian man who is hopelessly ill to choose eternal salvation before his soul's destruction ?

The daughter of *Aristippus* is dangerously ill ; she sends for her father, wishing to be reconciled to him, and to die with his blessing. Will this wise man, whose counsel the whole town respects, grant this reasonable request ? Will he go and take his wife with him, or will the influence of the confessor be required to move them ?

A mother, I do not say one who submits and yields before her daughter's evident vocation for a religious life, but a mother who makes her daughter a nun, takes upon herself the responsibility of another soul, and should be warned that she is answerable to God for it : if the daughter is not saved the mother is lost.

A man gambles till he is ruined : nevertheless he gets his eldest daughter married by giving her all he has left as her dower, the youngest has to take the veil, her only vocation being her father's gambling.

___

Some virtuous, fervent, healthy girls have had a good vocation, but were not rich enough to make a vow of poverty in a wealthy convent.

___

He who deliberates in his choice between an abbey and a simple monastery opens the old question of a popular or a despotic state.

___

To play the fool and marry for love, means marry *Melita,* who is very beautiful, wise, and prudent; whom you love, and who loves you, but who is poorer than *Ægina,* who is offered to you; and who, with a rich dowry, has also a rich disposition to spend it and your own wealth along with it.

___

Formerly marriage was a delicate matter : it was a long engagement, a serious affair, which deserved much thought, for a man was the husband of his wife during all the rest of his life, for better, for worse. There could be no question of a separate establishment; with a wife, children, and servants, a man could no longer enjoy the delights of his bachelor days.

___

To avoid the company of a woman who is not your wife is proper modesty; and not to frequent the society of persons whose reputation is open to attack, is not beyond my comprehension; but what false shame can make a man blush to be seen in public with his own wife, whom he has chosen for his inseparable companion, and who ought to be his joy and delight, his only society; she whom he loves and esteems, who is his chief ornament, whose wit, virtue, merit, and family, all do him honour! Why did he not begin by blushing at his marriage? I understand the power of custom, and how it tyrannizes over minds, and constrains manners, even without ground or reason. Yet I feel I should have the impudence to promenade in the most public place with her who should be my wife.

There is neither shame nor disgrace in a young man's marrying an old woman. He may do this from prudential motives, or to preserve himself from something worse. The infamy consists in treating his benefactress unworthily, and forcing her to see that she is the victim of a hypocritical, ungrateful man. If ever any pretence is excusable it is in such a case to feign kindliness; and if deceit be permissible, here is an occasion when it would be cruel to be sincere. Even if she lives longer than you expected, did you stipulate that she should enjoy life only long enough to give her time to make over her fortune to you, and pay all your debts? After this work was completed, did you expect she would have nothing more to do than to take a dose of opium or hemlock, and lie down and die? Is it a sin in her to live? If you were to die before her whose obsequies you have so well arranged, even to the bell-ringing and the funeral ornaments, would she be to blame?

For a long time it has been the custom for men to increase their wealth by bills and bonds; this method continues to be practised by some of the best men, and condemned by our most learned divines.

You have a piece of silver or even a piece of gold, but that is not enough; it is quantity which will be

effective ; make more if you can, amass a fortune and
leave the rest to me. You have neither birth, wit,
talent, nor experience; but no matter, keep up the pile :
and I shall place you so high that you may be your
master's equal, if you have one ; indeed, he must be a
very great man, if with all your precious metal
he does not some day lift his hat to you.

Oranta has had a lawsuit before the courts for ten
years, about the settlement of a very important affair
on which her whole fortune depends ; she may know
perhaps in five years more who her judges are to be,
and before what tribunal she is to plead for the
remainder of her life.

People seem to approve of a custom which has been
introduced into our courts of law, that of interrupting
the advocate in the middle of his speech, preventing
him ever warming into eloquence or wit, and forcing
him to confine himself to bare facts and simple proofs
to establish the rights of his clients ; and this very
rigid practice, which leaves an orator to deplore that
he had no opportunity to deliver the finest part of his
discourse, which banishes eloquence from its only
natural place, and is likely to make of our tribunal a
dumb show, is authorised by a solid reason against
which there is no appeal, namely, the quick despatch
of business. We can only wish that this reason were
oftener remembered in other places, that it held good
in other offices of the same court ; that it would put
some limit to written processes as it has done to
speeches at the bar.

The duty of a judge is to adminster justice ; his
trade is to delay it. Some judges know their duty, and
follow their trade.

He who solicits his judge does him no honour ; for he either mistrusts his wisdom and his probity, or he seeks to prepossess him in his favour, and obtain injustice.

There are some judges who even in a good cause are prejudiced if interest, friendship, relationship, or authority be brought to bear on them; they will rather be unjust than appear corruptible.

A magistrate who is a gallant man does more harm than a dissolute one ; the latter conceals his intrigues, and we do not frequently find him out ; the former has a thousand known weaknessess, through which he may be attacked by any woman he pays court to.

Religion and justice are almost equally respected in a republic, and the magistrate is almost as much an object of veneration as the priest. A counsellor would scarcely dance at a ball, be seen at a play, or forget simplicity and modesty in his dress, without bringing deserved contempt upon himself; and it is strange * that it was considered necessary to pass a decree to regulate his outward appearance, and force him to be grave and to command respect.

There is no trade which does not require an apprenticeship ; and in rising from smaller conditions to greater, there is always a certain time devoted to learning and practising that which is to be a profession, a time when mistakes are of little consequence, nay are rather helps to perfection. War itself, which seems to be the product only of confusion and disorder, has its rules. Men have to learn to kill each

---

* A judicial rule obliged counsellors to wear neckbands instead of cravats.

other methodically ; there is a school for soldiers, but where is the school for judges ? There are certain customs, laws, and practices, but when have they time, sufficient time to study them, to learn and digest them ? A young man passes from school to the bar, his money bags have made a judge of him,* and his first essay is to decide authoritatively the lives and fortunes of men.

The chief virtue of an orator is truth ; without it he degenerates into a declaimer. He disguises or exaggerates facts, libels, misquotes, espouses the animosity of his client rather than the justice of his cause. He is one of those advocates of whom the proverb says, " They are paid to abuse."

It is quite true that sum is due to him, he has a lawful right to it ; but there is some small formality he has to go through ; if he forgets that, he cannot persist in his claim, and consequently he loses the money, for he has undeniably waived his right ; now he is sure to forget this formality. This is what I call a lawyer's conscience. A good maxim for the law-courts, and one which would be equally useful, reasonable, and fair to the public, would be one exactly opposed to that which makes formality outweigh equity.

The rack is a marvellous invention, and an unfailing method of ruining an innocent weakly man and saving one who is robust and guilty.

The punishment of a guilty man is an example to others ; the condemnation of an innocent man is the concern of all honest people.

---

* In La Bruyère's time the position of judge was generally obtained by purchase.

I had almost said, as I am neither a robber nor a murderer, I shall never be punished as such; but that is too bold an inference.

It is a very grievous thing for an innocent man to be, through rash judgment, found guilty of a crime. Even the position of his judge is not more deplorable.

If I were to be told that at one time the public officer appointed to prosecute and root out thieves was a person who knew them well, and was aware of their misdeeds; was, indeed, himself often so deeply involved in their evil mysteries, that if some man of mark were robbed of a valuable jewel at night, as he left a crowded public place, this officer, to prevent a disturbance, would cause it to be restored to him; that one such affair became so notorious that the courts interfered and made a case against the officer; I would look upon such a story as one of those romances we read of in history, and which time has made incredible. How then can I believe that it may be presumed from fresh events, known and proved, that such a mischievous connivance exists at the present day, and that it is winked at or disregarded.

How many men there are who oppose strength to weakness, are firm and inflexible against the solicitations of the people, and, disregarding poverty, are rigid and stern in trifling matters; refusing all compliments, and remaining uninfluenced either by relations or friends; men whom women alone can corrupt.

It is not absolutely impossible for a person in great favour to lose his cause.

T

The last will of a dying man is listened to like an oracle ; there are many disputes over it, each one interpreting it in his own way, or, I should rather say, as his desires and interests dictate.

Were there no wills to regulate the rights of heirs, I doubt if there would be any need for tribunals to adjudge the disputes of men ; judges would be restricted to their dismal function of sending murderers, thieves, and incendiaries to the gallows. Who are those who dawdle about the chambers, crowding the floors and vestibules of the courts ? Are they heirs at law ? No, they are legatees, persons whose rights are established, but who still argue the meaning of a clause or of a word ; or disinherited persons who dispute a will made after careful thought and deliberation by some wise, good, conscientious man, assisted by able counsel; or they find flaws in a deed drawn up with all the lawyer's usual phraseology and skill ; it is signed by the testator and public witnesses, and although every formality has been attended to, still, perfect as it seems, it is rendered null and void.

Titius is present at the reading of a friend's will, his eyes are red and tearful, and his heart is heavy with grief at the loss of one by whose death he hopes to inherit a fortune. One clause makes him successor in office, by another he inherits property in town, by a third he is master of a country estate, while a fourth bestows on him a house in the best part of Paris, furnished and complete. His grief increases, unrestrained tears flow down his cheeks ; he is now a public officer with a place in the country and one in town, able to keep a good table and drive a carriage ; " Was there ever in the world a kinder man than the deceased?" But stay ! Here is a codicil which must be read ; and by

it *Mævius* is sole legatee, and *Titius* is sent back to
obscurity without either honours or money, and is again
obliged to go afoot. He dries his tears, and it is now
Mævius's turn to weep.

Does not the law which forbids murder include in it
poisoning, stabbing, burning, and drowning, assaults
and open violence; all modes, in fact, of destroying
human life? Did the law which deprives a husband
or a wife of the power of making over property to each
other not recognise that there are other less direct ways
of doing this? Has it neglected to make provision for
these indirect ways? Are trusteeships an evasion of
this same law, or does it even allow trusts?

When a man dearly loves his wife, does he not
leave his wealth to a faithful friend with every feeling
of confidence, and in the certainty that he will make a
right use of what has been entrusted to him. Would
he entrust his estate to one in whom he had
not perfect confidence that he would restore it
to the person for whom it is intended? Does he
even require a written promise or any oath or
agreement from his friend about this private understanding? Have not all men a prescience of what
they may expect from each other in such circumstances?
But since the property has devolved on this trusty
friend, can you tell me why he should lose his reputation if he kept it? What grounds would there be for
lampooning or abusing him? Why should you call
him a defaulter, or compare him to a servant who robs
his master of money he is sent to deliver to some one?
It is quite unfair to do this; for where lies the odium in
not being generous and in a man keeping to himself
what is his own? A trusteeship seems to involve much
perplexity, and to have many intolerable burdens
attached to it. If through respect for the law a man

appropriates the funds, he no longer passes for an honest man ; and if from respect to a deceased friend he carries out that friend's intentions and restores the legacy to his widow, he transgresses the law which differs much from the opinions of men ; it may be, however, that I should blame neither.

Typhon provides a certain nobleman with horses and dogs, and many things besides, and is in return patronised by the aristocrat, which renders him insolent, making him assume that he can do what he likes in the neighbourhood without fear of punishment ; so he commits all kinds of crimes till at last the prince has to take upon himself his chastisement.

Ragouts, liqueurs, entrées, entremets, are all words which ought to be unintelligible and barbarous to us ; and if they are not to be used in time of peace as only tending to encourage luxury and gluttony, why are they so well understood in times of war, or great calamity, during a siege, or the night before a battle ? Where do we find mention made of the table of Scipio or of Marius ? Do we read in any record that Epaminondas, Miltiades, or Agesilaus indulged in delicate or costly food ? I should not like to hear a great general praised for the taste, delicacy, or magnificence of his table till after the subject of his victories and bravery had been exhausted ; indeed, I should prefer that a general be deprived altogether of such praise.

THE PULPIT.

PREACHING has now become a mere show; that evangelical gravity, which was the very soul of it, no longer exists; and a good manner and delivery, finely-turned sentences, well-chosen words, and a long peroration, supply its place. No one listens seriously to the inspired words. Going to church is one amusement among many others; preachers emulate each other, and the hearers often make bets upon the best preacher.

Profane eloquence which, under Le Maistre, Pucelle, and Fourcroy was a powerful influence, has been transferred from the bar to the pulpit, where it ought not to exist.

Eloquent preachers vie with others even at the altar and in the very presence of the holy mysteries. The hearers judge him who preaches, condemn or approve, and are no more converted by the sermon of the man who pleases them than by the discourse of him they condemn. The orator pleases some and displeases others, but suits all in one point—that as he does not seek to make them better, so they do not trouble themselves to become so.

An apprentice is tractable, attentive to his master, profits by his instruction, and at last becomes a master himself.

The intractable man criticizes the discourse of the preacher as he does the writing of the philosopher, and so has neither religion nor sense.

Till there shall again appear a man whose method has been formed on the Holy Scriptures, who has studied them deeply, and is able to explain them simply and plainly, orators and declamators will be popular.

Quotations from secular authors, cold allusions, false pathos, antithesis, exaggerated symbols, are out of date. Imagery will soon follow, and give place to a simple exposition of the Gospel, accompanied by other advances which will inspire conversion.

This man for whom I so ardently longed, but dared not expect in our time, is at length come. The courtiers from their cultivated taste and knowledge of propriety approved of him, and, incredible though it seems, they left the king's chapel and went with the people to hear the Word of God preached by this apostolic teacher.* The city was not of the same opinion as the Court. When he preached there the parishioners deserted the church, even the churchwardens disappeared, the pastors remained, but the congregations dispersed, and neighbouring orators thus increased their audiences. I ought to have foreseen this, and not have said that such a man had but to show himself to be followed, but to speak to be listened to : I ought to have known the indomitable force of habit in men and in all things : and as for the last thirty years they have listened to rhetoricians, declaimers, enumerators, they care to run after those only who describe with exaggerated or minute detail ; not long since such lively turns and such witty expressions were used in sermons, that they might have passed for epigrams ; this style still exists, but softened, I own, till now they may be called

* Père Seraphin, a Capuchin preacher.

madrigals. But it is still considered quite indispensable and geometrically necessary to provide three
subjects for consideration. A certain thing has to be
proved in the first part of the discourse, another in the
second part, and yet another in the third. Thus you
will be at once convinced of a certain truth, and this
is the first head ; of another truth, and that is their
second point : and further, you must be convinced of
a third truth, and that is their third point ; so that the
first reflection will instruct you in one of the funda-
mental principles of your religion, the second of another
similar principle, and the last reflection of a third and
last principle, the most important of all, which, for
want of leisure, is put off to another time ; finally, they
take up and abridge this division and form a plan——
" More still," you say, " preparations for a discourse of
an hour longer ; the more they try to clear and unravel
all this the more they perplex me." I believe you.
indeed, and agree that it is the most natural effect of
all this mass of ideas which, while unmercifully burden-
ing the memories of the hearers, always come back
to the starting point. How those preachers pride
themselves on this method ! one would think that the
grace of conversion depends on such conditions:
nevertheless, how one can be converted by apostles
one can scarcely understand. I could almost ask
them in the midst of their impetuous discourse to
pause, breathe, and allow the congregation to breathe
also. What vain, useless words ! the time for such
homilies is gone by ; a Basil or a Chrysostom would not
restore them to favour, people would go to other
dioceses to escape from the sound of their voices, and
familiar lessons. The generality of men like phrases
and periods, admire what they do not understand, and
consider themselves clever in deciding between a first
and second point, or between the last sermon and the
last but one.

Less than a century ago a French book was composed of a certain number of Latin pages, in which a few lines or words in our language might be found. Ovid and Catullus were the arbiters in marriage settlements and wills, and the Pandects guarded the rights of widows and wards. No distinction was made between sacred and profane authors, both were quoted, and had even crept together into the pulpits; St. Cyril and Horace, St. Cyprian and Lucretius, spoke alternately; the poets expressed the sentiments of St. Augustine and all the fathers; for a long time they discoursed in Latin, even to women and churchwardens; and Greek was also spoken : much learning was necessary to produce such bad preaching. Other times, other customs; the text is still in Latin, but the sermon is French, and very fine French; the Gospel even is not quoted : very little knowledge is now required to preach well.

Scholasticism is at last banished from all the pulpits of the great cities, and consigned to the small towns and villages for the instruction and edification of the ploughman and the vinedresser.

A man must have talent if he hopes to please the people by a sermon of a florid style; a sprightly moral, frequent illustrations, brilliant passages and lively descriptions are not enough.

A higher mind scorns such extraneous embellishments as unworthy to advance the Gospel : he preaches simply, forcibly, and as a Christian.

An orator paints certain sins in such bright colours, introduces such delicate circumstances, endows him who sins with so much spirit and refinement, that if I have not a longing to resemble the portrait, I at least require some teacher who in a more Christian strain will disgust me with the vices which have been so agreeably depicted to me.

A fine sermon is a piece of oratory perfectly regu-lated, purged from all its faults, conformable to the precepts of human elegance, free from all the embel-lishments of rhetoric; those who have clear under-standings will not lose a single feature nor a single thought, they easily follow the orator in all his conclu-sions; it is an enigma for the people only.

What a deep and admirable discourse we have just heard. How well the most essential points of religion, and the most urgent motives for conversion have been handled; what a fine effect it ought to have had on the mind and soul of every hearer. They are persuaded, moved and touched to the point of resolving in their hearts that this sermon of *Theodorus's** is even finer than the last he preached.

It is a mistake to preach an easy, lax morality; there is nothing in it to awaken or stimulate the curiosity of the man of the world, who fears less than we think a severe doctrine, and who even likes the preacher who makes it his duty to proclaim it. It seems, then, that there are in the church, as it were, two sides ; one speaking the truth in all its breadth without fear or disguise ; the other listening eagerly with taste, admiration, and praise, and yet being made neither better nor worse by it.

Theodulus has been less successful than some of his hearers feared. They are pleased with him and

---

* Louis Bourdaloue, one of the most celebrated of French preachers.

his discourse, more so than if he had charmed their minds and ears, for he has flattered their jealousy.

Preaching and war resemble each other in one respect, there is more risk than in other things, and success is more rapid.

If you belong to a certain rank or class, and feel you possess no talent but for making dull discourses, preach, deliver dull sermons. Nothing hinders success so much as being unknown. *Theodotus* is well rewarded for his ill-turned phrases and his wearying monotony.

Large bishoprics have been obtained by pulpit oratory, which, however, have not always turned out so valuable to a man as a simple canonry.

The indolence of women, and the habit which men have of running after them wherever they assemble, make the reputation of dull orators, and support and sustain for a time those who are falling off in popularity.

Ought greatness and worldly power to bring a man praise in the pulpit of truth, and before God's holy altar? Ought such greatness to be extolled and celebrated at his obsequies? Is there no other greatness than that which is derived from authority and good birth? Why is it not the custom to eulogize a man who, in his life, has excelled in goodness, justice, gentleness, faithfulness, and piety? What we call a funeral oration is at the present day well received by the majority of hearers, only according to the distance they perceive in it from the Christian discourse; or, if you prefer, the nearer it approaches profane eloquence.

The orator looks for a bishopric through his discourses; the apostle seeks converts; he deserves to find what the other looks for.

We see some clerics return from a short sojourn in the provinces as vain of the conversions which they found already made, as of those which they could not succeed in making; already comparing themselves to the Vincents and Xaviers, believing themselves to be men of Apostolic merit; their great works and successful missions would not in their opinion be too well rewarded by an Abbey.

A man on a sudden impulse, not having previously thought about it, takes paper, pen, and ink, saying to himself, " I am going to write a book;" he is devoid of merit, except the need of fifty crowns. In vain I exclaim, "Take tools and saw, or turn, or make the spoke of a wheel, and you will earn the price of your labour," but he has not been apprenticed to those trades. "Copy then, transpose, correct proofs, but do not write ;" no, he wishes to write, to appear in print ; and because one does not send blank paper to the printer, he scribbles it over with anything he chooses; tells us that the Seine flows into Paris, that there are seven days in the week, or that the weather is rainy ; and as this is neither against religion nor the state, and as it will do no further harm to the public than to spoil its taste and accustom it to insipid, dull trifles, it passes muster and is printed, to the disgrace of the age, as if to humiliate good authors, nay, is reprinted. In the same way a man resolves in his heart, "I will preach," and he preaches; behold him in the pulpit with no other merit or vocation than his need of a benefice.

. A worldly or irreligious cleric, if he ascends the pulpit, is an orator. There are, on the other hand, holy men whose characters alone lead others to conviction ; they appear, and a whole congregation prepares to listen and is moved and influenced by their mere presence. The discourse which they are about to deliver will do the rest.

The Bishop of Meaux and Father Bourdaloue remind me of Demosthenes and Cicero. Both masters of pulpit eloquence have had the same fate as their great models ; one has made bad critics, the other bad copyists.

That proportion of pulpit eloquence which depends on the talent of the orator is a secret known to few, and difficult to attain ; what art is required to please and persuade at the same time. You must follow the beaten track, say what has been said and what you are expected to say ; the materials are grand, but worn and trite ; the principles are sure but the hearers at once arrive at the conclusions ; sublime subjects abound, it is true, but who can interpret the sublime. There are mysteries which ought to be expounded, but which are better explained by a lesson in the schools than in an oratorical discourse. The morality even of the pulpit, which comprises matter as vast and varied as the morals of men, still turns on the same pivot, reproduces the same imagery and prescribes itself limits much narrower than satire ; for after the usual invective against honours, riches, and pleasures, there is no more left to the orator than to hasten to the end of his discourse and dismiss the assembly. If sometimes we are moved to tears, let us analyse the genius and character of the preacher, and perhaps it will be allowed that our emotion has been caused rather by some per-

sonal interest in the matter preached than by the true
eloquence of the missioner.

The preacher is not supported, like the lawyer, by
ever new facts, by different events and unexpected
adventures. He does not discuss doubtful questions,
lays no stress on strong conjectures and presumptions,
all of which help to exalt genius, and give it power
and latitude ; rather establishing and directing eloquence than restraining it. The preacher must, however, take his discourse from a source common to all,
and if he departs from these common paths he is no
longer popular ; he is either too abstruse or he is
declamatory, he does not preach the Gospel. He requires only a noble simplicity, but that he must attain,
and it is a rare talent, and one beyond the capability of
most men ; for the genius, imagination, erudition, and
memory they possess is of no use to them ; it often
only hinders them.

The lawyer's profession is hard and laborious, and
he who exercises it must possess a fund of knowledge.
He is not merely primed like the preacher with a certain number of addresses, composed at leisure, and
delivered from memory, with authority, and without
fear of contradiction, which, with little alterations,
can be made to do him credit more than once. His
pleadings have to be spoken gravely before judges who
may command him to be silent, and in the presence of
adversaries who may interrupt him. He must be
quick and ready with his replies, able to speak in several
courts on different affairs in the same day. His house
even is no place of rest and shelter for him, nor a
refuge from his clients ; it is open to all who choose to
come and overwhelm him with their doubts and questions. He is no sooner in bed, refreshed and made
comfortable, than his room is crowded by people of all
conditions come to congratulate him on the grace and

charm of his language, making him remember one place where he nearly stopped short, or another case in which he has been doubtful if his pleading was as good as usual. His only repose after a long discourse is to begin to write a long document; he only varies his labour. I dare to say he is in his way what the early Apostles were in theirs.

Having thus distinguished the eloquence of the law and the function of the lawyer, from the eloquence of the pulpit and the office of the preacher, we can easily see that it is easier to preach than to plead, and more difficult to preach well than to plead well.

———

What an immense advantage an extempore sermon has over a written one. Men are swayed by eloquent gestures and by the solemnity of the congregation: if they have been, even in a small degree, prejudiced in favour of him who speaks, they will admire him and try to understand him. Before he has well commenced, they say to themselves, "This will be a good sermon;" then they go to sleep, and when he ends they wake up and say, "What a splendid discourse!" An author has less power to affect people, and his book is read in the retirement of the country, or in the quiet of a study. There is no crowded meeting to extol him, no partisans to sacrifice everything for his sake, and raise him to a prelacy; however excellent his book may be it is read with the intention of finding it indifferent. It is turned over and run through, then discussed and compared. Unlike sounds, which are lost in the air and forgotten, written words stand; sometimes publication is waited for impatiently only to condemn, and criticism is the greatest pleasure some find in it. They are annoyed to see passages on every page which ought to please, they will even go so far as to lay down the book at last because it is so good.

It is not every one who is fit to be a preacher; phrases, figures of speech, the gift of memory, the gown and the oath of a divine are not things every one desires or dares to appropriate, whereas every one imagines he can think, and still better, express on paper what he has thought; therefore, he is not a fair judge of another who thinks and writes as well as himself. In a word, the preacher is sooner made a bishop than the most intellectual writer is advanced to a small priory, and new honours are continually accorded to the former, while the latter has to be contented with his leavings.

If it happens that the wicked hate and persecute you, good men advise you to humble yourself before God, so that you may be preserved from the vain spirit which might arise in you with the feeling that you are not pleasing in the sight of such men. So when certain men, who habitually exclaim against indifferent work disapprove of a book you have written, or of a discourse you have delivered, be it at the bar, or in the pulpit, or elsewhere, humble yourself, for there is no greater or more personal temptation to pride.

A preacher ought, I think, in each sermon he delivers to make choice of some great truth, one of the deadly sins which may move to terror or yield instruction; handling it deeply and exhaustively; omitting all the divisions and subdivisions which are so far fetched, involved and perplexing; he should not take for granted what is not the case, that the great and fashionable world understands the religion it professes or the duties it ought to perform. He should not be afraid to instruct these grand, refined people in their catechism; let him employ the time others take to write a long sermon in making himself master of his subject, so that his eloquence will flow from his heart and soul, growing as he speaks; let him after careful preparation abandon himself to his own genius and to the emotions a great subject will inspire him with. Let him spare himself those great efforts of memory which are more like reciting for a wager than a solemn occasion, and which spoil all the grace of delivery; let him, on the contrary, by his own fine enthusiasm shoot out conviction into souls and alarm into hearts, and inspire his hearers with some other fear than that of seeing him halt in his rhetoric.

———

Let not him who is not yet confident enough to forget himself in the ministry of the holy word be discouraged by the austere rules which are prescribed to him, as if they robbed him of the means of showing his own talent and attaining to the dignity to which he aspires. What finer talent can a man possess than that of preaching like the Apostles? and what can better deserve a Bishopric? Was Fénelon unworthy? would he have missed his Prince's choice but for another choice?

Do those whom we call bold thinkers know that they
are so named in irony? For what greater weakness
can exist than to be doubtful of the principle of our
being, of life, sense, knowledge? and of how all these
things must end? What can be more discouraging for
a man than doubts and questionings as to whether his
soul is material like a stone, corruptible as the
vilest worm? Is it not bolder and greater to accept the
idea of a being superior to all other beings, by whom
all things were made, and to whom all things
must yield; of a being supremely perfect, infinitely pure, who is from everlasting to everlasting,
and of whom our soul is the image, and, if I may dare
so to say, a part, being spiritual and immortal?

Worldly, earthly, gross, I call those persons whose
minds and hearts are bound to one little portion of
the world they inhabit, which is the earth; who
value nothing, love nothing beyond; people whose
minds are narrowed to the limits of what they call
their own dominions and possessions. I am not surprised that men, whose support is an atom, stumble
over the smallest efforts they make to fathom the
truth; with such short-sighted vision they are unable
to pierce beyond the heavens and the stars to God;
and perceiving nothing of the excellence of that which
is spiritual or of the dignity of the soul, they are still
less sensible of any difficulty in satisfying its aspira-
tions, or of feeling how much the whole earth is

U

inferior to the soul, and the longing the soul comes to have for one supreme being who is God, or of the absolute need of a religion which will show them God, and be a sure pledge of His reality. On the contrary, I understand very well that it is natural for such men to fall into a state of unbelief or indifference ; and to make use of God and of religion only when it suits their policy, that is to say, as far as it serves to regulate and improve the world, for this, according to them, is the only thing worth thinking about.

Some men, after much travelling, end in being perverted, and lose the little religion left to them ; from day to day they meet with new forms of worship, new rites and ceremonies ; they are like the people who go into a shop undetermined as to what they wish to buy, and who are made more indifferent still from the variety of choice offered to them ; each thing pleases them in some way ; but they are unable to decide, and come away without having purchased anything.

A man should examine and prove himself well and seriously before declaring himself an unbeliever, so that he may at least act up to his principles, and die as he has lived ; or if he does not feel his convictions strong enough to carry him as far as this, he should resolve to live as he would wish to die.

I should expect that those who act differently from other people, and contradict the usually accepted principles of mankind, should know more than other men, and be ready with clear reasons and convincing arguments.

Should a good, just, well-governed, sober man assert

that there is no God, I should at least think his judgment impartial; but such a man is not to be found.

The difficulty I find myself in to prove that there is no God makes me perceive the existence of one.

I feel that there is a God, and I do not feel that there is none; this is enough for me, all the world's reasoning is useless to me. I conclude that God exists; this conclusion is in my nature. I received the principles of my belief involuntarily in my childhood, and I have preserved them too naturally in my later life to suspect them of falsehood; but there are minds which renounce these truths. I question their existence, but if it be so, this proves only that there are monsters.

There is no such thing as atheism. Great men who are most apt to be suspected of it are too lazy to decide in their own minds that there is no God. Their indolence is so extreme as to render them cold and indifferent on this important question, as also upon the nature of their own souls and the significancy of a true religion. They neither deny these things nor grant them; they never think about them.

Are men good, faithful, and just enough to deserve our whole confidence, and not to make us wish for the existence of a God, to whom we can appeal from their injustice, and whom we can petition when they persecute or deceive us?

If it is the grandeur and sublimity of religion which dazzles and confuses unbelievers, they cannot be called freethinkers, they are only weak-minded, feeble, geniuses; if, on the contrary, it is its humility and simplicity which makes them reject it, they must indeed be strong in their unbelief; stronger than all the great and learned men who, nevertheless, were so faithful, such as the Leos, the Basils, the Jeromes, and the Augustines.

Man is born false; truth is simple and honest, and he desires gilding and ornament. Truth or reality is not one of his natural qualities; it comes direct from Heaven in all its perfection, and man loves only his own work, fiction, and fable. Just look how people invent and add to a tale, and load it with vulgarity and foolishness. Ask even the most honest man if his conversation is always truthful, if he does not sometimes even surprise himself by the distortions he indulges in through vanity or levity, if to make a story better he does not often find himself making a few additions to some event which seems to require a little more circumstance. Something happens to-day and, perhaps, under our own observation. A hundred people who have seen it will relate the fact in a hundred different ways; what credence then can I give to the relation of facts which are separated from us by so many centuries? What foundation have I for believing the greatest historians? What is history? Was Cæsar really murdered before the Senate? Was there ever a Cæsar? "What strange ideas," you exclaim; "what doubts and questions!" You laugh and think me scarcely worth an answer; and, indeed, I believe you are right. But I must be assured that the book which speaks of Cæsar is not a profane book, written by the hands of men who are liars; that it was not found by chance among other manuscripts containing histories, some of which are true and others doubtful; but that, on the contrary, the book is inspired, holy, divine, that it bears the marks of its holy origin, that it has been believed for nearly two thousand years by an innumerable society of men who have never all this time allowed the smallest alteration in it, and who have made of it a religion which they have preserved in all its integrity ; that there is even a solemn and indispensable obligation to believe in all the facts contained in the volume which speaks of Cæsar and his Dictatorship. Confess, *Lucilius*, you will doubt that there ever was a Cæsar.

All music is not fit for the praise of God, and to be heard in the sanctuary. Every kind of philosophy does not speak worthily of God, of His power, of the principles of His mighty works, and of His Holy mysteries. The more subtle and ideal that philosophy is, the more vain and useless to explain these things which only require from men a right reason to be understood up to a certain point, and which, beyond that, cannot be explained at all. To pretend to give a perfect explanation of God, of His perfection, and, if I dare so to speak, of His actions, is to go beyond the ancient philosophers, the apostles, or first teachers of the Gospel, without being so prudent or exact; it means searching long and digging deeply, and failing to find the springs of truth. If we abandon the terms goodness, mercy, justice, omnipotence, which present to us such sublime and beautiful ideas of God, we are only able by great efforts of imagination to borrow dry, barren, senseless expressions, to admit strained original ideas, or at least, ideas which are subtle and ingenious, and which, as they gradually teach us new metaphysics, will take away our religion from us.

To what extremes will men not be carried in the interests of a religion of which they are so little convinced that they practise it so badly.

If all religion is a respectful fear of the Divine Being, what shall we think of those who dare to offend Him in His delegate here on earth, who is the king?

———

Were we to be assured that the secret motive of the embassy from Siam* was to incite the most Christian king to renounce Christianity, and to consent to their priests entering his kingdom, who, being allowed to penetrate into our households, would try by their books and discourses to persuade our wives and children, and even ourselves, to accept their religion; afterwards, raising their pagodas in our midst for the adoration of their images, with what scorn and derision would we listen to such an extraordinary project. Yet we ourselves make a voyage of six thousand leagues for the conversion of the Indies, and to teach Christianity in Siam, China, and Japan; that is to say, to propound seriously to these nations doctrines which must appear to them equally foolish and ridiculous. Nevertheless, they endure our religion and our priests; they listen to them sometimes, and allow them to build churches and to perform their mission. What is the cause of this difference in them and in us? Does it not demonstrate the force of truth?

———

It is not seemly that any kind of person should set up his banner as almoner, and have all the beggars of the town gathered round his door, each receiving his alms. But, on the other hand, who is there among us who does not know of some hidden case of dire necessity which he is able to try to relieve either at once from his own purse or through his mediation with others? In the same way all are not qualified to go into a pulpit, and from thence to preach the Word of

———

* Sent to France in 1680.

God; but who at some time has not had it in his power
to try by gentle winning words to lead some erring
soul to believe? If, during all his lifetime, a man has
taught the gospel message to only one man, he has not
lived in the world in vain, nor has he been but a cum-
berer of the earth.

There are two worlds : one in which our sojourn is
short, and which we must soon leave never to return
to again ; the other into which we must soon enter to
abide there for ever. Interest, authority, friends, a
great name, and great riches, are useful in the first ;
but scorn of them all is of the most use for the second.
It is our own concern to choose which is of greatest
importance.

He who has lived a single day has lived a century :
the same sun, the same earth, the same universe, the
same sensations ; nothing is more like to-day than to-
morrow. To die would be a new sensation, to be no
longer a body, but a spirit ; but man, impatient as
he is for novelty, has no curiosity to experience this
change. However restless and wearied he is of everything, he is never tired of life, and would probably
consent to live for ever ; for what he sees of death
more violently impresses him than what he knows of
it. Sickness, pain, the grave, take from him the desire
to go to another world ; it requires all the earnestness
of religion to reconcile him to death.

Religion is either true or false. If it is no more than
a vain fiction, I grant that the honest man, the monk,
and the ascetic recluse, waste sixty years, but they run
no other risk ; therefore, if it is even founded on truth,
what an unutterable misfortune for the wicked man :
the mere thought of all the woe he is preparing for

himself makes me miserable; imagination is too feeble to conceive it, words are vain to try to express it. Even supposing our faith in the truth of religion were less sure than it is, surely the paths of virtue are the best.

I almost think that those who dare to deny God do not deserve that we should strive to prove to them His existence, or at least that I should handle the matter more earnestly than I have already done in this chapter; the ignorance of their natures makes them incapable of understanding the clearest and most natural inferences. Still I am willing that they should read what I am about to write, provided they do not persuade themselves that this is all one could say on such a glorious subject.

Forty years ago I was not: neither was it in my power that I should ever exist, even as now that I do exist, I have no power to cease from being: therefore, I had a beginning and I continue to be, through some influence apart from me, and which will continue after me, because it is better and more powerful than myself; if this something is not God, will you tell me what it is?

You say, "Perhaps I exist as I am only through the power of a universal nature which is and has been from all eternity." But this nature is either spiritual, and is God; or it is material, and consequently could not have created my soul; or it is a compound of spirit and matter: and whatever is spiritual in nature, I call God.

Or again, perhaps, you add that what I call my soul is only a portion of matter which exists through the power of a universal nature, which also is material, always was and will be for ever just as we see it now,

and is not God; but at least you must admit that what I
call my reason, whatever it may be, is something which
thinks, and that, if it is matter, it is necessarily matter
which can think; for no one will ever persuade me
that whilst I thus reason with you, there is not something within me that thinks ; now this something which
is in me and which thinks; if it owes its being and its
preservation to a universal law, which always was and
ever will be, which it acknowledges as its cause, must of
necessity be either a universal something which thinks,
or else a nobler and more perfect nature than that
which thinks; and if this something thus formed is
matter, we must still conclude that it is a universal
material law which thinks, or that it is nobler and more
perfect than that which thinks.

To continue, I maintain that this matter, being such
as we have supposed it to be, if it be not chimerical,
but real, cannot be imperceptible to all our senses ;
and that if it is not apparent in itself, it would at least be
perceived in the diverse dispositions of those parts which
constitute all bodies, and which make the difference
between them. Matter, then, is itself all these different
bodies ; and since according to the supposition, matter
is a something which thinks, or is better than that
which thinks; it follows that it is such at least as regards
some of these bodies, and consequently that it
thinks in stones, in minerals, in the earth and sea,
and also in myself, since I am only a body. I therefore
owe this something within me which thinks, and which
I call my soul, to the union of all these gross, earthy,
corporeal parts, which together form the universal
matter of this visible world ; an absurd argument.

If, on the contrary, however, this universal nature,
whatever it may be, cannot be all these bodies, nor any
of these bodies, it follows from that cause that it is
not matter, and cannot be perceived by any of our

senses. If, nevertheless, it thinks, or is more perfect
than that which has the faculty of thinking, I still conclude that it is spirit, or something better and more
complete than spirit; if, moreover, there remains no
more of that which thinks in me, and which I call my
mind, than that universal nature to which we must go
back to find its first cause and sole origin, inasmuch as
it does not find its principle in itself, and still less in
matter, as has just been demonstrated, I did not then
dispute about names, but this original source of all
understanding which is the soul itself, and which is
more excellent than all reason, I call God. In a word,
I believe then that God exists; for that which thinks
within me I have not bestowed on myself, since it was
no more in my power to create it at first than it is now
to be the preserver of it for a single moment. Nor do
I owe this gift to a material being superior to myself,
since it is impossible that matter can be superior to that
which thinks; therefore, I must have received it from a
being who is superior to me, and who is not material,
and that Being is God.

The soul sees colour through the medium of the eye,
and hears sounds by medium of the ear; but if those
subjects or objects were removed, seeing and hearing
would cease, and yet being would not cease, because
the soul is not only that which sees or hears, it is that
which thinks. Now, how can such power cease? It
is not from want of organism, since it is proved that
the soul is not material; nor from want of objects so
long as there is a God and eternal truths; therefore it
is incorruptible.

I cannot conceive that a soul which God has filled
with the idea of His infinite and all-perfect being can
be annihilated.

Look, *Lucilius,* this spot of earth* is better cared for, more adorned than any of the other parts which are near it. Here we find spaces watered by smooth as well as spouting waters. There are endless sheltered walks lined with fruit-laden palisades. On one side a leafy wood, which shelters from the strongest sun, and on the other a lovely view. Lower down a Yvette or a Lignon, which once ran unnoticed among willows and poplars, is now an adorned canal. There long, cool, shady avenues traverse the fields and lead you to a residence built by the water's brink. Do you exclaim, "What a lucky chance! How many beautiful effects have happened to unite here!" No, on the contrary, you will doubtless say, "How well all this has been contrived, arranged, and executed, what great skill and intelligence have been displayed in this conception." I agree with you, and would add that this must be the dwelling-place of one of those men who, from the first day they are in a place, think only of beautifying it. And yet after all what is this piece of earth thus disposed, and on the embellishment of which so much art has been lavished, if all the earth be but an atom suspended in the air, and if you pay any heed to what I am about to say?

You, *Lucilius,* are placed somewhere on this atom of earth, you must, therefore, be very small, for you occupy so little space; however, you have eyes which are two almost imperceptible points : do not forget to raise them towards the heavens. What do you sometimes see there? Is it the full moon? She is beautiful and very luminous, although her light is in reality but the reflection of the sun; she appears as large as the sun and greater than the other planets, or any of the stars ; but be not deceived by external appearance,

---

* Chantilly.

for there is nothing in the sky so small as the moon ;
its surface is thirteen times smaller than the earth's
surface, and it is forty-eight times less solid. The
earth has four times its diameter of seven hundred and
fifty leagues, and the truth is, it is only its nearness to us
which makes it appear so large and brilliant, for its
distance from us is scarcely thirty times the diameter
of the earth, or about a hundred thousand leagues. Its
course is very insignificant compared with the vast
tour the sun makes in the firmament of heaven ; for
we know the moon's course is only five hundred and
forty thousand leagues a day ; this is equal to twenty-
two thousand five hundred leagues each hour, or three
hundred and seventy-five leagues a minute. In order to
accomplish this course, however, the moon must travel
five thousand six hundred times quicker than a post
horse, which covers four leagues in an hour ; she must
fly eighty times more rapidly than sound, than the
noise, for example, of a cannon, and of thunder, which
travels two hundred and seventy-seven leagues an
hour.

But indeed there is no comparison between the moon
and the sun with respect to its distance from us, its
size, or its course. Only think of the diameter of the
earth ; it is three thousand leagues ; that of the sun is
a hundred times more ; it must therefore be three hundred
thousand leagues. Now, if this be its extent, what must be
its surface, what its solidity ? Do you understand clearly
the immensity of this dimension, and that the earth a
million times over would not be larger than the sun ?
" What an immense distance, then, it must be from us,"
you say, " if we are to judge from its appearance." You
are quite right, the distance is tremendous. It is com-
puted that the sun's distance from the earth is no less
than ten thousand times the diameter of the earth, or
in other words, thirty million leagues ; and it may even

be four, six, or ten times further ; there is no exact method of determining this distance.

In order to help your imagination to realize this, let us suppose a mill-stone falling from the sun to the earth : let us allow it to fall with the greatest speed possible to conceive, a rapidity greater than any falling body has ever attained, let us farther suppose that this rapidity is maintained unceasingly and uniformly, never either gaining or losing in speed, that it travels fifteen fathoms every second, which is half the height of the highest steeple, and in a minute it advances nine hundred fathoms. But to make this calculation easier we shall make it a thousand fathoms, and a thousand fathoms are equal to half a league, so in two minutes the mill-stone would travel a league, and in an hour, thirty leagues, and in a day, seven hundred and twenty leagues ; now to reach the earth the stone would have to travel thirty million leagues ; therefore it would take forty thousand, six hundred and sixty-six days, which are more than a hundred and fourteen years, to complete this journey. Do not be alarmed, *Lucilius,* attend to what I say : the distance from the earth to Saturn is at least ten times that of the earth's distance from the sun, that is to say, it cannot be less than three hundred million leagues, so this stone would take more than eleven hundred and forty years to fall from Saturn to the earth.

Now try to realize this elevation of Saturn, and if you can, raise your imagination to consider the immensity of his daily course. Saturn's orbit is more than six hundred million leagues in diameter, and consequently more than eighteen hundred million leagues in circumference ; so that an English horse, which would travel ten leagues an hour, would take twenty thousand five hundred and fifty-eight years to make this journey.

I have not said all, *Lucilius,* that could be said about the wonders of this visible world, or, to use your frequent expression, on the marvels of chance, which only you will admit as the primary cause of all things. There is yet another workman more wonderful than you imagine; try to understand chance, instruct yourself in the power of your God. Do you know what a small thing this distance of thirty millions of leagues from the earth to the sun, and that of three hundred millions of leagues from the earth to Saturn, is, compared to the distance from the earth to the stars. No one knows the height of a star, it is, if I may say so, immeasurable; angles, lines, and parallaxes, are useless to compute it. If a man in Paris were observing a fixed star, and if in Japan another man were looking at the same star, the two lines which would reach from their eyes to the star would not form an angle, but would be confounded and mixed into a single line, so far short of space is the whole earth in comparison with this distance. But the stars have this in common with Saturn and the sun: and I must add something more ; if two astronomers, one on the earth and the other in the sun, were observing the same star at the same time, the two visual rays of these two astronomers would not form a sensible angle. To explain this otherwise, if a man were in a star, our sun, our earth, and the thirty millions of leagues which separate them, would appear to him the same point ; this is clearly demonstrated.

Nor is the distance between one star and another known, although to us they appear so close. The Pleiades, judging from our sight, almost touch each other, and in the line of stars which form the tail of the Great Bear one star seems to lie on another; sight can scarcely discern the space of sky which separates them, to the eye it seems a double star ; now if all the science of astronomy is useless to discover the distance between them, what can we conceive of the space between two stars, which even to us seem remote from each other, and what again of the two polar stars. How tremendous the line which reaches from one pole star to another, and how immense the circle of which this line is the diameter. Is it not worse than trying to sound a bottomless abyss to attempt to imagine the solidity of the globe of which this circle is only a section. Can we still be surprised that these stars, though so immeasurably great, seem to us no larger than sparks? Shall we not rather admire that from such a boundless height they still preserve a form and are not invisible? There are many which escape our vision. We fix the number of the stars, but how can we number those which are unseen ; those, for example, which make the Milky Way, that track of brilliant light which from North to South on clear nights is observed in the sky. Our eyes cannot pierce to their infinite height, we cannot distinguish any particular star as we gaze at that white and shining pathway in the heavens.

We are placed then on this earth as on a grain of sand suspended loosely in the air ; a multitude of fiery globes of infinite size are for ever revolving round this grain of sand, and for more than six thousand years they have been crossing the vast immensity of the heavens. If you prefer another system, one no less marvellous, the world itself is turning round the sun, the centre of the universe, with inconceivable rapidity. I try to imagine to myself all these globes, those alarming bodies always moving on in such marvellous order ; with no confusion, no coming into contact one with the other ; if the smallest of them all were to deviate and but touch our earth, what would become of it? But all keep their

places, remaining in their prescribed order, following
the paths assigned to them ; and this so quietly, as far
as we know, for human ears are not formed to distinguish any sound from that ceaseless march of stars, while
the ignorant scarcely know of their existence. Oh, what a
marvellous economy of chance : could intelligence even
have done better ? There is only one thing, *Lucilius*,
I cannot understand : these great bodies are so exact
and constant in their courses, in their revolutions, and
in all their relations to each other, that an insignificant
animal, confined to a corner of that immense space, a
corner which is called the world, having carefully
observed them, has evolved an infallible method of predicting in what degree of their respective courses all
these stars will be to-day, or two, three, four, or twenty
thousand years hence. This is my difficulty, *Lucilius* : if it
is by chance that they observe such unchanging rules,
what is order? what are rules?

'I would even like to ask you what is chance, is it a
body, or is it a spirit ? Is it a being distinguishable
from other beings, one having a particular existence
somewhere ? Or rather is it not a mode or a fashion of
being ? When a bowl runs against a stone, we say it
was chance ; but does that mean anything more than
that these two bodies accidentally hit each other ? If
by this chance or this hit the bowl does not now
run straight, if its direct aim is weighted, if it no longer
rolls on its axis, but turns and whirls like a top, shall I
from this infer that from this same chance motion is in
general in this bowl ? Shall I not rather suspect that
the bowl owes motion to itself, or "to the impulse of
the arm which threw it." And because the wheels of a
clock are regulated one by the other to a certain time,
shall I examine less curiously what may be the cause of
all these movements, if they act of themselves or
through the moving force of a weight which sets them

in motion. But neither these wheels nor that bowl have the power of producing movement of themselves, nor could they change this motion unless they could change their own nature ; it seems, then, that they are moved otherwise, by some power which does not belong to them. And the celestial bodies, if they could change their motions, would they change their nature ? Would they cease to be bodies ? I cannot believe this. They still move, and if not of themselves and by their own nature, we must search and examine, O *Lucilius*, if there be not principle independent of them which causes their motion; and whatever you may discover, I call this principle God.

If we could suppose these great bodies to be motion-less, we should not require to ask who gives them motion, but we should still be ready to ask who made these bodies, as we should inquire who made these wheels or this bowl ; and if each of these great bodies were supposed to be but a heap of atoms which have accidentally knit themselves into shape and form, I would still take one of these atoms and I should say, Who created this atom ? Is it matter or is it spirit? Did it conceive its own being before it came into being ? Then it existed a moment before it came into being ; it was and it was not at the same time ; and if it be the author of its own being and of its manner of being, why did it create itself a body rather than a spirit ? More than this, had the atom no beginning, is it eternal ? is it infinite ? Will you make a God of this atom ?

The mite has eyes, it turns aside from any object that could hurt it. Place it on a black surface that you may observe it better: if while it moves to the other side you lay the most tiny straw in its way it will alter its course. Now do you believe that the optic

X

nerve, the retina and the crystalline humour, which are the mediums of light, are given to this little creature by chance?

God condemns and punishes those who offend Him. He is the only Judge of His own motives; this we might resist if He were not Himself justice and truth; that is, if He were not God.

If you assume that every man in the world, without exception, lives in plenty and wants for nothing, my deduction from your proposition would be that no man has plenty, that all want for everything. All wealth is reduced to two kinds, money and land; if all were rich who would cultivate the ground and excavate the mines. Those who live far away from mines could not dig up their treasures; and those who live in barren lands which produce only minerals would not be able to reap fruits from the earth. People would depend on commerce, you suppose: but if all men had abundance of wealth, and none were obliged to live by labour, who would transport the gold and silver and all kinds of commodities from one place to another? Who would prepare the ships and guide them across the seas? and who would convey goods by land? Everyone would be in want of necessaries and of all useful things. If there were no necessaries, there would be no arts or sciences, no inventions, no machinery. Besides, this equality in wealth would lead to equality in condition, would banish subordination; men would have to be their own servants, and would render no help to each other: law would be worthless, and useless, and universal anarchy and violence would produce outrage, murder, and impunity from the punishment of crime.

If, on the other hand, you would assume all men to be poor, in vain the sun would shine on our horizon,

warm the earth and render it fruitful; in vain the
heavens would pour out refreshing rains upon it, or the
rivers water it with streams carrying to all countries
wealth and abundance. In vain the seas, the rocks,
and the mountains open and let us dig into their depths
for all the hidden treasures they contain. But if you
will lay it down as a law that of all men scattered
throughout the whole world, some must be rich, some
poor, and some intelligent, you will then bring about
another law, a law of necessity which will draw men
together and bind them in a union of fellowship and
content; some to serve and others to obey, and some
to perfect labour and invention; while others rule, protect, succour, and sustain, and enjoy; thus order is
established, and God is manifested.

Some inequality in the conditions of men for the
maintenance of order and subordination is the work of
God, and sets forth the divine law. Any great disproportion which we remark among men is their own
work, brought about by the law of violence. All
extremes are corrupt, and originate with man : the law
of compensation is just, and comes from God.

If these characters are not liked I shall be surprised ; if they are liked, I shall be surprised even
more.

Henderson & Spalding, Printers, Marylebone Lane, W.

Mr. David Stott's

Publications

370 Oxford Street

LONDON W.

June 1890

The Stott Library.

UNDER this title I am now issuing a Series of Books by the best Writers, in 32mo size, elegantly printed on toned paper, in a beautifully clear type. Each Volume contains an Etching as frontispiece, and is published at Three Shillings, and any Volume can be had separately.

ESSAYES OF MONTAIGNE.

FIRST BOOK. Translated by JOHN FLORIO. Introduction by JUSTIN H. MCCARTHY, M.P. Two Volumes. With a Portrait in each.   [Now Ready.

SECOND BOOK. Two Volumes. With an Etching in each.
[Now Ready.

DE QUINCEY.

A Selection of his best Works. Introduction by W. H. BENNETT. Vol. I. Confessions of an English Opium-Eater. Suspiria de Profundis. With Etched Portrait. Vol. II. Murder considered as one of the Fine Arts. The English Mail-Coach. The Last Days of Kant. Recollections of Charles Lamb. With View of De Quincey's Cottage at Lasswade.   [Now Ready.

ESSAYS OF ELIA.

By CHARLES LAMB. Two Volumes. With Two Illustrations specially Engraved for this Edition.   [Now Ready.

EMERSON'S ESSAYS.

Introduction by RONALD J. MCNEILL. Two Volumes. With Portrait and View of Emerson's House at Concord.   [Now Ready.

BACON'S ESSAYS.

Collated with all the best Editions. With View of Bacon's House at Gorhambury.   [Now Ready.

FAMILIAR LETTERS OF JAMES HOWELL.

Edited, with Biographical Introduction, by W. H. BENNETT. Two Volumes. With an Etching in each.   [In June.

SIR THOMAS BROWNE'S RELIGIO MEDICI.

[In the Press.

One Hundred Copies of each are being issued on Large Paper.

Other Volumes in preparation, which will be duly announced.

The Stott Library.

Opinions of the Press.

SATURDAY REVIEW.—The miniature "Stott Library," a charming set of bijou reprints, now includes Lamb's "Essays of Elia," in two volumes, with two beautiful etchings of Edmonton Churchyard and Lamb's Cottage at Edmonton. This is the prettiest of all pocket editions of "Elia."

THE SPECTATOR.—Elegant little volumes, truly fitted to the capacity of the shallowest pocket; well printed, and on good paper.

ST. JAMES'S GAZETTE.—The miniature library to which the publisher, Mr. David Stott, gives his own name, hardly needs further commendation, and might either "take place in the most sumptuous drawing-rooms of all the 'wreaths' and 'Flora's Chaplets' of the book shops," or fill the last vacant space in one's travelling bag.

THE ATHENÆUM.—The pretty little series he has baptized with his own name.

PUNCH.—As to books, there's a lot. Mr. David Stott sends the "Essays of Elia" in compass tiny :
But although compact, 'tis a pleasant fact, that the type is clear and the paper shiny.

THE SCOTSMAN.—His dainty "Stott Library," one of the neatest editions a lover of books could desire, clearly and elegantly printed, and illustrated with good frontispieces. The series is sure of success.

MORNING POST.—Printed in type of a size and clearness which must satisfy all who are fortunate enough to have average powers of vision.

THE NEW YORK CRITIC.—Just the sort of thing to slip into your pocket next summer when you go fishing or walking. A model of neatness, compactness, cheapness, and unpretentiousness. The most desirable edition of Lamb on grounds of appearance and convenience.

The Stott "Montaigne," one of a series of typographical tit-bits.

THE EVENING POST.—"The Stott Library," a charming little series. One could not desire a daintier get-up.

THE STAR.—All true lovers of literature should be grateful to Mr. Stott for these handy and pretty little volumes, daintily bound and exquisitely printed.

THE BOOKSELLER.—Dainty little volumes, which, with their tasteful binding and clear reprint, will recommend themselves to the bibliophile.

DAVID STOTT, 370, OXFORD STREET, W.

A PRETTY RADICAL,

And Other Stories.

By MABEL E. WOTTON.

Crown 8vo, price 5s.

Athenæum :—"A collection of really good short stories. Very well worth reading."

Scotsman :—"Neatly and gracefully told."

St. James's Gazette :—"Pleasantly told and happily conceived."

The Daily News :—"Miss Mabel E. Wotton has got a happy knack of turning off short stories. For some strange reason the British public, unlike the Parisian public, do not like short stories, but they ought to like Miss Wotton's."

The Pictorial World :—"A really good collection of short stories. The best and most powerful and pathetic tales in this entertaining volume, according to our judgment, are 'Monsieur le Curé' and 'Beauty and the Beast;' good examples of opposite types."

The Speaker :—"Miss Wotton's stories are really clever —some of them astonishingly clever. The situation in 'Almost a Tragedy' is exceptionally strong, and, if elaborated in a play, should give a clever actress such a chance as is seldom found. Guess, then, our delight when in reading on we found in 'My First Patient' another as good. 'Told in the Firelight' is dramatic, too ; and over 'Beauty and the Beast' and 'Told in the Studio' we came very close to real tears."

Daily Telegraph :—"Miss Wotton ought to be heard of again."

Pall Mall Gazette :—"Neat, pointed, and well put together. Full of interest."

SAPPHO:
Memoirs, Text, and Translation.
BY
H. T. WHARTON, M.A.

*With Etched Portrait of Sappho and Autotype of Fragments
of Sappho's MS.*

Parchment, Fcap. 8vo. Second Edition. PRICE 7s. 6d.

THIS BOOK IS NOW OUT OF PRINT.

"A pretty volume, in which Mr. H. T. Wharton has collected all
the extant fragments attributed to the Greek poetess, together with a
prose translation and a liberal selection of the English verse translations and imitations which have appeared since the time of Addison.
. . . . The chief novelty of the book is a series of translations,
written expressly for it by Mr. J. A. Symonds."—*Athenæum*, June
13th, 1885.

"A valuable addition to classical literature. . . . The work
cannot but prove interesting, both to scholars and to those whose
ignorance of Greek debars them from a study of the Lesbian's frag-
mentary works in the original."—*Graphic*, June 13th, 1885.

"The little book will be treasured by all lovers of poetry, and, we
may add, by all bibliophiles, for its intrinsic beauty. . . . As for
Mr. Wharton's prose translations, they are characterized by admirable
fide'ity and self-restraint."—*The Literary World*, Boston, August
22ud, 1886.

SIR PHILIP SIDNEY'S
ASTROPHEL AND STELLA:
Wherein the Excellence of Sweet Poesy is concluded.
Edited from the Folio of 1598.
BY
ALFRED W. POLLARD.

With Portrait. Parchment, Fcap. 8vo. PRICE 7s. 6d.

" E lited with great care."—*Athenæum.*

" Mr. Pollard's beautiful little volume should attract many lovers
of fine verse."—*Spectator.*

"A very pretty and scholarly edition of a sonnet-cycle, which well
deserves all the care that editor and printer can bestow. Mr. Pollard's
introduction is a capital piece of literary workmanship."—*Pall Mall
Gazette.*

"A pretty, an exact, and a presentable edition of Sidney's sonnets."
—*Manchester Guardian.*

"Put forth in a way that does credit to both editor and publisher."
—*Literary World.*

Enigmas of the Spiritual Life.

By the Rev. A. H. CRAUFURD, M.A.,

Author of " The Unknown God."

Crown 8vo, Price 6s.

"In a volume of essays and sermons, unusually full of real thought and fine feeling, Mr. Craufurd takes hold with firm grasp of the intellectual difficulties of the age."—*Scotsman.*

"It is a service to the cause of religion to present, as is here done, the many-sidedness of Christianity. Some of these discourses were delivered from the pulpit to an 'unusually thoughtful congregation,' and assuredly they had their mind full of thought."—*St. James's Gazette.*

"Very thoughtful and often very wise essays. . . . Their teaching is always sober. . . . His intellectual caution and lucidity of thought are always remarkable."—*Spectator.*

"The moderate, yet ardent, phase of belief to which the volume before us gives an eloquent voice. . . . The style of the book is excellent. It is more incisive than that of either Robertson (of Brighton) or Service; and Mr. Craufurd says, comparing volume with volume, more in less space than either. Out of the book we might compile a cento of aphorisms, clear, crisp, often conclusive, always suggestive, and frequently recalling those of Emerson. This volume rises far above the standard of common pulpit oratory, and asserts its place in English literature."—*Glasgow Herald.*

"This is a series of extremely able sermons or essays. Mr. Craufurd's chief characteristics appear to be a genuinely Christian width of sympathy and profound emotional tenderness."—*The Academy.*

THE UNKNOWN GOD.

Sermons preached in London. Second Edition. Crown 8vo, 6s.

RECENTLY PUBLISHED BOOKS.

MEMOIRS OF THE MARGRAVINE OF BAIREUTH.
Translated and Edited by Her Royal Highness PRINCESS
CHRISTIAN. With Portrait. Post 8vo. Price 12s.
Uniform with the above.

THE MARGRAVINE OF BAIREUTH AND
VOLTAIRE. By Dr. GEORGE HORN. Translated by H.R.H.
PRINCESS CHRISTIAN. Post 8vo. Price 7s. 6d.

FREDERICK, CROWN PRINCE AND EMPEROR.
A Biographical Sketch by RENNELL RODD. With an Introduction by H.R.H. the Empress Frederick. Crown 8vo, 6s.

SAPPHO: MEMOIRS, TEXT, AND TRANS-
LATION. By H. T. WHARTON, M.A. Second Edition. With
Etched Portrait of Sappho, and Autotype of Fragment of
Sappho's MS. Parchment, Fcap 8vo. Price 7s. 6d. Out of
print.

SIR PHILIP SIDNEY'S ASTROPHEL AND
STELLA, WHEREIN THE EXCELLENCE OF SWEET POESY
IS CONCLUDED. Edited from the Folio of 1598. By ALFRED
W. POLLARD. With Portrait. Parchment, Fcap 8vo. Price
7s. 6d.

THROUGH ROMANY SONGLAND. By LAURA
ALEXANDRINE SMITH. Crown 8vo. Price 5s.

THE PREACHER OF ST. JUSTIN'S. By A. M.
ROSE. Crown 8vo. Price 3s. 6d.

AFTER PARADISE; or, Legends of Exile, with other
Poems. By ROBERT, EARL OF LYTTON. Second Edition. Small
Fcap 8vo. Price 3s. 6d.

THE EARLY LIFE OF JESUS. By Rev. STOPFORD A.
BROOKE, M.A. Crown 8vo. Price 6s.

THE UNITY OF GOD AND MAN, and other
Sermons. By Rev. STOPFORD A. BROOKE. Second Edition.
Fcap 8vo. Price 4s.

SUNSHINE AND SHADOW. Meditations from the
Writings of the Rev. STOPFORD A. BROOKE. Arranged for Daily
Use. With Portrait. Second Edition. Revised. Fcap 8vo.
Price 6s.

ENIGMAS OF THE SPIRITUAL LIFE. By the
Rev. A. H. CRAUFURD, Author of "The Unknown God." Small
8vo. Price 6s.

THE UNKNOWN GOD. Sermons preached in London
by the Rev. A. H. CRAUFURD. Second Edition. Crown 8vo.
Price 6s.

TRUE RELIGION; being a Series of Short Essays
touching the intimate Relation of Religion to some Matters of
Common Life. By the Rev. JOHN W. DIGGLE, Vicar of Moseley
Hill, Liverpool. Crown 8vo. Price 5s.

FEDA, and other Poems, chiefly Lyrical. By RENNELL
RODD. Crown 8vo. Price 6s.

POEMS IN MANY LANDS. By the same Author.
Second Edition. Crown 8vo. Price 5s.

THE UNKNOWN MADONNA, and other Poems.
By the same Author. With Frontispiece by W. B. RICHMOND,
A.R.A. Crown 8vo, cloth. Price 5s.

RECENTLY PUBLISHED BOOKS.

FROM WEST TO EAST. By HENRY ROSE, Author of "Three Sheiks." Crown 8vo. Price 3s. 6d.

VERONA. By Mrs. L. ORMISTON CHANT. Fcap. 8vo, cloth. Price 5s.

CHILDREN'S FAIRY GEOGRAPHY; or, A Merry Trip Round Europe. By Rev. FORBES E. WINSLOW, St. Leonard's-on-Sea. New and Cheaper Edition. Tenth Thousand. Price 6s. "One of the most charming books ever published for young people."

THE CHILDREN'S FAIRY HISTORY OF ENG-LAND. By Rev. FORBES E. WINSLOW, Author of "The Children's Fairy Geography." 4to, with 200 Illustrations, cloth elegant, Price 6s.

FINGERS AND FORTUNE; A Guide Book to Palmistry. By EVELINE M. FARWELL. Eighth Thousand. Fcap. 8vo, cloth. Price 1s.

LOVE AND SELFISHNESS.. By OSSIP SCHUBIN. Translated from the German by HARRIET F. POWELL. Crown 8vo. Price 5s.

A NEW REVIEW OF NATIONAL EDUCATION. By HEATHER BIGG, F.R.C.S., &c. Fcap. 8vo. Price 2s.

WHAT MUST I DO TO GET WELL? AND HOW CAN I KEEP SO? By One who has done it. Fourth Edition. Revised and greatly enlarged. Crown 8vo. Price 5s.

ELECTRO-HOMŒOPATHIC MEDICINE. A New Medical System, being a Popular and Domestic Guide founded on Experience. By COUNT CESAR MATTEI. Translated by R. M. THEOBALD, M.A., M.R.C.S. Demy 8vo. Price 6s.

LETTERS TO A PATIENT ON CONSUMPTION AND ITS CURE BY THE HYPOPHOSPHITES. By JOHN FRANCIS CHURCHILL, M.D. Demy 8vo. Price 5s.

CHELSEA WINDOW GARDENING; or, Some Notes on the Management of Pot Plants and Town Gardens. By L. M. FOSTER. Price 4d. sewed, 6d. cloth.

NOTES ON HANDWROUGHT LEATHER FOR RECREATION CLASSES. By L. M. FOSTER. Price 6d. sewed.

IN THE PRESS.

BALLADS FROM "PUNCH."

BY

WARHAM ST. LEGER.

Foolscap 8vo. Price 3s. 6d.

The Renaissance of Music.

BY

MORTON LATHAM.

Crown 8vo. Price 6s.

Odes from the Greek Dramatists.

Translated into Lyric Metres by English Poets and Scholars.

EDITED BY

ALFRED POLLARD.

Parchment, Foolscap 8vo. Price 7s. 6d.